William Sheldon

The Millennium

The Good Time Coming

William Sheldon

The Millennium
The Good Time Coming

ISBN/EAN: 9783337778613

Printed in Europe, USA, Canada, Australia, Japan

Cover: Foto ©Andreas Hilbeck / pixelio.de

More available books at **www.hansebooks.com**

THE

MILLENNIUM:

THE

GOOD TIME COMING.

WITH A

HISTORY OF EXPERIMENTS

ON THE

ODIC FORCE.

BY THE AUTHOR OF

MILLENNIAL INSTITUTIONS, THE SEVENTH VIAL, AND THE THEOLOGICAL MYSTERY

SPRINGFIELD, MASS.:

SAMUEL BOWLES & COMPANY, PRINTERS.

1862.

THE MILLENNIUM, &c., &c.

I. INTRODUCTORY.

I TRUST I shall not be suspected of levity. Something of the kind might be suggested by my title—THE MILLENNIUM—THE GOOD TIME COMING. It was merely designed however, to contrast the ideas suggested by the respective designations—the secular and the scriptural. Most people of reflection, it is probable, throughout the *so called* Christian world, are looking for a glorious future. But how different the views of him who is imbued with the teachings of scripture, and of him who is not. The one looks for a future where righteousness—RIGHTEOUSNESS—will prevail universally. Where humility and meekness will take the place of the haughty, punctilious, resentful, or, as the case may be, servile, spirit of the world. Where the love of acquisition is repressed or diffused. Where emulation is regulated and chastened. Where faith, virtue, knowledge, temperance, patience, godliness, brotherly kindness and charity will be attributes of all, and will "abound;" where plenty will be the heritage of all; where to each one will be secured the substantial advantages of wealth, without its temptations; where the enjoyments of this life will be sought and partaken of with moderation, and in all good conscience; and where spiritual mindedness, (as opposed to worldly mindedness,) or that earnest desire for the perfected nature and enjoyments, and the glory, of a blessed future state of existence, will shed a sacred calm, like that of a holy Sabbath, on the minds of all. Of course, those who are on the right side, will not all attain equal degrees of these gifts and graces.

Shall I venture to attempt a delineation of the views of the future, entertained by the men of this world ? Such a delineation would be difficult ; for, while the scripture account is well defined, the notions of those who reject the scriptures, or but slightly regard them, are diverse, like those of the ancient schools of philosophy, while philosophy was truly "vain," as according to scripture—little more than hypothesis built upon conjecture.

Some of the plans of the *social reformers* are sufficiently simple and direct, for I conclude that those of agrarians and radicals, if not those of red republicans, should be included. In England there are such as believe that deposing the hierarchy and abolishing the House of Lords, placing all religious denominations on an equality, and rendering offices of public trust accessible to all, would be the great panacea. The attention of many of these is fixed more upon pulling down than upon building up.

Then there are great numbers, extensively diffused, but having their chief abiding place in the United States, who hold that a purely representative government, religion being left to itself, and in which the freest scope is afforded to the worldly passions of acquisition, emulation and ambition ; a very liberal morality being accorded in the matter of electioneering, to say nothing of the license assumed in transactions of business, is the *chief hope of mankind.* An overweening patriotism would almost seem to be the principal religion of many of these. Events now rapidly transpiring in the United States — July, 1861—surprisingly manifest this, and will ultimately perhaps, modify the current of opinion as to the "hope of mankind." Though this system does not oppugn religion, it appears to contemplate little if aught but worldly advantages.

In advance of these systems, somewhat primitive, or at least crude and immature, as they are regarded by many, are others, not yet extensively reduced to practice, embracing a wide range of thought, and some of them rising to theories of great refinement. Among these may be mentioned the theory of the *perfectibility of human nature*, so prevalent about the time of the French revolution, and that of the late Robert Owen. Mr. Owen is extensively known as an advocate of communism. But he has other claims to attention : first, arising from the circumstance, set forth in the work entitled Millennial Institutions, that he is *perhaps*, expressly alluded to in prophecy.* In addition to his teachings in socialism, Mr. Owen provided for his followers, a religion, such as it was. He also deemed amusement and relaxation, of sufficient importance to be included as an integral part of his system. His religion, if that may be so called which rather ignores or sets aside all religion, is known under the name of the Doctrine of Circumstances. This system teaches, if I comprehend it perfectly, that no one can be more guilty than any other, since another, under *similar circumstances*, would act precisely as he does. This was probably regarded by Mr. Owen as irrefragable ; and at first view it seems quite plausible. It causes a glimmering of the mental vision, which prevents our at once seeing its fallacy. Does it find, or appear to find confirmation in the teaching of scripture, that he who is guilty of one of the commandments is guilty of all ? He who violates one, *under circumstances equally favorable*, would violate any other. It need not be said that it is inconsistent with scripture. It is opposed by the phenomena of conscience

---

* Those who have read the work referred to, will understand me when I say, that it is difficult to fix with certainty, *on the map*, the precise situation of the *north court*—Ezek. 40 : 35–19. According to one method, the table towards the north-east—verse 39—is precisely on the site of Lanark, the seat of Mr. Owen's socialist experiments. According to other methods it is at a greater or less distance.

and remorse, *original principles*, implanted in our natures, by the great author of our being, for the regulation of our conduct. The metaphysical answer perhaps is, that God has made each individual accountable for his actions, *under the circumstances in which he is placed*. It was indispensible for those to whom it was appointed to bear the heat and burden of the day, to labour and be faithful; while those who were called at the eleventh hour, would not fail of their reward. The practical influence of the doctrine must be antinomian and demoralizing, in a high degree; though it will not be questioned that Mr. Owen, and many others, whose teachings have conflicted with scripture, (most or many of whom, however, have taught some kind of morality,) have been quite sincere in their views.

The science of metaphysicks, (which teaches first principles,) is unquestionably, one of the noblest that can occupy the attention of the human mind. Regarded collectively however, like all things else since the fall, in which man is a *particeps*, with the exception perhaps, of the pure mathematicks, it is imperfect. This is evinced by the discordant notions entertained by religious sects, all supported by subtile metaphysicks. Most of these discrepancies however, would be avoided by a more just and philosophic metaphysical training. God has vouchsafed *two revelations* to man : that of *intuitive truth*, and that of the revealed word. And it has been the fault in the reasoning of most religious sects, that they seem to have regarded the teachings of the revealed word, *and as according to their own interpretation*, as the only infallible truth, instead of the verities of intuitive certainty ; not considering apparently, that upon these the truths of the word must ever rest, as a basis. I will not affirm that no amount of cumulative evidence, of a lower grade is not sufficient to neutralize an intuitive certainty ; but as a general rule, that which presents itself to the mind as a primary idea, self-evident, and the converse of which cannot be clearly apprehended, is in all cases to be received as truth, unless opposed by another *apparent truth*, of the same character.

It was not my intention however, to offer a treatise on the rules of metaphysical reasoning; but, from the acknowledged imperfection, and unsatisfactory results of metaphysical speculation heretofore, to deduce the importance of a *right spirit*, in the quest after truth. To some extent this is of more importance than the discovery of truth itself. It appears to be ordained as the great compensating power for the unavoidable imperfections of all copies of the scriptures. Christ says, *Suffer little children to come unto me, and forbid them not : for of such is the kingdom of God. Verily I say unto you, whosoever shall not receive the kingdom of God as a little child shall in no wise enter therein.* In the earliest and best ages of the church, the Apostles and their cotemporaries and successors, embraced the doctrines of the gospel with the singleness of view and the confiding trust of little children. Metaphysical difficulties had not yet arisen. When these appeared, faith became, not less confident perhaps, but less satisfactory, natural, consolatory and vital. It is needless to inquire here, how far the views of the apostles were finally enlarged, and their mental vision rendered more clear, by inspiration. Such a disposition is of more value than a stern, ungenial bending of the intellect to a supposed inexorable logick. An over confident, dogmatic, positive temper on the one hand, and an unfaltering, unswerving adherence to party lines on the other, unreasoning it may be added, except in the prescribed methods, and after the received formulas—might there not be danger that these would sometimes lead to a "form of godliness without the power ?" Viewed as adapted to the circumstances which surround him, man is evidently in a most imperfect condition. The dislocations and disadjustments, which are observable in every direction, seem to prove that he is in a lapsed and fallen condition. Have any of those who reject the Bible, avowedly or practically, offered a theory of man, bearing the least comparison, for sublimity and probability, to that proposed in the scriptures ? the account there given of the creation, and of the fall of man, and of the method devised for his recovery? Under a more logical system of exegesis than has generally prevailed, and observing the simple rule of holding the mind in suspense, where objections are *as yet* insuperable, instead of rushing to a premature conclusion, most of the alleged difficulties will vanish. Even geology, I believe it will appear hereafter, instead of being reconcilable with the Mosaic account, only after much violence to language, singularly confirms it. If there be any who hold that man was created as he is, and that therefore he is not accountable, such a doctrine would perhaps find its best support in the fact that mere morality has hitherto done little for restoring or bringing him to a state of purity, righteousness, peace and happiness.

In the year 1833 I published a work entitled Millennial Institutions. It consisted principally of a comment on the fortieth chapter of Ezekiel. It was supposed to be proved that the six courts of which the "frame of a city," verse 2, consists, properly arranged, form a map, representing the continents of the old world, together with England. In this delineation, under architectural emblems, are represented, more especially, the civil and social institutions of the millennial period. Most of these emblems are found in the court, ver. 35—49, representing England. Here are the emblems of government, and of social and domestick arrangements. Here are the chambers of the *singers*, and of the *priests the keepers of the charge of the house*, and of the *priests the keepers of the charge of the altar. These are the sons of *Zadok among the sons of Levi, which come near to the Lord to minister unto him.* The altar, ver. 47, is in front of this court, towards the east; while at the north gate are " tables, whereupon they slew " *their sacrifices ;* intimating perhaps, in the connexion, both the

*Priest in the time of David.

prevalence of socialism, in the millennial period, *as when the tribes went up to Jerusalem*, and that one form of the true religion had been superseded by another. Hence it is inferred that England is the kingdom spoken of, Matt. 21: 43: *Therefore I say unto you, The kingdom of God shall be taken from you,* and given to a nation bringing forth the fruits thereof.* It appears to follow that pure christianity, millennial christianity, and the civil and social institutions of the Millennium, are to proceed from England.

During the considerable period, which has intervened since the publication of the work referred to, I have seen no reason to change my opinion as to the principal meaning of the emblems set forth in the description of the "frame of a city." This is confirmed by various passages in the Old Testament, in addition to that cited from the New.

For a number of years, commencing early in 1852, I was engaged in a series of experiments on the recently discovered imponderable element, od-force or odyle. These experiments led to interesting results. A number of important discoveries, concerning the nature and properties of the new element, were achieved. Some of these throw unexpected light upon the statements of scripture. The new element is intimately connected with all the processes of life, whether animal or vegetable; and it can be made to exercise a controling influence in the prevention of some of the most formidable diseases. It will also subserve various economic and useful purposes.

I propose, in the following work, to give an account of some of these discoveries; especially of those which illustrate the scriptures. They tend generally, to confirm the authority of scripture; and will hereafter, if I am not mistaken, be intimately connected with human, or, in other words, with millennial progress. The entire work

---

*The Jews.

may be regarded as supplementary to that mentioned above, entitled Millennial Institutions.

Heaven grant that I may be enabled to proceed with the work, in a spirit of humility, in the fear of God, and in a manner which may be well pleasing in his sight. In Christ's name, Amen.

II. THE MILLENNIUM.

THE question may arise whether the thousand years, or millennium as it is popularly called, of Revelation, is the same period as that, described in such glowing language, by the writers of the Old Testament. By comparing and adjusting a few leading particulars, the several statements may perhaps be harmonized.

The book of Revelation is supposed to consist, not of a single consecutive series, but of several such. The series, of which the chapter giving an account of the millennium is a part, appears to commence, either with chapter fifteen or seventeen. The question which, will depend upon the meaning of the two last verses of chapter sixteen. But it is not essential to my present purpose, to determine where the series commences; it is sufficient that chapter seventeen is included. This chapter gives an account of the "judgment" of Mystical Babylon, or, as her name is expressed in scriptures, MYSTERY, BABYLON THE GREAT, THE MOTHER OF HARLOTS AND ABOMINATIONS OF THE EARTH.

In chapter 18 it is emphatically declared that Babylon is fallen, meaning that she is ready for destruction; God's people are commanded to come out of her, lest they become partakers of her sins, and receive of her plagues; and her final destruction is described.

Chapter 19 commences with great rejoicings, both in heaven and on earth, on account of the destruction of Babylon: verses 1—7.

Then follows the announcement, verses 7—10, of a sacred rite, called the marriage of the Lamb. And he saith unto me, Write, Blessed are they which are called unto the marriage supper of the Lamb. The angel who here speaks, appears to be the one who communed with John, at the beginning of chapter seventeen.

After this an august procession issues forth, consisting of the armies in heaven upon white horses, led by one who is called Faithful and True, and whose name is called The Word of God. The power and offices of this being are described. Verses 11—16.

The apostle then saw an angel standing in the sun, ver. 17, who calls upon all the fowls that fly in the midst of heaven, to gather themselves together to the final contest of the powers of light and of darkness. The result of this contest is described.

The first verses of chapter 20, verses 1—3, give a brief account of the imprisonment of Satan for a thousand years.

Then follows the description of the millennium: verses 4—6.

Here we have a regular series of events, in immediate, or near preparation for the millennium. More remotely the series commences, perhaps, with the pouring out of the sixth vial, at verse 12 of chapter 16.* This vial is supposed to represent the discoveries of America, and of the passage to India, by the Cape of Good Hope. Three unclean spirits like frogs—in the water and out of the water—on the water and on the land—went forth to the kings of the earth and of the whole world, to gather them to the battle of that great day of God Almighty.

We have, above, as has been said, a regular series of prophetical events, evidently in immediate or near preparation for the millennium. Before attempting any exposition of this most important portion of scripture, I will give my views as to the structure of the book of Revela-

---

*Still more remotely perhaps, as has been said, with chapter 15.

tion; or rather of the second part, commencing at the fourth chapter. Chapter 4, ver. 1. *After this I looked, and behold, a door was opened in heaven: and the first voice which I heard was as it were of a trumpet talking with me; which said, Come up hither, and I will shew thee things which must be hereafter.* However repugnant it may be to the feelings of those who regard the theatre as of most evil tendency, it cannot be denied that this part of Revelation is essentially dramatick. A few particulars will render this evident. There is an auditory. The fields of heaven, or a visionary structure above them, afford a theatre, suitable for representing the events of prophecy, *as on the earth.* Still above this there is an arrangement, representing a relative heaven. Different places and various objects, as mountains, the wilderness, the sea, &c., are actually represented. There is frequent change of scene. The *action of the piece,* so to speak, comprises the prophetical events of a most important period, in the history of the human race. There is a plot, not involved, perhaps, after the manner of the secular drama, but displaying God's judgments; and resulting in the triumph of the righteous, and the destruction of the wicked. The different series of events are so many acts, and the changes of place, time, &c., in these, are scenes. There are expressive emblems. Various characters are introduced. Neither pantomine nor dialogue are wanting, but the language (of the speakers,) is principally monologue. There is a chorus far transcending in sublimity, all that the Greek dramatists ever imagined. All this is *described* by the apostle. He relates what he saw, and gives the words of the different speakers.

The language is commonly figurative, but becomes literal, by an easy transition, when circumstances require. When a prominent word is employed in some special figurative sense, there is always a suspicion that it is employed in the same sense thereafter, but this is not in all instances the case.

Babylon is obviously pre-eminent, chiefest, among the powers of evil, that oppose the gracious and beneficent designs of God, towards the children of men. It becomes therefore, a subject of the highest interest, what Babylon is, what is meant by her emphatick, almost startling designation. And there is a time in prophecy, when the question becomes one of momentous importance, in view of the command, cited above, and given by a voice from heaven, *saying, Come out of her, my people, that ye be not partakers of her sins, and that ye receive not of her plagues.* I propose to endeavor to investigate the question, by considering the principal evidence on the subject, which is to be found in Revelation; and then to refer to some of the most considerable passages, which are supposed to be illustrative or explanatory, in the Old Testament. A complete examination of the subject, would far exceed my limits. This inference may be safely drawn from the passages, which have thus been passed in brief review, that, previous to the millennium, the powers of evil will not relinquish the world, which they have possessed so long, without a desperate struggle.

III. MYSTICAL BABYLON—IS THE INDIVIDUAL SYSTEM—IS UNIVERSAL.

In the work referred to in the introductory section—Millennial Institutions, 1833—I propose the theory that Babylon is the individual system. This is a term employed by Mr. Owen to denote the individual tenure of property, or, more generally, the organization of society by families. During the long period which has intervened since, I have seen no reason to doubt the correctness of that hypothesis, so far as it extends; though I have seen abundant reason for believing that another and darker element, not sufficiently regarded then, is essential to the constitution of this mysterious and baleful influence.

Babylon is mentioned twice in Revelation, previous to chapter seventeen. Ch. 14: 8. *And there followed another angel, saying, Babylon is fallen, is fallen, that great city, because she made* ALL NATIONS *drink of the wine of the wrath of her fornication.* I believe it will be found that the statements concerning Babylon can be rendered consistent, only in one way. By supposing that the term, *that great city*, is put, by synecdoche, for all the cities of the earth.* Without any violent figure of speech, *commercially* speaking, and as respects their universal influence upon all, whether *kings of the earth* or *peoples, and multitudes, and nations and tongues*, they may be regarded as one city. A merchant in London sends to Smyrna, or Surat, or Canton, for articles, which they respectively produce, as he would send to a remote street, or streets, of London itself. When the Sultan has exhausted the resources of the money-lenders, or money *holders*, of his own capital, he borrows of a banker in Naples or Amsterdam.

Babylon is fallen, is fallen. This form of expression, (as above) the particular style of repetition, as well as the words employed, is not used in scripture, I believe, concerning any state, nation, kingdom, organization or influence, except Babylon. It is used concerning Babylon, both in the Old and the New Testament. And it is observable that it seems to be employed, in the Old Testament, in a double sense, referring both to the ancient and the prophetical Babylon; and also with a reference to our own time. See Is. 21: 9. The other instance in which it is employed in the New Testament, is at ch. 18: 2. It was the purpose, as I believe, in all these instances, to convey an idea of the universal extent, and duality of the sway of Babylon, spreading over the east and the west, the old continent and the new.

---

* The term *great city* is employed in a similar sense, when first used in Revelation: see ch. 11: 8. It there can mean nothing less than the Turkish empire. See also, 16: 19.

In addition to the instance above, Babylon is mentioned in Revelation, previous to chapter seventeen, at chapter 16: 19, in the description of what followed on the pouring out of the seventh vial. And this instance is entirely confirmatory, in the connexion, of the views above. To understand the connexion, it will be needful to refer, once more, to the account of the sixth vial. Verse 12. *And the sixth angel poured out his vial upon the great river Euphrates; and the water thereof was dried up, that the way of the kings of the east might be prepared.* The waters of the Euphrates were dried up, as the waters of the Adriatic were, at the same time. Commerce had taken another direction, in consequence of the discovery of the passage to India, by the Cape of Good Hope. Caravans no longer crossed the Euphrates, or started from the cities on its banks, with the commodities of Persia, India and Cathay, for the marts of the west. Verse 13. *And I saw three unclean spirits like frogs come out of the mouth of the dragon, and out of the mouth of the beast, and out of the mouth of the false prophet. For they are the spirits of devils, working miracles, which go forth unto the kings of the earth and of the whole world, to gather them to the battle of that great day of God Almighty.* From the Roman Empire, which still existed in spirit as well as in name, from feudal Europe, and from an imperfect, and probably a corrupt and deteriorated church, went forth discoverers, adventurers, conquerors, founders of states, merchants, and missionaries, *accompanied, as we shall see in another section, by literal " spirits of devils."* Verse 16. *And he gathered them together into a place called in the Hebrew tongue, Armageddon. He* gathered them, that is, the angel of the sixth vial. The pouring out of the seventh vial, and what immediately followed, is described in the two next verses, 17, 18. It then follows, ver. 19, *And the great city was divided into three parts, and the cities of the nations fell.* The *great city.* Keeping in mind that Babylon is called the *great city,* (" *that* great city,") when first mentioned in Revelation, ch. 14: 8, that made ALL NATIONS drink of the wine, &c., that the three unclean spirits, ch. 16: 13, 14, went forth to *the kings of the earth and of the* WHOLE WORLD, *to gather them to the battle,* that they, or the *sixth angel,* gathered them together to Armageddon—see verse 16—and that the seventh angel, evidently in continuation, poured out his vial into the air, which surrounds the earth, and that nothing which follows conveys the least intimation that the field of vision is contracted, can it be doubted that the great city, or Babylon, that was *divided into three parts,* comprises all the cities of the earth ? The *cities of the nations—and the cities of the nations fell,* ver. 19,—are not then, without but within the *great city,* constituting perhaps, one of the three parts, into which the city is divided. *And the cities of the nations fell: and great Babylon came in remembrance before God, to give unto her the cup of the wine of the fierceness of his wrath.* The judgment of Babylon, and her final destruction, are described in the two next chapters, 17, 18.

Chapter 17. I trust it is proved, above, that the influence of Babylon is universal. I will proceed to consider evidence tending to prove that Babylon is the individual system ; including, of course, other combinations and influences, that naturally result from this organization of society. Babylon is personified in chapter 17, as a splendid harlot, arrayed in gorgeous apparel, and decked with gold and precious stones, and having in her hand, a *golden cup, full of abominations and filthiness of her fornication.* It is said in Jeremiah, 51: 7, of *ancient Babylon,* renowned for commerce and wealth,—Jer. 51: 13, *O thou that dwellest upon many waters, abundant in treasures :*—that *Babylon hath been a golden cup in the Lord's hand, that made all the earth drunken : the nations have drunken of her wine, therefore the nations are mad.* See also, in connexion, Rev. 17: 2. *With whom the kings of the earth have committed fornication, and the inhabitants of the*

earth have been made drunk with the wine of her fornication. Need the reflection be made, that much the same
things are predicated of the ancient, as of the prophetical
Babylon?

Verse 3. *So he carried me away in the spirit into the
wilderness: and I saw a woman sit upon a scarlet-coloured beast, full of names of blasphemy, having seven
heads and ten horns.* It is evident that Babylon is perfectly
conversant with the dwellings and the affairs of men.
Why then is her chief seat in the wilderness? Is it because she has made, by her enchantments, a wilderness of
all the earth? How many, alas, have found it such; and
who had they been endowed with a spirit of observation
and of judgment, would have perceived that all their desolation and unhappiness might be traced to the great fact
of the individual tenure of property, whether they could
claim any portion of this world's goods, or otherwise.
But is there not a more special adaptedness of the figure?
A wilderness, a forest of native trees, unreclaimed, that
have not been meliorated by culture, not *domesticated*, affords a most perfect emblem of society, in its *primitive
stage*, consisting of an aggregate of separate families.
This will be seen, when it is recollected that physiologic-
ally speaking, every tree is either a family, or one of the
heads of a family. That such is the true interpretation,
may be inferred from the figurative use, which appears to
be made of the tree, in other portions of Revelation, and
in the Old Testament. Rev. 7: 1—3. *And after these
things I saw four angels standing on the four corners of
the earth, holding the four winds of the earth, that the
wind should not blow on the earth, nor on the sea, nor on
any tree. And I saw another angel ascending from the east,
having the seal of the living God: and he cried with a loud voice
to the four angels, to whom it was given to hurt the earth and the
sea, Saying, hurt not the earth, neither the sea, nor the trees, till
we have sealed the servants of our God in their foreheads.*
Here, as I understand the passage, the angels of the

3

nations* are commanded to see that in all the revolutions of nations, nominally christian, and of christian belief, (described with such power, in Matt. 24 : 6, and following verses,) no change shall be made in the institution of marriage, in family relations. Rev. 8: 7. *The first angel sounded, and there followed hail and fire mingled with blood, and they were cast upon the earth: and the third part of trees was burnt up, and all green grass was burnt up.* Does this passage speak of the diffusion of polygamy, and of the banishing of the sweet amenities of virtuous youthful courtship, during the spread of the Mahometan power? Rev. 9: 4. *And it was commanded them that they should not hurt the grass of the earth, neither any green thing, neither any tree; but only those men which have not the seal of God in their foreheads.* After the above, this passage will require no comment. I will only observe, that if an exposition of the entire passage, given some years since, in a former work, were the true one, the command, first of verse 4, seems to have been observed, notwithstanding the polygamy of the Mormons, and the changing "affinities" of the Spiritualists. There is another passage, in the Old Testament, which appears to be still more decisive. Is. 61 : 3. *That they might be called Trees of righteousness, The planting of the Lord, that he might be glorified.* Here is an allusion, doubtless, to particulars, which may be gathered from various scriptures. The time will come when the days of man will equal the days of a tree. Is. 65 : 22. *For as the days of a tree are the days of my people.* Their children will all be righteous. "*For they are the seed of the blessed of the* LORD, *and their offspring with them.*" Ver. 23. But there is a *family* resemblance in this, that during the life of many, the number of their descendants will equal that of the blossoms of a tree.

The name given to *Babylon* is singularly descriptive and appropriate on the supposition that Babylon is the indi-

*See Dan. 10: 13, 20.

vidual system. Verse 5. *And upon her forehead was a name written*, MYSTERY, BABYLON THE GREAT, THE MOTHER OF HARLOTS AND ABOMINA- TIONS OF THE EARTH. MYSTERY. Every trade, art, profession, calling, has its mysteries, which enable the professors to circumvent others. Then there are in- numerable associations, combinations of men, more or less formal and regular, and known by various designa- tions, or without name, the object of which, it is to be feared is, to enable those concerned to obtain undue ad- vantage over those without. The most considerable of these is the ancient Masonic fraternity. And again, the several callings are practiced under laws, *founded on the individual tenure of property*, which are themselves a mystery, inasmuch as it requires the labours of a life, thoroughly to comprehend them. Their obscurity and uncertainty, the delays incident to legal decisions, and their frequent reversal, may perhaps be classed among the abominations of the earth. I believe that at least one, and one of the most distinguished of the Lord Chancel- lors would admit this to be true.

But there are mysteries more perplexing, more dread than any yet mentioned, interwoven in the very texture of society, as at present constituted. Of these I propose to speak hereafter.

BABYLON THE GREAT. Various prophetical per- sonifications of scripture comprise large portions of the earth, vast empires, but the term *great* is not applied to any of them, at least with such emphasis, so distinguish- ingly, as to Babylon.

THE MOTHER OF HARLOTS AND ABOMINA- TIONS OF THE EARTH. What harlotry can be men- tioned, literal or figurative, which does not claim Babylon, (as the term is understood above,) as its *mother?* Of course, *evil concupiscence*, incident to our natures, is the father.

It is not desirable perhaps, to know much of *the abominations of the earth*. In the dark chambers, in the hideous recesses of the " great city," what deeds without a name are perpetrated. But some of the *abominations of the earth*, are sufficiently apparent to all who will observe. Among these are the acknowledged corruption, and unalloyed, narrow selfishness, of the legislatures of the several states of our glorious republick.* How happens it that in New York, *the chief seat of Babylon in this western world*, naturally one of the healthiest spots on the globe, the mortality of infants is greater than in any other city ? I think I have seen lately an account of an orphan asylum, in another land, in which not one of the " wee unchristened bairns "—perhaps they *were* all christened—survived the period of infancy. I remember some notice of a burial association, various members of which, murdered near relatives, members of their own families, for the sake of the miserable pittance, which could be saved from the burial fee. But there is one of the abominations of the earth, which, from its enormity, its extensive prevalence, and the boldness with which it is practiced, should be denounced by all who can in some sort comprehend the evils which it is likely to inflict upon humanity. I am old enough to remember with what enthusiasm the advent of chemical science, in the United States, was hailed by intelligent men. What a field was here opened for its benefits. And yet, such is the blighting, blasting influence of the Babylonian constitution of society, that while the *real advantages* are quite doubtful, all the resources of this noble science have been employed in debasing every article of food, and domestic use, and even of medicine, that would admit of it. If this is too strong a statement I rejoice at it, but unquestionably enough is true to evince the necessity of legislative· interference, which however, is hardly to be expected.

---

* See note (A).

But enough. While abominations of the earth, those which are more apparent, and are admitted to be such, meet us on every side, it will be difficult to convince men that these are owing to the structure of society; to convince those who respect the Bible, that Babylon, by far the most memorable of the evil personifications of scripture, whose prophetical history occupies two entire chapters of the twenty-two of Revelation, with other notices, merely represents the SPIRIT of the laws and usages, which regulate property, and the practices which have grown up under them. And yet what else answers, without forced construction, to all the specifications? What other power has exercised such a potent influence upon *all nations;* what other power, that could be personified as a splendid harlot, with a golden cup in her hand, has made all nations to drink and be drunken with the wine of her cup?*

And yet men of the world will be amazed at these allegations against property, as the term is commonly understood, against the medium of exchange, and against individual possession. We should be reminded of the sacred rights in worldly possessions, as according to scripture, of the incentives given to industry and enterprise, by the hope of possession, of the indispensibleness of a medium of exchange; of the numerous passages in the scriptures of the Old Testament, at least, where riches are spoken of as a blessing, and the reward of good conduct, of the maxims inculcating this truth; of the innumerable benefits conferred by wealth in the hands of the benevolent, and even by the pursuit and accumulation of wealth, by those who are confessedly of worldly minds. This may be true, yet it is equally true that the evils, which have been specified, and innumerable others, are to be ascribed to the method of distributing the products of industry, which has ever prevailed. What is required, is, a

---

*See ch. 14 : 8 with 17 : 2.

mode of accomplishing this, which will secure the advantages, without the evils. And this, in God's good time, and with God's blessing, the organization of society by small communities, instead of families, will accomplish. There is a *mutual protection*, and a *perpetuity* in the one case, which cannot be afforded by the other.

What is national prosperity, the highest prosperity, under the individual system? Prosperity such as was that of the United States, till a recent period?* Look around in all charitableness. . What do you behold but a glittering, spiritual necropolis, constantly reminding you of the solemn and awful words of the Saviour, *Enter ye in at the strait gate : for wide is the gate, and broad is the way, that leadeth to destruction, and many there be which go in thereat : Because strait is the gate, and narrow is the way, which leadeth unto life, and few there be that find it.* All honour to men of true beneficence, who, having of the good things of this world committed to their charge, endeavour to approve themselves as faithful stewards in the solemn trust. God grant that they may be enabled to keep in mind the injunction : *Make to yourselves friends of the mammon of unrighteousness ; that when ye fail, they may receive you into everlasting habitations. If therefore ye have not been faithful in the unrighteous mammon, who will commit to your trust the true riches ?*

IV. BABYLON—A LOCAL AND UNIVERSAL JUDGMENT OF—THE SUPERIOR BEINGS CONCERNED.

It may be questioned if the dramatick element, in the two chapters describing the judgment of Babylon, has ever been sufficiently regarded. It throws much light on the actual purport of the various descriptions. Ch. 17 : 1, 2:

---

*Nov. 4, 1861.

And there came one of the seven angels which had the seven vials, and talked with me, saying unto me, Come hither; I will shew unto thee the judgment of the great whore that sitteth upon many waters: With whom the kings of the earth have committed forni- cation, and the inhabitants of the earth have been made drunk with the wine of her fornication. Doubt- less there were special reasons ·for selecting one of the angels of the seven vials for this purpose. The reasons appear to have been these: to set forth and keep in mind, the connexion between the series of the seven vials, especially the three last, and the judgment of Babylon described in this chapter. And also to signify, (in the entire connexion,) by contrast with the agents and *expositors* and conditions of the final and universal judgment of the woman, in the next chapter, that the judgment here described, is but partial and local. The passage cited above is evidently preliminary; and it appears, (as it is *primary*,) to be *substantive* and *inclusive.* On comparing it with verse 15, and with ch. 14: 8, and 18: 3, it will be evident, (if any doubt could have existed before,) that the *kings* and the *inhabitants* of *all the earth* are designed, whatever individual exceptions there may have been.

After the preliminary address, the angel carried John into the wilderness, where he saw a woman sitting upon a scarlet-coloured beast, having seven heads and ten horns. The appearance of the woman is described, and the name is given, which was written upon her forehead. John then saw her *drunken with the blood of the saints and with the blood of the martyrs of Jesus, and wondered with great admiration.* Ver. 7. *And the angel said unto me, Wherefore didst thou marvel? I will tell thee the mystery of the woman, and of the beast that carrieth her, which hath the seven heads and ten horns.** The *judgment* of the beast is de-

---

*Verse 8 and following. Of these verses I shall speak directly.

scribed first. He goeth into perdition. Ver. 8, with 11. The judgment of the woman is that inflicted upon her by the ten *kings* represented by the ten horns of the beast. *These shall hate the whore, and shall make her desolate and naked, and shall eat her flesh, and burn her with fire.* Ver. 18. *And the woman which thou sawest is that great city, which reigneth over the kings of the earth.* Of all the earth, as has been shewn; a recognizing, at the close, of what might have been inferred from the two first verses, that the final judgment of Babylon will be far more extensive than that here described; that the judgment here described, as has been said, is but partial and local, though it may be central and have the lead.

The mission of the angel who talked with John—*one of the angels which had the seven vials*—here ceases. He has described, as might have been anticipated from his being one of the angels of the seven vials, the progress and judgment of Babylon, in her connexion with what might be called *prophetic ground*, or the Roman empire. This appears from her having been drunken with the blood of saints and martyrs of Jesus, and from other particulars, which will be mentioned in the sequel. In the next chapter, which describes the final judgment of Babylon, as has been observed, other agents and expositors are introduced, and other conditions exist. The angel, whose appearance is the commencement of this solemn and august transaction, is evidently of the highest order of angelick excellence. A voice of warning and of judgment is heard from heaven; and instead of the comparatively narrow circuit of the Roman empire, it is proclaimed that Babylon has exercised a dire influence over *all nations*. But hear the words of the book.

Ch. 18 : 1–3. *And after these things I saw another angel come down from heaven, having great power ; and the earth was lightened with his glory. And he cried mightily with a strong voice, saying, Babylon the great is fallen, is fallen, and is become the habitation of devils, and the hold of every foul spirit, and a cage of every unclean and hateful bird. For all nations have drunk of the wine of the wrath of her fornication, and the kings of the earth have committed fornication with her, and the merchants of the earth are waxed rich through the abundance of her delicacies.—And the earth was lightened with his glory.* Whether this is to be understood literally or figuratively, it can hardly be the former, it appears to intimate that the influence of Babylon has been universal. *And is become the habitation of devils, and the hold of every foul spirit.* See ch. 16 : 12—14. The two passages leave no doubt of the great and increasing prevalence of diabolick influence, after the event which followed the pouring out of the sixth vial. This is that *darker element* of which I have spoken, at the commencement of section 3, as being essential to the constitution of Babylon. Well may one of the names of Babylon be Mystery.

After the angel above has proclaimed the fall of Babylon, together with the reason which seems to have especially contributed to it, a voice is heard from heaven. God himself condescends to warn his people, and to declare the judgment of Babylon. As my readers, should I have readers, may not be disposed to turn to the Revelation, I will give the whole of this sublime chapter, in its several divisions. It is questionable perhaps, whether the voice from heaven ceases at the close of verse 8, or continues so as to include the first clause of verse 17. If it ceases with verse 8, the remaining verses are merely declaratory, in the inspired language of the apostle.

Ver. 4—17. *And I heard another voice from heaven, saying, Come out of her, my people, that ye be not partakers of her sins, and that ye receive not of her plagues. For her sins have reached unto heaven, and God hath remembered her iniquities. Reward her even as she rewarded you, and double unto her double according to her works: in the cup which she hath filled, fill to her double. How much she hath glorified herself, and lived deliciously, so much torment and sorrow give her : for she saith in her heart, I sit a*

4

queen, and am no widow, and shall see no sorrow. Therefore shall her plagues come in one day, death, and mourning, and famine; and she shall be utterly burned with fire; for strong is the Lord God who judgeth her. And the kings of the earth, who have committed fornication and lived deliciously with her, shall bewail her, and lament for her, when they shall see the smoke of her burning, Standing afar off for the fear of her torment, saying, Alas, alas, that great city Babylon, that mighty city! for in one hour is thy judgment come. And the merchants of the earth shall weep and mourn over her; for no man buyeth their merchandise any more: The merchandise of gold, and silver, and precious stones, and of pearls, and fine linen, and purple, and silk, and scarlet, and all thyine wood, and all manner vessels of ivory, and all manner vessels of most precious wood, and of brass, and iron, and marble, And cinnamon, and odours, and ointments, and frankincense, and wine, and oil, and fine flour, and wheat, and beasts, and sheep, and horses, and chariots, and slaves, and souls of men. And the fruits that thy soul lusted after are departed from thee, and all things which were dainty and goodly are departed from thee, and thou shalt find them no more at all. The merchants of these things, which were made rich by her, shall stand afar off for the fear of her torment, weeping and wailing, And saying, Alas, alas, that great city that was clothed in fine linen, and purple, and scarlet, and decked with gold, and precious stones, and pearls! For in one hour so great riches is come to naught. Ver. 11. And the merchants of the earth shall weep and mourn over her, for no man buyeth their merchandise any more. When the social system is efficiently organized, on a scale of adequate magnitude, they will not need to buy of those who still follow the mysterious devices of Babylon. What relevancy or appropriateness can there be, in the catalogue of merchandise, which follows, verses 12, 13, on the supposition that Babylon is the Papacy or aught else but the individual system.*

---

*All the things here mentioned may have been purchased for the Papacy, *as such*, to support her state and magnificence, for her processions and other pub-

Ver. 17—19. *And every shipmaster, and all the company in ships, and sailors, and as many as trade by sea, stood afar off, And cried when they saw the smoke of her burning, saying, What city is like unto this great city! And they cast dust on their heads, and cried, weeping and wailing, saying, Alas, alas, that great city wherein were made rich all that had ships in the sea, by reason of her costliness! for in one hour is she made desolate.* These verses are narrative, and evidently are not uttered by the voice from heaven.

Ver. 20. *Rejoice over her, thou heaven, and ye holy apostles and prophets; for God hath avenged you on her.* The voice from heaven is here perhaps again heard. *For God hath avenged you on her.* This passage and various others that will be noticed* shew that the influence of Babylon has been most hostile to true religion, to man's best interests.

Ver. 21—23. *And a mighty angel took up a stone like a great millstone, and cast it into the sea saying, Thus with violence shall that great city Babylon be thrown down, and shall be found no more at all. And the voice of harpers, and musicians, and of pipers, and trumpeters, shall be heard no more at all in thee; and no craftsman, of whatsoever craft he be, shall be found any more in thee; and the sound of a millstone shall be heard no more at all in thee; and the light of a candle shall shine no more at all in thee; and the voice of the bridegroom and of the bride shall be heard no more at all in thee: for thy merchants were the great men of the earth; for by thy sorceries were all nations deceived.* Still another mighty angel has a part, by a most emphatick testimonial, in this final judgment of the mystick harlot. Observe his concluding words addressed to her. *For by thy sorceries were* ALL NATIONS *deceived.*

---

lick displays; but would the loss of the entire traffick impoverish any considerable number of the *merchants of the earth?* and on the other hand, can this extended list of merchandises, represent the sale of masses, indulgences, &c.? as if the *merchants of the earth,* ver. 11, were factors of the church.

* See verses 6—8; 23.

Ver. 24. *And in her was found the blood of prophets, and of saints, and of all that were slain upon the earth.* The language in this last verse, once more assumes the narrative form. The statement in this verse proves, first, the universal extent of Babylon. But is it not true in another sense: that Babylon has either directly caused, or influenced, *modified*, or to some extent given form and shape, to all murders, all assassinations, all wars, from the first murder to the present time?

V. BABYLON—IS NOT SPIRITUAL ROME.

In the two chapters, some of the more prominent particulars of which we have now considered, there are two judgments of Babylon; as she sitteth upon the scarlet-coloured beast, and upon many waters, which last are explained, in the text, to mean all nations and peoples, or perhaps all without the limits of the Roman Empire. The second and final judgment incomparably exceeds the first in extent and dignity, in the sublimity of the descriptions, and the eminency of those by whom it is conducted, rising from exalted angels, to the Supreme Majesty of Heaven. It is proved then conclusively, and so as not to admit of a question, that Babylon is not Spiritual Rome. But there is abundant internal evidence to this effect, in the seventeenth chapter, and which, as I proposed, I will now consider. If it can be shown that Babylon is not Spiritual Rome, it will go far toward proving, in the Protestant mind at least, that Babylon is indeed the individual system.

Babylon, as has been noticed, is first introduced as sitting upon many waters. This statement is probably definitive, including that which directly follows, in which a personification of Babylon is described, and as sitting upon a scarlet-coloured beast. Both Catholicks and Protestants admit that this beast is the Roman empire; only the

Catholicks hold that it is merely heathen Rome. What is comprised in the Roman empire? Does it consist of the surface, the buildings, the valuables, and the inhabitants; or of the inhabitants only? On either supposition, how utterly incongruous is the metaphor, which supposes that seven moderately sized hills, the mere hills, are the heads of the beast. The term employed in the text to describe the heads, *seven mountains*, cannot include the city upon the hills, for that is the woman. *And the woman, which thou sawest, is that great city which reigneth over the kings of the earth.* Ver. 18, with 9. The ten horns of the beast are explained to be ten kings; and it is intimated that each of them is to receive a kingdom. If these originate at Rome, either from its political or religious influence, they proceed, not from the heads of the beast, but from the woman. Is this hypercritical? All difficulty will be obviated by another mode of interpretation. It is said, somewhat abruptly, ver. 10, that there are *seven kings*. But for these nothing is said concerning kingdoms. As the number is the same as that of the heads, is it not probable that these are the kingdoms? The term mountain then, *seven mountains*, is used in the sense in which it is so often employed in the prophetical writings of the Old Testament, as denoting kingdoms, or some other aggregate of men; and the literary connexion between the Old and the New Testament will not be questioned. Is. 2 : 2. *And it shall come to pass in the last days, that the mountain of the Lord's house*—the church—*shall be established in the top of the mountains, and shall be exalted above the hills; and all nations shall flow unto it.* Many other instances might be cited. The seven kings, *or governments*, exist, not contemporaneously, but in succession. The seven mountains then, or heads of the beast, are seven kingdoms, or people, or possibly the chief cities of such, which at different times, have become predominant, within the limits of the Roman empire. What is said of the succession of the kings, or governments, is true of the kingdoms; though it

is to be observed that after their predominance ceases,
(which constitutes them heads of the beast, in the more considerable sense,) they still continue to exist. As is said of
the beasts in Daniel, that *they had their dominion taken
away, yet their lives were prolonged for a season,* &c., &c.
Of the kings or kingdoms in Revelation, it is said, *five are
called.* There are different ways of enumerating these,
but the following will perhaps be as satisfactory as any.
The Assyrian monarchy, the Egyptian, (which in the time
of Sesostris came as near to being a universal monarchy
as others so accounted,) the Babylonian, the Persian,
the Grecian. Five are fallen, *and one is.* The Roman
was the existing monarchy, or empire as it was called,
in the time of John. When the Roman empire was
established on the ruins of those which had fallen, the
Roman people, or possibly the city of Rome, became the
sixth head. If the city of Rome, it was only as one of the
heads; the septenary is found only in the seven hills, and
these, it has been shewn, cannot be the seven heads.
When the bishop of Rome assumed the supremacy in the
church, which was permanently conceded by the western
division of the empire; the religious element (whether
genuine or otherwise is a question which I will not here
attempt to determine,) manifested itself locally, after an
unwonted sort, but not as a principal. The splendid Hierarchy and the multiplied religious houses, or monastic establishments, gave a peculiar phase to the social constitution; but Babylon, the worldly Babylon, the same Babylon that ruled in India and China, as well as in the
kingdoms of the west, was predominant.

Ver. 10. And there are seven kings: five are fallen,
and one is, *and the other is not yet come ; and when he cometh,
he must continue a short space.* In the work referred to
above—Millennial Institutions, 1838—I advanced the
hypothesis, that this "ascendency" or government, is
"the popular imperial, founded by Napoleon." The Roman empire has continued, in some sort, to our own times,

and France is within its ancient limits. But the restoration of the French empire, by Louis Napoleon, renders this hypothesis more than doubtful. I now incline to the belief that the seventh government may be described as that of atheistical, republican France, or perhaps of the French revolution. It continued a *short space*, or perhaps till the restoration by the first Napoleon, of publick Christian worship.

It will not be needful here, to consider farther, the prophetical divisions of the Roman empire, and the transactions within its limits—it being my object at present, merely to prove that Babylon is not Spiritual Rome; but events are rapidly transpiring—Dec. 2, 1861—which may render it expedient to return to this obscure portion of scripture, at the close of the present work.

VI. BABYLON—RELATIVE CLAIMS OF ROME AND CONSTANTINOPLE TO THE TITLE—THE CIVIL LAW —ŒCUMENICAL BISHOP—GRANT OF THE EMPEROR PHOCAS—BABYLON EARLIER THAN THE TIME OF JOHN—SITTETH A QUEEN—THE TWO CITIES SINCE THE CAPTURE OF CONSTANTINOPLE BY THE TURKS—ST. GEORGE.

It is remarkable that Protestant commentators, after having determined that Babylon is a corrupt Christian power, established in a city which is seated on seven hills, should so lightly set aside the claims of Constantinople, also seated upon seven hills. Mr. Scott, the author of the popular commentary, merely says, "This is the well-known situation of Rome: " (upon "seven mountains,") "and though Constantinople is also built on seven hills, they are comparatively obscure, *and no other mark of the beast answers to it.*" The italicks are mine. Bishop Newton expresses himself briefly, to much the same effect. It would altogether exceed my limits to go into a full examination of the subject, but I will mention a few particulars.

Admitting that the sixth "king," in the passage of Revelation, which we have been considering, represents the imperial Roman government, (in which Protestant commentators, and the plan proposed above, agree,) it is quite observable that immediately after the Roman empire became Christian, the emperor to whom this change was owing, removed the seat of empire from Rome to Constantinople.* This, it will be observed, in view of Babylon being, as alleged, a corrupt Christian power, seated at Rome. The *successors and representatives* of the sixth "king "† as above, continued to reign at Constantinople for 1123 years, while the empire of the west terminated in 146 years. A writer speaking of the fall of Constantinople says, it was "once the metropolis, and long the sole existing remnant of the Roman empire. It fell a prey to the Turks 1043 years after Rome was taken by Alaric, and 977 years after the entire subversion of the western empire."

Byzantium, on the site of which Constantinople was built, had been reduced to a village, by war, a little previous; but it still contained idol temples, which Constantine destroyed, and built Christian churches in the new city. I do not learn that there was ever an idol temple in Constantinople; while some authors "attribute Constantine's choice of a new capital to a dislike which he had conceived against Rome, on account of the enthusiastic attachment of that city to Paganism."

Notwithstanding the alleged "obscurity" of the seven hills of Constantinople, they appear to be sufficiently well defined. In a description of the city it is said, "The palace and garden of the seraglio occupy the eastern

---

*The emperor Constantine embraced Christianity about the year 312, and transferred the seat of the empire from Rome to Constantinople, in the year 330.

†Not, of course, as Pagan emperors.

promontory, the first of the seven hills." Five of the
seven hills, " rise like terraces one above another;" and
it is said that the seventh hill and the " narrow ridge of
the sixth hill," were not covered with buildings till about
a hundred years after the death of the founder of the city.

If the influence of Babylon extends over " all nations,"
how is this, if Babylon be Rome, to be reconciled with the
following? " The doctrine of the eastern or Greek
church, which is unquestionably, the most ancient, prevails at this day over a greater extent of country, than
that of any other church in the Christian world." And
then, after mentioning numerous countries where the
Greek religion prevails, the writer adds, that " it will be
evident that the Greek church has a greater extent of territory than the Latin, with all the branches that are sprung
from it." It is of no consequence to the present argument, that the spiritual supremacy of the patriarch of
Constantinople does not exist in any particular country.
The Greek faith will shut out the influence of Rome.
The supremacy of the Patriarch over the Russian church,
continued for more than a hundred years after the cap-
ture of Constantinople by the Turks.

It appears, by the facility with which the Greek emperors disposed of the patriarchs, and the patriarchal
office, that the emperor was the virtual head of the
church.* The temporal and spiritual power, then, of the
emperor, with the conceded power of the patriarch, may
be placed in opposition to the spiritual and temporal power
of the pontiff of Rome; and the wealth and magnificence
of Constantinople may be opposed to that of the Roman
see; though in this respect it would lose nothing by a
comparison with secular as well as spiritual Rome. It is
said that in less than a century after Constantinople was

---

* Constantine declared himself to be the head of the church; as Henry VIII.
subsequently declared himself to be the head of the Church of England, and
Peter I. of the Russo-Greek church.

founded, it "disputed with Rome itself the pre-eminence
of riches and numbers." Constantine, with lavish expen-
diture, adorned the new city with the choicest specimens
of art that could be found in the cities of Greece and
Asia. The imperial palace, as built by Constantine, " ri-
valled the palace of the Cæsars on the Palatine Mount;"
and with the improvements and additions to its magnificence, made by his successors, continued, "during eleven
centuries, the admiration of all who visited the East."
The "church of St. Sophia is thought, in some respects, to
exceed in grandeur and architecture St. Peter's at Rome."
When, in the eleventh century, Constantinople was plundered, almost nine hundred years after the city was founded, and after it had been for several centuries declining,
the treasure that was divided by the captors, was greater
than had ever been found in any conquered city, previous
to that period; and yet "notwithstanding the penalties
of excommunication, and even of death, denounced
against any one who should secrete any part of the spoil,
the secret plunder is supposed to have exceeded what was
produced in public." And this, it will be recollected, after
the plunderings of Rome by Alaric, and other barbarian
conquerors. Bishop Newton, T. Scott, and Doddridge
express the opinion that the description in the twelfth and
thirteenth verses of Rev. 18, includes both actual merchandise, and those spiritual wares, that have been a
source of wealth to Rome. We have seen that Constantinople has equalled, if she did not exceed Rome, in material wealth and magnificence. Those who are acquainted
with the pages of Gibbon, will remember to what extent
criminal intrigue, violence, reckless selfishness, and dire
cruelty prevailed in the eastern capital. Can it be doubted that the power and influence of religious station, and
the opportunities of religious pretence, had their value
and their price, in this mart of wickedness. The wealth
of Rome was derived originally from the plunder of conquered nations, and the rapacity and extortions of the

local governors placed over them, while that of Constantinople was derived from commerce; and Babylon, it need not be said, was pre-eminently commercial. Rev. 18 : 17, 19. *And* EVERY *shipmaster, and* ALL *the company in ships, and sailors, and* AS MANY AS TRADE BY SEA, *stood afar off—and cried, weeping and wailing, saying, Alas, alas, that great city, wherein were made rich all that had ships in the sea.* Need it be said that this is not applicable to Rome, except in a remote sense, while it is eminently applicable to Constantinople? If the words in capitals are to be understood literally, they can be applied only to what is supposed to be the real Babylon.

Rev. 17 : 18. *And the woman which thou sawest is that great city, which reigneth over the kings of the earth.* Considered by itself, this passage must mean the kings of all the earth. And I find nothing opposed to such a construction, it being remembered that there are two judgments of Babylon, the one partial, and the other universal. But I will not insist upon this, here, in the comparison of the two cities. The rule of Babylon is unquestionably *commercial,* or intimately connected with traffick, and the only question is, what kind of traffick is intended. Bishop Newton says, " *Fornication,* in the usual style of scripture, is idolatry:" the inference being that as *Rome is an idolatrous church,* Rome is Babylon. But he cites no decisive proof of this from scripture, and there is negative proof to the contrary. Coloss. 3 : 5. *Mortify therefore your members which are upon the earth ; fornication, uncleanness, inordinate affection, evil concupiscence, and covetousness, which is idolatry.** Covetousness, the love of the world, is idolatry, but *not* the other offences, which are mentioned. It appears a more natural supposition that fornication represents unlawful or dishonest dealing, incited by worldly-mindedness. But however this may be, and whatever Babylon may typify, the chief engine of

*See also Ephes. 5 : 5.

government, in all extended rule, even despotic, in Christian nations, is civil law.

The Civil or Roman law, especially so called, which has served to so great an extent, as the basis of all law, in Europe, and the nations derived from Europe by colonization, was compiled and composed in Constantinople, and thence disseminated, by imperial edict, throughout the Roman world. And it may be doubted whether all that is popularly alleged against Rome, her sale of indulgences, her absolution, confession, penance and masses for the dead, her interference in the affairs of nations, whether by intrigue, by interdict or actual war, has been productive of so much evil, so much wickedness and misery, as the civil law. Should it be alleged that this was unavoidable, are we not furnished with a powerful argument, considering the slow progress of reform, for the necessity of a change in the very mechanism of society? And again, should it be urged that *some law* is indispensable, and that the civil law was the best that could be had, this may be true in a sense, but yet is rather a begging the question. All honour to the noble purpose and zeal of the emperor Justinian; but his minister Trebonian, though in some respects most admirably qualified for the great work, seems to have been a very *composite* character. I have reasons for according to him a general rectitude of purpose, in the prosecution of the task, entrusted to him by the emperor, but this was consistent with his introducing into an immense work, of this description, executed in haste, antiquated and venerable.pedantries of mischievous tendency. And if, in a course like his, he could preserve the original keen perception of natural justice from being blunted or *dispersed*,* it would be difficult to avoid being influenced by the *esprit du corps*. But the principal defect in the Justinian code was perhaps, the want of a simple

---

* Notwithstanding his immense knowledge of law, he is *said* to have had little practical notion of equity.

and practical method of disposing, permanently, of *new cases*, that bugbear to those who doubt the value of all written codes: perhaps thus; by giving, throughout the entire jurisdiction, to the *earliest decision*, in all such cases, with due precautions, (especially employing the briefest and most precise language,) the *force* of law, rather than merely the *authority* of precedent. Slight injustice might sometimes have been perpetuated, but this would have been a trifling evil, compared with others which would have been prevented. Such a course would have tended to prevent litigation on the one hand, and the "law's delay" on the other. It would have exercised a powerful control over corrupt judges; and have tended greatly to check the abuses of power. In our own times, when it is not even surmised that a judge can be bribed, the frequent reversals in the higher courts, (which appears to be a part of the system,) however advantageous to lawyers, are a stain on modern jurisprudence, and tend greatly to throw discredit on the science of law; as do the frequent delays, and perhaps denials of justice, on the most paltry technicalities. Good sense should prevail in courts of law, as well as in the transactions of business. Can it be that the crying, the almost intolerable defects popularly ascribed to the English high court of chancery, are attributable to the circumstance that the proceedings in that court, "are to this day, in a course much conformed to the civil law?" But alas, while society remains as it is, while human nature, trained in the school of individual selfishness remains as it is, while the MYSTERY of Babylon continues, can any considerable and permanent reform be expected, in either of the departments of government? May we indulge a hope that the judgment of Babylon will be the prelude to a better state of things, in which but little law, and that of a paternal character, will be required?

The Patriarch of Constantinople first assumed the rank or office of œcumenical or universal Bishop; and subsequently, the Bishop of Rome, (by way of rejoinder perhaps,) set up the claim of being the successor of St. Peter.

The bishop of Rome was declared universal bishop, by an edict of the Greek emperor Phocas, of the date of 605; not improbably, (considering the character of Phocas,) the result of political calculation, perhaps designed to curb the pride of the Greek Patriarch. At that time, and for 146 years subsequently, Rome was governed, as a dukedom, (such was the style) of the eastern empire, by an officer appointed by the Exarch of Ravenna, who was, in turn, appointed by the Greek emperor. The edict of Phocas could hardly have been regarded as valid, unless he had been recognized as the head of the church. Under these relations of the two seven hilled cities, the *exclusive* claim is set up, for the bishop of Rome, or the Roman hierarchy, (including of course, the seven hilled city,) and commencing with the period above mentioned, of being the alone mystical and spiritual Babylon. Nothing is said, in scripture, to the effect that Babylon increases from feeble beginnings. On the contrary, when first introduced,* *seemingly as cotemporary with John*, she appears in full splendour, *arrayed in purple and scarlet colour, and decked with gold, and precious stones, and pearls ; having a golden cup in her hand*, &c. Purple, it will be recollected, was worn by the Roman emperors. The language of the angel, who proposed to John to shew him the judgment of the great whore, is also remarkable ; *I will shew unto thee the judgment of the great whore* THAT SITTETH UPON MANY WATERS : *with whom the kings of the earth* HAVE *committed fornication, and the inhabitants of the earth* HAVE *been made drunk with the wine*, &c. All the difficulties will be obviated, by supposing that the seven mountains, upon which the woman sitteth, are different portions of the territory of the Roman empire, as at different periods. The Assyrian monarchy being regarded as the first, in point of

---

* Rev. 17. 3—5.

time, the wealth and magnificence of that monarchy, even at an early period, might well have represented Babylon.

Rev. 18 : 7. *For she saith in her heart, I sit a queen, and am no widow, and shall see no sorrow.* How utterly inapplicable is this, to both Rome and Constantinople. Both have experienced great reverses, it can be said of both, that their queenly vestments have been trampled in the dust, that they have been widowed from all most dear to their hearts, of earthly good ; both have been visited with cruel fears, and dire sorrows. For more than four centuries, the Patriarch has exercised his functions under sufferance of a haughty conqueror, an enemy to his faith. On the other hand, some time before this period, Rome was forsaken by the Pontiff, who exercised the duties of his office, and held the papal court, for more than seventy years, in a foreign land : " to the great detriment of Italy and Rome, in which city many of the churches fell to ruins." During the four centuries above mentioned, the Pope was *entirely deprived* of a large portion of his spiritual domain, by the reformation ; and Rome was once more plundered by an invading army, and " subjected to greater calamities than she had ever endured from the northern barbarians." In our own time, the Patriarch and his trembling followers, have been subjected to the fury of the enraged Moslems ;* and Rome has been again conquered, and despoiled of her choicest treasures, of more costliness than ornaments of gold, or jewels of price ; and the venerable Pontiff dragged, with little reverence, from the seven hilled city. The present successor of St. Peter has been compelled to flee to a place of refuge from the violence of his own people ; and is, at the present moment, protected, in his capital, by the troops of a foreign power.

The course of the argument, in the above paragraph, is this. The Babylon described in chapter 17, is the same as that whose final destruction is spoken of in chapter 18.

---

*At the commencement of the Greek revolution.

See chapter 17 : 1, 2; 15; 18, in the entire connexion. Various circumstances, however, in the history of the Roman empire, and of the nations within its limits, required a separate notice of Babylon, as there existing. Babylon, whose catastrophe is described in the eighteenth chapter, *sits a queen, is no widow, fears no sorrow.* But Rome and Constantinople have been unqueened, and widowed, and overwhelmed with fears and sorrows. Therefore, neither of those cities is Babylon, in any primary or individual sense. Just so far as they have made a traffick of spiritual things, or devised evil things, and given them a sacred name, for the purpose of gain, or oppression, &c., just so far they have been identified with the true Babylon; only, as has been observed, presenting a phase of peculiar malignity. As simony may be worse than ordinary bribery, and the sale of indulgencies to sin, than that of incentives to sin; though even here, all would depend upon circumstances. The truth is, spiritual and secular Babylon were inextricably mingled; as the monks of a monastic establishment might exchange their spiritual *merchandise* for the products of the field and the loom. But the secular Babylon greatly predominated, perhaps in the city of Rome; at any rate, throughout the spiritual domain of both Rome and Constantinople. Every city within the limits of the empire, was a seat of Babylon, but Rome and Constantinople being political and commercial centres, as well as places of religious influence, were representative cities. It is only the true, secular, mystical Babylon, considered as an universal system of individual possession, that can say, *I sit a queen, and am no widow, and shall see no sorrow.* Even if we descend to apparent local exceptions, (which however, are hardly more than the bite of an insect, and scarcely worthy of notice,) as when a city is plundered by a vindictive enemy, the spirit of individual possession is intensified, the system, as a principle of evil, is triumphing.

I trust it has been made to appear that Babylon is not a corrupt Christian power, nor any single city; but as I have drawn a comparison between Rome and Constantinople, to shew that under the general system of interpretation adopted by Protestants, the claims of Rome to the bad eminence, are not so complete and exclusive, as has been supposed, it is proper to add, that while, for many centuries after Constantinople was founded, after the bishop of Rome became universal bishop, and after Jerusalem, the "holy city," was conquered by the Turks, Constantinople appears, in many respects, to have had the advantage; yet that since Constantinople was conquered by the Turks, the balance has, seemingly preponderated towards the west. Since then, Rome, notwithstanding her dismemberment at the reformation, has seen a period of great prosperity and splendour, in which she exercised an important influence, in the affairs of the world, and in the midst of events, which seemed tending toward the consummation of the predictions of scripture. The revival of learning, the art of printing, the magnetick needle, and the discoveries of Columbus and De Gamma, introduced a new era. The revival of learning however, was owing in great measure, to the labours of scholars, who had fled, with their books, from Constantinople, where, principally, learning had been cultivated, during the dark ages. Rome once more revived. St. Peter's was finished. Wealth poured in from various sources. A very distinguished writer, cited by bishop Newton, says of the treasures displayed at Loretto, they "as much surpassed my expectation, as other sights have generally fallen short of it. Silver can scarce find an admission, and gold itself looks but poorly amongst such an incredible number of precious stones." The glittering splendours and treasures of art of Rome, were the admiration of Europe. The *Babylonian civilization* of the west, subverting or destroying every thing with which it came in contact, went forth in great measure, at first, from nations under the spiritual domain of Rome. The society of the Jesuits acquired and retained immense influence, in the courts of the kings of Europe, and in the most distant regions; Rome became at least a secondary, a *reflex* Babylon. It seemed as if she were about to acquire more than she had lost by the reformation. But soon a wondrous change came over the scene. Within little more than one hundred years past, the productions of infidel writers, the American and French revolutions; the multiform and ever increasing influence of the press; the new power of *worldly democracy*, as opposed to the *fanatical democracy* of an earlier period;* practical infidelity, semi-belief and indifferentism; philosophical " self-righteousness "; the extension of the colonial power of England; and last, though not least, neological christianity, or infidelity, it is not very material which term is employed, have wrought an entire change, in the condition of the governing nations of the earth. The temporal power of Rome, has dwindled to insignificance; and its spiritual power, though nominally more considerable, is probably more nominal than real. The days of superstition, and implicit belief, are rapidly passing away. Are we on the eve of great prophetical developments?

Little appears to be said, in the more accessible books of reference, concerning the history of the Greek church, since the Turks became possessed of Constantinople. It has been intimated that during this period, the Russo-Greek church has withdrawn from the spiritual jurisdiction of the Patriarch, and that Peter I. declared himself the head of the church. He attempted considerable reforms. It is said that there is more unanimity in the Russian church, than in any other considerable body of Christians. They have not fallen into different denominations, like the Protestants, nor into different schools, so to speak, like the Catholicks. Previous to the Greek revo-

---

*I trust I shall not be misunderstood in the use of these terms. I employ them, as general expressions, in the sense in which I suppose they would be employed, by those best informed. I judge no man.

lution, and perhaps still, the Patriarch at Constantinople, dwelt in a palace; and there were 23 churches of the Greek communion, in the city. The patriarchal church was dedicated to St. George. I will not here insist upon Providential coincidences, signs of the times; it is sufficient that unavoidable association conducts the mind to a kingdom whose patron saint is St. George, and which is the first commercial nation on the globe. Whose chief city, as I have seen it affirmed, like Rome and Constantinople, is seated on seven hills. However this may be, London, the commercial metropolis of the world, must be regarded as the representative city of the Babylon of scripture. St. George was also chosen the patron saint of that nation which discovered the modern route to the wealth of the East; and his name is perhaps connected with more orders of chivalry than that of any other individual. And if the historic record be true, what a worthy patron for the scripture Babylon. In homely parlance, a *trading character*, and "money catcher." An army contractor, and one of the worst of his class. Accused of peculation, he fled from a suit commenced against him, with his ill gotten wealth. Possessed of talent, versatility and energy, he became bishop of Alexandria. Here his avarice and rapacity were such that he was expelled from the city, the people rising against him as one man. Recovering his authority, with much difficulty, he continued his career, till he was ignominiously dragged to prison. Here, after a few days, he was slain in a tumult of the "Pagan populace," (perishing much like the founder of the Mormons,) and thus acquiring the honours of martyrdom. Of course, Pope Gelasius, "who placed him among the martyrs of the churches, rejects his acts as spurious, and the composition of heretics."

VII. BABYLON—IS NOT HEATHENDOM.

Aside from a corrupt christianity, and the individual system, the only other power on earth, I believe, which it can be surmised answers to the description of Babylon, is Paganism. But Paganism can be disposed of in few words. There may be some resemblance, in Paganism, to the traffick, the sorceries, and the persecutions of Babylon; but Babylon is too exclusively and splendidly commercial, and too rich, to represent Paganism. There is a unity about Babylon, which cannot be predicated of Paganism. Instead of being represented by all the gods and goddesses of the pantheon, and many others without the pale of classical mythology, she is personified by a single splendid and wealthy harlot, who sometimes persecutes, but who is greatly *admired* by the *merchants of the earth*, and *all the company in ships, and sailors, and as many as trade by sea—all that had ships in the sea, were made rich, by reason of her costliness*—but none *worshipped* her. Nothing *appears* to be said of worship, in the entire connexion; or nothing but what is quite as susceptible, or more so, of another explanation. Babylon appears to become *more and more* an habitation of devils, instead of *less and less*. See Rev. 18: 2. *All nations* have drunk of the wine of her cup, she reigneth, as has been shewn, over the kings of *all* the earth; but there are nations, like the United States, that have never been Pagan. Her name, *Mother of abominations of the earth*, when so many of these have commenced in nominally christian lands! It is not true of Paganism, that she *sits a queen, and is no widow, and fears no sorrow,* but notoriously the reverse. It is not true that in her will be found at her final destruction, the *blood of prophets, and of saints, and of all that were slain upon the earth.*

*Rev. 18:7.   †Rev. 18:24.

VIII. BABYLON—ADDITIONAL EVIDENCE THAT
BABYLON IS THE INDIVIDUAL SYSTEM—PROOFS
OF THE SOCIAL OR COMMUNITY SYSTEM FROM
THE OLD TESTAMENT.

There is another proof that Babylon is the individual
system, which of itself is well nigh sufficient. It is this.
That if the individual system should be superseded by the
social, there will be a destruction of the former, throughout the earth, very similar, (figuratively speaking,) to that
described in the eighteenth chapter of Revelation. That
the individual system is to be superseded by the social,
there is abundant evidence in the Old Testament, some of
which, as I proposed in a former section, I will now consider. And first, of the vision in the nine last chapters of
the prophet Ezekiel. This, or the first chapter, has already been referred to, but we will go somewhat more into particulars.

No one, at all conversant with the scriptures, can read
this description, without being convinced that it relates to
the glorious period so often referred to, by the prophets of
the Old Testament. Civil government is recognized, but
with few particulars, other than the mention of the prince,
and injunctions to the princes of Israel, in figurative language, to justice and religious observances. See ch. 45:
9—25. The descriptions relate, for the most part, to the
religious establishment, and the social, domestick, and
economick arrangements. Chap. 43: 1, 2; 4—7. *Afterward he brought me to the gate, even the gate that looketh
toward the east: And, behold, the glory of the God of
Israel came from the way of the east: and his voice was
like a noise of many waters: and the earth shined with
his glory. And the glory of the Lord came into the house
by the way of the gate whose prospect is toward the east.
So the spirit took me up, and brought me into the inner
court; and, behold, the glory of the Lord filled the house.
And I heard him speaking unto me out of the house;
and the man stood by me.*

And he said unto me, Son of man, the place of my throne, and the place of the soles of my feet, where I will dwell in the midst of the children of Israel forever. In chapter 47, mention is made of the *healing waters*, which *issued out of the sanctuary*, by which it appears, all vegetable and animal life is *healed*, or, restored to the paradisaical state. At the conclusion, chap. 48: 35, it is said, *And the name of the city from that day shall be, The Lord is there.* That the social organization prevails, is shewn more especially in the fortieth chapter, in which is described *the frame of the city;* but there are not wanting, in the second part of the vision, intimations to the same effect. The cherubim and palm trees on *all the walls of the house round about* seem to indicate a permanent and unfailing supply of food and clothing.* In the vision of the healing waters, ch. 47, and of the *very many trees* on the banks, *all trees for meat*, it is said, ver. 12, *neither shall the fruit thereof be consumed.* Here again permanent and unfailing supply seems to be intimated. Immediately after the above, commences an account of the distribution of the land among the tribes; and it is said, ver. 14, *ye shall inherit it, one as well as another.* If this refers, as seems probable, to individuals, it need not be insisted that the social arrangement can alone, permanently secure this result.†

In chapter 40, verses 35—49, describing the north court, which represents England, we find that while the entire

---

*See ch. 1: 11, and 46: 19—24. As the literal temple at Jerusalem was ornamented with cherubim and palm trees in a similar manner, might there not have been an allusion to the shew-bread, or *continual bread* as it is called, Numb. 4: 7? Twelve loaves, equal to the number of the tribes, were placed upon the golden table of the shew-bread, by the priests of the week, every Sabbath, where they remained during the week. The shew-bread could be lawfully eaten by the priests, but by none else. The meaning of the Hebrew, which is translated shew-bread, is "*bread of faces,*" or " *bread of the faces.*" Does not this designation lead to the *true* or *ultimate* purport of the sacred rite?

†See ch. 47: 21—23. The *lot* here spoken of, especially as concerning an inheritance for strangers, may refer to various things, other than individual possession, sufficient for the maintenance of a family. Indeed, in a small country

structure is called the *frame of a city*, this court is called a *house :* see ver. 45, 46, 47. The length of the ranges of buildings surrounding this and the other courts, is over seven hundred feet, with two tiers of rooms. The height is not specified, but as the height of the gates is over 90 feet,—fifty cubits, doubtless the sacred cubit—the height of the building could hardly have been less than eight or ten stories, affording space for from 600 to 1,000 inhabitants, numbers, perhaps, "which it would not be expedient to fall short of or exceed, in the organization of a social community, designed to assemble together for public worship." The emblems of civil government are at the east gate of this court,* shewing that while considered as part of the *frame of a city,*† this court is a *house,* considered as part of a map of the eastern world, it is a MODEL KINGDOM. A striking evidence of the intent of the vision appears to be found in verses 4, 5, of this chapter, (40): Ver. 4, *And the man* (Ezekiel's conductor, mentioned in the verse preceding,) *said unto me, Son of man, behold with thine eyes, and hear with thine ears, and set thine heart upon all that I shall show thee ; for to the intent that I might show them unto thee, art thou brought hither: declare all that thou seest to the house of Israel.* After this impressive injunction, designed to signify that every particular had an important meaning, the narrative proceeds. Ver. 5. *And behold a wall on the outside of the house round about, and in the man's hand a measuring reed of six cubits long by the cubit, and an hand breadth : so he measured the breadth of the building, one reed ; and the height, one reed.* The length of the reed, (if measured by the sacred cubit,) was very nearly eleven feet. The building was therefore about eleven feet square ; and was surrounded, as appears probable, by a wall, though the language is not perhaps, entirely un-

---

like Palestine, progressive subdivisions of land, would soon render this impossible; not to mention that under a general and comprehensive system of husbandry, (well administered,) the land would be far more productive, than under individual superintendence.

*Ver. 48, 49. See Millennial Institutions. †Ver. 2.

equivocal. The building was undoubtedly intended to represent a dwelling of the smallest size, of those designed for the individual form of society; and thus, by the way of contrast, to place beyond doubt, the principal meaning of the vision of the city. If the building were surrounded by a wall, this would strikingly represent the isolation of the individual system.

Mention has been made, in a former section, of the sacrificial tables at the north court; and of the chambers of the singers, those of the priests, the keepers of the charge of the house, and of the priests the keepers of the charge of the altar. We have seen that the visionary temple, and also the literal temple at Jerusalem, were profusely ornamented with figures of cherubim and palm trees. In the frame of a city there are no cherubim, and the palm trees are employed sparingly. They are found only on the posts of the gates: see ver. 16, 22, 26, 31, 34, 37. And it is a noticeable circumstance that while at all the gates, with one exception, the posts are turned towards the entries of the gates, at the north gate, they are turned outward, towards the north, and of course toward the sacrificial tables. The absence of the cherubim seems to prove that the emblem of the palm trees is to be understood as having a secular meaning. They are placed only upon the posts of the gates to signify that the emblem relates to ordinary life. An idea is also conveyed of permanence and stability. While the obvious connexion of the posts and the palm trees at the north gate, with the sacrificial tables, shews that *the burnt offering, the sin offering, and the trespass offering*—see ver. 39—43—*the burnt offering and the sacrifice*, denote ordinary food, prepared, not by *the priests the keepers of the charge of the altar*, but by *the priests the keepers of the charge of the house*. The altar, it will be perceived—see ver. 47—was before the house, or in front of the east gate. See ver. 42. What are the *instruments wherewith they slew the sacrifices*, but the ordinary furniture of the table? Ver. 43. *And within were hooks, an hand* *broad, fastened round about.* The alternative reading is *and-irons,* or, *the two hearth stones.** That the palm trees refer in the present instance to common food, appears from the circumstance that the fruit of the palm, (the date palm is undoubtedly intended,) is not mentioned, though in the East "constituting an important article of food," among the sacred offerings, under the Jewish ritual. " A distinguished naturalist remarks ' the region of palms is the first country of the human race, and man is essentially *pal-mivorous.' "*

The additional evidence of the social system, which I have observed in the Old Testament, is found, in two chapters, consecutive, of Isaiah, of which more hereafter. In a considerable number of passages, more or less obscure, but the meaning of which, it being granted that the individual system is to be superseded by the social, is sufficiently evident. And lastly, there are a few passages, which afford internal evidence that the introduction of the millennium is to be preceded or accompanied by such a change. I will here refer to some of these, premising that I shall limit myself for the most part, to the questions at issue, the downfall of the individual, and the rise of the social system ; with little regard to the extraneous matters, which are mingled, or more or less directly associated with the passages which will be cited ; though I may refer, as occasion requires, to the context.

Is. 4 : 5, 6. *And the Lord will create upon every dwelling-place of Mount Zion, and upon her assemblies, a cloud and smoke by day, and the shining of a flaming fire by night : for upon all the glory shall be a defence. And there shall be a tabernacle for a shadow in the daytime from the heat, and for a place of refuge, and for a covert from storm and from rain.* That this passage relates to the millennium appears from verse 3 of the same chapter. *And it shall come to pass that he that*

---

*Andiron. "Irons at the end of a fire grate, in which the spit turns."—Eng. Dic.

is left in Zion, and he that remaineth in Jerusalem, shall be called holy, even every one that is written among the living in Jerusalem. It also appears from ver. 4, in connexion with ver. 16—26 of the chapter preceding, that before this change will happen, the vanities of emulation in dress, fashion, and display, will have ceased. This alone well nigh proves a radical change in the constitution of society. Ver. 5. *And the Lord will create upon every dwelling-place of Mount Zion, and upon her assemblies, a cloud and smoke by day, and the shining of a flaming fire by night.* Here the *dwelling-places* and the *assemblies* are put in opposition. A *cloud,* (which could hardly rest upon *every dwelling-place* designed for a single family,) rests upon each dwelling, by day; as a smoke, to pursue the figure, (and alluding to the pillar of smoke in the wilderness,) leads the inmates up to the place of the solemn assembly, resting upon it.* *And the shining of a flaming fire by night.* Here again, is an allusion to the journeying in the wilderness. The *fire by night* was moving or stationary, as the Jews were travelling or at rest. *For upon all the glory shall be a defence.* Not a defence from external enemies, for there will be none to *molest, or make afraid;* but from anxious cares, from want, and probably may be added, from pestilence. This view is fully confirmed in the next verse. *And there shall be a tabernacle for a shadow in the day-time from the heat, and for a place of refuge, and for a covert from storm and from rain.* A *tabernacle,* not *tabernacles.* There is not a single expression, which seems, (in the connexion,) to recognize the existence of dwellings, designed for single families.

Is. 14 : 29—32. *Rejoice not thou, whole Palestina, because the rod of him that smote thee is broken: for out of the serpent's root shall come forth a cockatrice, and his fruit shall be a fiery flying serpent. And the first-born of the poor shall feed, and the needy shall lie down in safety: and I will kill thy root with famine, and he shall slay thy remnant. Howl, O gate; cry, O city; thou, whole Palestina, art dissolved: for there shall*

*See Ex. 13 : 21, 22; 33 : 9; Numb. 9 : 15—23, ver. 19 with ch. 1 : 53, 3 : 5—8.

come from the north a smoke, and none shall be alone in his appointed times. What shall one then answer the messengers of the nation? That the Lord hath founded Zion, and the poor of his people shall trust in it. Verse 29 relates to vicissitudes in the Jewish nation, which it is not within my present plan to consider. Ver. 30. *And the first-born of the poor shall feed.* Provision is made for the first-born of the poor, *though they should marry young.* It will not be needful for them to labour, to accumulate a store, previous to marriage. *And the needy shall lie down in safety.* Free from the fear of want, whether arising from lack of employment, or inability to labour. Ver. 31. *Thou whole Palestina art dissolved.* This undoubtedly alludes to the dispersion. *For there shall come from the north a smoke, and none shall be alone in his appointed times.* If the *frame of a city,* which the prophet Ezekiel saw in the *land of Israel,* includes England; and if there is allusion, under appropriate emblems, to culinary *and sacrificial* fires, and to a union of the people, in which *none would be alone,* can there be a doubt of the meaning of this passage? Ezek. 40: 2. *In the visions of God brought he me into the land of Israel, and set me upon a very high mountain, by which was as the frame of a city on the south.* The frame of a city was, it seems, to the south of the very high mountain. The high mountain then, represented England, so plainly indicated in the frame of a city, considered as a map. Is. 2: 2. *And it shall come to pass in the last days, that the mountain of the Lord's house shall be established in the top of the mountains, and shall be exalted above the hills; and all nations shall flow unto it.* The true, millennial, social union is to be established in England, is to be copied thence, in Palestine, after the restoration, and to proceed thence throughout the earth. Ver. 32. *What shall one then answer the messengers of the nation? That the Lord hath founded Zion, and the poor of his people shall trust in it.* Some nation sends messengers to Palestine, after this great change in their condition, to inquire concerning their prospects. Some particular nation is referred to, which coincides with, and confirms the above. See verses 22—27. There is a purpose of the Most High, connected with ancient Babylon, which relates to the *whole earth*, to *all the nations*. How singularly this confirms our exposition, above, of the Babylon of Revelation, if we suppose that the *yoke*, ver. 25, relates to unjust and oppressive rule, and the *burden* to the social and worldly customs and practices, of which Babylon was the centre, and great example.

Is. 32: 13—20. *Upon the land of my people shall come up thorns and briers; yea, upon all the houses of joy in the joyous city: Because the palaces shall be forsaken; the multitude of the city shall be left; the forts and towers shall be for dens forever, a joy of wild asses, a pasture of flocks; until the spirit be poured upon us from on high, and the wilderness be a fruitful field, and the fruitful field be counted for a forest. Then judgment shall dwell in the wilderness, and righteousness remain in the fruitful field. And the work of righteousness shall be peace; and the effect of righteousness, quietness and assurance for ever. And my people shall dwell in a peaceable habitation, and in sure dwellings, and in quiet resting places; When it shall hail, coming down on the forest; and the city shall be low in a low place. Blessed are ye that sow beside all waters, that send forth thither the feet of the ox and the ass.* Verses 13, 14 clearly indicate a radical change in the *form* of society. Ver. 14. *The multitude of the city shall be left.* As those without gradually adhere to a better social organization, in which industrial arts are practised, without the evils incident at present, to factories, and in which more rational employments and amusements are cultivated, they will resort less and less to the city. While the city, notwithstanding the extremely artificial condition, which at present prevails, even in the lowest haunts of ignorance and destitution, will gradually lapse in the direction of primitive barbarism; till it becomes a *joy* only to those who obstinately adhere to the earliest "social compact," now becoming obsolete, and in which the individual tenure is guarded, so to speak, with military precautions and vigilance. Ver. 15. *Until the Spirit be poured upon us from on high.* The partial reformation, indicated above, will prepare the way for the blessed influences of God's Holy Spirit. *And the wilderness be a fruitful field, and the fruitful field be counted for a forest.* Here is an allusion to the *tree husbandry,* spoken of in Ezek. 47: 1—12. Ordinarily a *wilderness* is too extensive for individual possession, or to be called a *field,* in the sense in which the word is employed, when it is said that men *add field to field.* But under the improved, millennial husbandry—arboriculture—with community of interest, the *wilderness* becomes a *fruitful field,* and the *fruitful field* a forest. Ver. 16. *Then judgment shall dwell in the wilderness, and righteousness remain in the fruitful field.* The highest science will prevail in the new system of husbandry; and the few and simple laws regulating the distribution of the labour, and of the product of the *fruitful field* will be founded in equity—millennial equity. Ver. 17. *And the work of righteousness shall be peace; and the effect of righteousness, quietness and assurance forever.* Has such righteousness as has prevailed hitherto, produced any such results? or *would any such as can prevail under the individual system,* &c.? 18. *And my people shall dwell in a peaceable habitation, and in sure dwellings, and in quiet resting places.* Observe the language: a peaceable *habitation,* not peaceable habitations. 19. *When it shall hail, coming down on the forest.* Here apparently, is an allusion to some especial excellence, or advantage, in the system of tree husbandry. See ch. 45: 8. *And the city shall be low in a low place.* The alternative reading, in the margin, and there can be little doubt, the true reading, is, *and the city shall be utterly abased.* 20. *Blessed are ye that sow beside all waters.* Here is an allusion to the true system of vegetation, and to some most interesting particulars in the new system of husbandry. I hope to be able to speak of both hereafter. *That send forth thither the feet of the ox and the ass.* Domestick animals first, and finally, (as we shall soon see, in another portion of scripture,) all the lower orders of the creation, as they were made partakers, by the curse, of the consequences of the fall, so will they partake of the advantages of a renovated husbandry.

Is. 65: 17—25. *For, behold, I create new heavens and a new earth: and the former shall not be remembered, nor come into mind. But be ye glad and rejoice for ever in that which I create: for, behold, I create Jerusalem a rejoicing, and her people a joy. And I will rejoice in Jerusalem, and joy in my people; and the voice of weeping shall be no more heard in her, nor the voice of crying. There shall be no more thence an infant of days, nor an old man that hath not filled his days: for the child shall die a hundred years old; but the sinner being a hundred years old shall be accursed. And they shall build houses, and inhabit them; and they shall plant vineyards, and eat the fruit of them. They shall not build, and another inhabit; they shall not plant, and another eat: for as the days of a tree are the days of my people, and mine elect shall long enjoy the work of their hands. They shall not labour in vain, nor bring forth for trouble; for they are the seed of the blessed of the Lord, and their offspring with them. And it shall come to pass, that before they call, I will answer; and while they are yet speaking, I will hear. The wolf and the lamb shall feed together, and the lion shall eat straw like the bullock: and dust shall be the serpent's meat. They shall not hurt nor destroy in all my holy mountain, saith the* LORD. It is very probable, see ver. 17, that the terrestrial heavens, or the atmosphere, will be improved and meliorated,* by the action of the imponderable elements, under the direction of science, in processes of greater extent than has hitherto been dreamed of. Concerning the *new earth*, something has already been said. There is a character of permanence, in the domestick institutions described in this passage, which is

---

*Can it be doubted that the atmosphere was affected by the curse, or the deluge, or perhaps by both? That it is now very different from that of Paradise?

utterly inconsistent with any results which the individual system has yet afforded. See ver. 21—23. Ver. 25 seems to intimate that there will be a surprising improvement in vegetable products. Carnivorous animals can now be inured by degrees, to the use of a proportion of vegetable food; and modern chemistry informs us that the difference between animal and vegetable food, is not so great as might be supposed. But an entire change seems to be wrought in the disposition of the savage and carnivorous animals. Discipline, and the fear of man, as men increase, with abundance of vegetable food, *bearing a still nearer resemblance to animal food*, might accomplish considerable; but is it too much to suppose that the change will be effected, in part at least, by influences from above? The power which preserved Daniel in the den of lions, will perhaps be employed to effect an enduring change, at least in the temper and disposition of the savage animals, either without or in addition to secondary means, such as this description supposes. *And dust shall be the serpent's meat.* Is the serpent to be an exception? Is it quite sure that the translators have supplied the omission in this passage correctly? Might it not read, And dust *shall* NOT *be* the serpent's meat? Especially in view of what immediately follows. *They shall not hurt nor destroy in all my holy mountain.* The occasional presence, in the haunts of men, of animals that had previously been fierce and wild, seems to be here implied; *somewhat perhaps, as in Paradise.*

Jer. 23: 4. *And I will set up shepherds over them which shall feed them: and they shall fear no more, nor be dismayed, neither shall they be lacking, saith the Lord.* This passage will require no comment.

The following section was written, or commenced near the close of the year 1859, as the beginning of a work, which I then contemplated. After having made considerable progress, I found myself entirely disabled from writing. When I again commenced, the reasons for a change of plan were such that I began anew. The following section however, chimed in so well with my present purpose, that I have concluded to give it entire, (or perhaps with very slight variations,) though this will involve some repetitions, and perhaps some want of logical arrangement.

X. BABYLON—ADDITIONAL EVIDENCE FROM THE OLD TESTAMENT, RESPECTING THE INDIVIDUAL AND SOCIAL SYSTEMS—FAITH IN THE MILLENNIUM—DESCRIPTION OF THE MILLENNIUM—THE "WAY"—DESTRUCTION OF THE INDIVIDUAL SYSTEM—THE INDIVIDUAL SYSTEM A REGULAR PREPARATION FOR THE MILLENNIUM—SOCIAL SYSTEM, MEANS, INTERPOSITION — DEMONIAC POSSESSION—ODIC FORCE—SOCIALISM AN INDISPENSIBLE CONDITION OF THE MILLENNIUM —SOCIAL UNION—INSTANCES OF SOCIAL COMMUNITIES.

Some there are who, in consequence of a religious education, have a dreamy, shadowy belief that in the distant future there will be a time when all will be just and honest—religious—when abundance will universally prevail, when existing civil, political and social institutions will be only of beneficent tendency. But this truth is one with which they have no practical concern, it belongs to another period, to quite another generation of men. But where are they who possess an abiding, practical belief; who obey the great injunction to watch? It is a solemn question, *Nevertheless when the Son of Man cometh, shall he find faith on the earth?*

There are many who believe in what is popularly denominated, *the good time coming;* but their notions are variant, and devoid of coherence; *each one forms an idol for himself;* as no two see the same rainbow, so no two see the same good time coming. There are also philosophists or philosophers so called, who believe in the *perfectibility of human nature*, and a corresponding perfectibility of art and science. But their theories are also diverse, and they are perhaps for the most part, unbelievers in revelation.

In contrast with the above the "good time coming" of the scriptures, has the advantage of being determinate, of being circumstantially and accurately described. We are told that the growth of Eden will be restored. *For the Lord shall comfort Zion : he will comfort all her waste places ; and he will make her wilderness like Eden, and her desert like the garden of the Lord ; joy and gladness shall be found therein, thanksgiving, and the voice of melody.* Is. 51 : 3.* This restoration is to be brought about by the application of scientifick principles. *There shall be an handful of corn in the earth upon the top of the mountains ; the fruit thereof shall shake like Lebanon, and they of the city shall flourish like grass of the earth.*† Those who have seen the magnificent cones of the Lebanon cedars, will be able to appreciate the reference to Lebanon. See Is. 28 : 23—29. The improved and restored products of the earth, by improving the human organism, *material and spiritual*, will tend to *produce righteousness, to cause salvation—Drop down ye heavens, from above, and let the skies pour down righteousness ; let the earth open, and let them bring forth salvation, and let righteousness spring up together ; I the Lord have created it.* Is. 45 : 8. The same cause will aid in producing such a change in the stamina, the temperament and *morale* of the lower orders of the crea-

---

* Some might contend that this language was *only* figurative, that it described the rejuvenescence of THE CHURCH, or perhaps of *the Jewish church;* but I incline to believe that it relates to material as well as spiritual restoration. See, in the connexion, ver. 1: *Hearken to me ye that follow after righteousness, ye that seek the Lord: look unto the rock whence ye are hewn, and to the hole of the pit whence ye are digged.* The *rock* may represent the earth as after the curse—Gen. 3 : 17—19—and *the hole of the pit* will describe the state of sin and death to which man was reduced by the first transgression.

† City: see Ezek. 40 with 47 : 1—12.

tion, that they will dwell together in peace, will no longer hurt or devour one another. *The wolf also shall dwell with the lamb, and the leopard shall lie down with the kid ; and the calf and the young lion and the fatling together ; and a little child shall lead them. And the cow and the bear shall feed; their young shall lie down together :* AND THE LION SHALL EAT STRAW LIKE THE OX. Is. 11: 6, 7. *The wolf and the lamb* SHALL FEED TOGETHER, and THE LION SHALL EAT STRAW LIKE THE BULLOCK :—*They shall not hurt nor destroy in all my holy mountain, saith the Lord.* Is. 65 : 25.

The poor will be abundantly provided for: or rather there will not be any poor. *For the needy shall not always be forgotten : the expectation of the poor shall not perish forever.* Ps. 9 : 18. *And in this mountain shall the Lord of hosts make unto all people a feast of fat things, a feast of wines on the lees, of fat things full of marrow, of wines on the lees well refined. And he will destroy in this mountain the face of the covering cast over all people, and the vail that is spread over all nations. He will swallow up death in victory : and the Lord God will wipe away tears from off all faces ; and the rebuke of his people shall he take away from off all the earth : for the Lord hath spoken it.* Is. 25: 6—8. *And the work of righteousness shall be peace ; and the effect of righteousness, quietness and assurance forever. And my people shall dwell in a peaceable habitation, and in sure dwellings, and in quiet resting places.* Is. 32: 17, 18. Righteousness will universally prevail. *They shall not hurt nor destroy in all my holy mountain : for the earth shall be full of the knowledge of the Lord, as the waters cover the sea.* Is. 11: 9. See also, above. Of the Jews, after the restoration, it is said: *Thy people also shall be all righteous.* Is. 60: 21. Wars shall cease. *And he shall judge among the nations, and shall rebuke many people : and they shall beat their swords into ploughshares, and their spears into pruning-hooks : nation shall not lift up sword against nation, neither shall they learn war any more.* Is. 2 : 4. The "days of the years" of men will be extended, so as to equal the age of the patriarchs before the flood. *For as the days of a tree are the days of my people.* Is. 65 : 22. All will be "kings and priests"; but in a sense how different from that of some modern politicians, and their deluded followers; how different, as respects worldly advantages, from that of the early periods of the church, of which it is said; *Unto him that loved us, and washed us from our sins in his own blood, And hath made us* KINGS AND PRIESTS *unto God and his Father; to him be glory and dominion forever and ever. Amen. Behold he cometh with clouds; and every eye shall see him, and they also which pierced him: and all kindreds of the earth shall wail because of him. Even so. Amen.* Rev. 1 : 5—7. There is most important instruction in this sublime passage. It should teach us to strive to be prepared for the coming, whenever it shall be; for, *of that day and hour knoweth no man.*

This glorious state of the church, of the world, in which every one will have all the solid advantages of wealth, will be instructed in righteousness, and will have abundant opportunities for exercising all legitimate influence, and for doing good, is to be brought about, under Providence, by means. *And a highway shall be there,* AND A WAY, *and it shall be called The way of holiness; the unclean shall not pass over it; but it shall be for those: the wayfaring men, though fools, shall not err therein. No lion shall be there, nor any ravenous beast shall go up thereon, it shall not be found there; but the redeemed shall walk there: And the ransomed of the Lord shall return, and come to Zion with songs and everlasting joy upon their heads: they shall obtain joy and gladness, and sorrow and sighing shall flee away.* Is. 35 : 8—10.*

What is this WAY, in addition to the *highway,* which is called *the way of holiness?* Consider the uses of a highway. It leads to solitary dwellings, to hamlets, villages,

---

*See also Is. 62 : 10, 11. *To be accomplished in due time.*

towns, cities. It leads to lands held under the individual tenure of property. I cannot doubt that this *way*, is a social union, which seems to be predicted in various places in the scriptures, which is somewhat elaborately described in the fortieth chapter of Ezekiel, and portions of the chapters following, under architectural emblems, and those of the tenure and cultivation of land; and of which, various social arrangements, especially those of Meacham, the founder of the social and economical polity of the Shaking Quakers, or Millennial Church, and of Robert Owen, are a dim foreshadowing. An examination of the entire section, from which the passage above is cited, comprising chapters thirty-four and thirty-five of Isaiah, will I believe shew this conclusively; and as this social union is believed to be an indispensible preliminary of the millennium, it may be not inappropriate to give a brief analysis of the two chapters.

Chapter thirty-four commences thus : *Come near, ye nations, to hear ; and hearken, ye people : let the earth hear, and all that is therein ; the world, and all things that come forth of it. For the indignation of the Lord is upon all nations, and his fury upon all their armies : he hath utterly destroyed them, he hath delivered them to the slaughter. Their slain also shall be cast out, and their stink shall come up out of their carcasses, and the mountains shall be melted with their blood. And all the host of heaven shall be dissolved, and the heavens shall be rolled together as a scroll : and all their host shall fall down, as the leaf falleth off from the vine, and as a falling fig from the fig tree. For my sword shall be bathed in heaven : behold it shall come down upon Idumea, and the people of my curse to judgment.* Here, at the close, there would seem to be a lamentable anti-climax, were it not for the concluding words: *and the people of my curse to judgment.* It must be supposed that Edom, or Idumea, on account of some specialty, is put emphatically for all the nations of the earth. There are three or four circumstances in the history of Edom, which will require to be considered in this connexion. First, the inhabitants were descended from Esau; and it is not improbable that by reason of blood, of tradition, of example, and precept, the characteristics of Esau were transmitted to his descendants. Obadiah, verse 6. *How are the things of Esau searched out! how are his hidden things sought up.* Second, Herod, who was king of the Jewish nation, under the Romans, at the time of the birth of the Saviour, and who slew the children at Bethlehem; and his son, who beheaded John the Baptist, were princes of Idumean descent. See, third, Obadiah, verses 10—16. But it is the remaining circumstance which appears to claim particular attention. The capital of Idumea, Petra, (capital of western Idumea, as Bozrah was the chief city of the eastern division,) has been visited somewhat latterly, for the first time perhaps, since the revival of letters, by intelligent Europeans. It is situated in a rocky gorge, and on the face of the steep rock, there are still visible, artificial excavations, which were formerly used as dwellings. Hence the exclamation of the prophet of woe to Edom: *The pride of thine heart hath deceived thee,* THOU THAT DWELLEST IN THE CLEFTS OF THE ROCK, *whose habitation is high; that saith in his heart, Who shall bring me down to the ground.* Obadiah verse 3. Is there, on the face of the earth, another such emblem of the "individual system"? The rocky gorge, representing communities, and the various tenements, that exclusive and carefully guarded *selfishness*, which must form the basis of the individual tenure.

We will now advert to some of the passages in the section under consideration, which seem to shew, (in the entire connexion,) that the *way*, which is *the way of holiness*, consists, (so far as it is external, and tangible,) in the advantages of a *scriptural* social union.

And first, observe the remarkable similarity of chapter thirty-four, to the eighteenth chapter of Revelation. There Babylon is put for a *somewhat*, that has exercised a hurtful, and most extraordinary influence, in the affairs of men, from the earliest periods : *And in her was found the blood of prophets, and of saints, and of all that were slain upon* ₊ *the earth.* Rev. 18 : 24. Here Edom appears to be a representative, in like manner. In a former work, (Millennial Institutions,) I have endeavored to shew that the chapter in Revelation describes the downfall of the individual system. A comparison of the two chapters will make it very probable that they refer to one and the same thing. *And in her was found the blood of prophets, and of saints, and of all that were slain upon the earth.* It is worthy of observation perhaps, that the first murder was connected with the individual holding of property. Had Cain and Abel offered a mutual sacrifice, there would have been more fraternal feeling, and much less likelihood of that jealousy, which led to the fatal result. The same cause has been productive, of course more or less directly, of all wars, all revenges that have led to slaughter and murder, all publick executions, all homicides.

Is. 34 : 1, cited above. Why is the *earth* called upon, so emphatically, to hear, in addition to the *nations*, and in connexion with the *world*, unless this solemn call, this call of doom, refers to the *soil*, and the arrangements of men concerning it. Verse 5. *For my sword shall be bathed in heaven.* This extraordinary expression can hardly refer to the *justice* of heaven. Must it not rather allude to the perfect social arrangements of the blest? *The sword of the Lord is filled with blood.* Ver. 6. That is, after it descends to the earth. See the remainder of the verse. Verse 7. *And the unicorns shall come down with them.* What can represent more perfectly than the one horn of the unicorn, the singleness of purpose, and the somewhat aggressive and belligerent attitude of individual selfishness? *And the bullocks with the bulls.* Here, by an odd figure of speech, *families* seem to be intended. Verses 8, 9. *For it is the day of the Lord's vengeance, and the year of recompenses for the controversy of Zion. And the streams thereof shall be turned into pitch, and the dust thereof into brim-*

stone, *and the land thereof shall become burning pitch.* It
seems not quite clear whether the words above, *the streams
thereof,* refer to the word Zion, in the verse preceding, or
to the words *land,* and *land of Idumea* in verses 6, 7. I
incline to believe that all should be included ; for until the
change, the great destruction here described, the affairs of
the *Spiritual Zion,* under whatever designation, are inextricably connected with the individual regime. Towards the
close of the continuance of the individual system, upheld
by worldly-minded and desperate adherents, its *current
will become clogged,* as would a river, if its stream were con-
verted into pitch ; while its minor transactions will be rendered repulsive, to those who are becoming acquainted
with a better arrangement; till at last the whole substra-
tum is, as it were, in flames. How similar are the figures
in Revelation. Rev. 18 : 8. *And she shall be utterly burned
with fire.* Ver. 17, 18. *And every shipmaster, and all the
company in ships, and sailors, and as many as trade by sea, stood
afar off, and cried when they saw the smoke of her burning.*

Verses 9—17, of the chapter in Isaiah, speak of the final,
and irretrievable destruction of the individual form of society ; and describe a number of the more prominent varieties of character, which are inevitably formed under its
influence. Doubtless there will be memorials of the
earlier social arrangement, long after the millennium has
commenced : architectural, monumental, including mor-
tuary inscriptions, works of art, libraries, museums of various sciences, publick records, archives of families, and
cherished mementos, which have descended, perhaps from
the time of the crusades, or a still earlier period. But
with little exception, a few immortal dreams :

> All save immortal dreams that could beguile
> The blind old man of Scio's rocky isle.—*Byron.*

and a few immortal discoveries, with what an indescribable
sense of desolateness, will the most of these strike the
heart; like the arrow heads, and stone axes of our aborig-

inal inhabitants, which the plough sometimes reveals. But this is not the everlasting desolation spoken of in the text, and which will exist only in the historic record, (doubtless an *enlightened* historic record, illumining the dusky memorials of an earlier period;) and the traditions, the minds, of men; and fully justifying the language of the inspired page. Ver. 9, 10. *And the land thereof shall become burning pitch. It shall not be quenched night nor day; the smoke thereof shall go up forever: from generation to generation it shall lie waste; none shall pass through it forever and ever.* Ver. 11. *He shall stretch out upon it the line of confusion and the stones of emptiness.* This is already done in the minds of those who understand the evils of the individual system. In like manner to the above, the different classes of character which are described, *shall possess it forever: from generation to generation shall they dwell therein.*

These are described in a strain of sacred poetry, of almost unrivalled grandeur, and replete with the very spirit of desolation. It is said of them as described under the several emblems, verse 16, *Seek ye out of the book of the Lord, and read: no one of these shall fail, none shall want her mate.* The list commences thus: verse 11, referring to verse 10, cited above. *But the cormorant and the bittern shall possess it.* The former of these is proverbial for his rapacity; the bittern ranges about in fenny places, and is distinguished by a peculiar cry. Of these only is it said that they shall *possess* the realm of desolation. This is perhaps worthy of remark, and may help us to assign to them their *mates*, as according to the language of the text. Mention is then made of the *owl* and the *raven;* of *dragons* (winged serpents,) and of *owls;* marginal reading, or *ostriches.* Ver. 14. *The wild beasts of the desert shall also meet with the wild beasts of the island, and the satyr shall cry to his fellow.* Have we here the devices and secret understanding of the larger commerce, and its accompaniment, unrestrained licentiousness? *The screech owl also shall rest there, and find for herself a place of rest.* The screech owl may perhaps represent the more immediate getters-up of *panics.* The list concludes with *the great owl* and *the vultures.* Is the great owl put for the Lord Chancellor; and also perhaps, generally, for the chiefs of the higher judicatories? That his presence is really suggestive, appears by a recent circumstance, the death, in England, of an aged owl, one of a succession of owls that have been kept in an ancient tower, for many generations, and the more eminent of which have borne the names of different chancellors. The venerable individual recently deceased, was known as chancellor Thurlow. The writers of fiction, who seem, from the days of Smollet, and I know not how much earlier a period, to have had an hereditary or prescriptive dislike of lawyers, might imagine that the vultures meant them.

Chapter 35 : 1, 2. *The wilderness and the solitary place shall be glad for them; and the desert shall rejoice and blossom as the rose. It shall blossom abundantly, and rejoice even with joy and singing: the glory of Lebanon shall be given unto it, the excellency of Carmel and Sharon; they shall see the glory of the Lord, and the excellency of our God.—The wilderness and the solitary place shall be glad for them.* That is, for the different varieties of character described in the preceding chapter. They will prepare the way for that better state of things, which is predicted.

My limits will not admit of going into a more particular examination of this extraordinary portion of scripture —(chapters 34, 35.)—I will conclude by citing the words of the text: *Seek ye out of the book of the Lord, and read.*

I will add a few words as to the social organization of society, or socialism, or the social or community system. It is a curious circumstance that nearly all the more staid, and respectable, and "religious" portion of the community, are exceedingly hostile to the social system, if, indeed, they do not regard it as a basis for infidelity and license. May not a principal reason be that these, owing to favorable circumstances, enjoy most of the advantages of the individual organization, while they are comparatively exempt from its evils; and that they ascribe the evil and misery, which they witness around them, *too exclusively* to depravity, "bad conduct," and want of foresight, without allowing sufficiently for the inherent defects, and inevitable tendencies of the individual arrangement? the integral constitution of society by private families instead of small communities or "families"—FAMILIES—as they are called by the Shaking Quakers. Doubtless, in a sense, all moral evil is owing to *depravity ;* or, to state it a little more clearly to the apprehension of some, to liability, in our present existence, to numerous temptations on the one hand, and to frailty, the consequence of an imperfect nature, or organization, on the other. But, some circumstances are more favorable, beyond comparison, to the development of the depraved tendency, than others. Every discreet parent, who endeavors to "train up his child in the way he should go," understands this. The chief of the unfavourable circumstances are, first, an imperfect and ill balanced organization.* The next in order, of the unfavourable circumstances, is want of instruction and discipline in early life, when the character is formed ; (though indeed, the whole train of evil influences, is sometimes combined, in that period ;) then come idleness and want of employment, bad example, innumerable .temptations, with the facilities for gratification, afforded by the individual organization of society, destitution, and misery.

In a former work—Millennial Institutions, 1833—I propose the theory that since, in a well planned, and faithfully conducted social organization, most of these unfavour-

---

* By this I mean, not merely that organization liable to irregular and unreasonable feelings and passions, to pain, sickness and death, which our first parents necessarily transmitted, after their own organization was reduced to this condition, by eating the forbidden fruit ; but an organization which is an unspeakable descent from this ; and which is owing in most cases, to a violation of natural laws, through a succession of generations.

able circumstances might be obviated, the people would be, in an equal ratio, prepared to receive those influences of the Spirit, which alone form the true basis of the Christian character. I recognized the momentous truth, (which social reformers, for the most part, it is to be feared, overlook,) comprised in the well known declaration, *Not by might, not by power, but by my Spirit, saith the Lord of hosts.*

Metaphysicians will differ greatly, as to the positive value of second causes, of that class or series known in the affairs of men, by the designation of "means," more especially. My own opinion is, that they have a real value, conferred upon them, accorded to them, by the great Disposer of events; that their influence, however subtile and occult, is exercised in accordance with laws, no less determinate and infallible, than those which govern the revolutions of the heavenly bodies. If there be any exception to this rule, it is found in the *voluntary decisions of moral agents*—FREE AGENTS—for men, in their present state, are able to *decide*, and often do, in opposition to motive, as well as in accordance with it; (having thus *more liberty* than the angels, who have not sinned;) and I apprehend it will be found to be a fatal defect in the Edwardean philosophy, that passion, appetite, the various irregular and unreasonable impulses to which men are subject, are confounded with *motive*.

In addition to the influences, which ordinarily govern in the affairs of men, it appears that in consequence of the irregularities introduced into the system of *the earth and the world*, by the fall, the righteous government of God requires occasional interposition; differing from miracle in this, that there is no apparent or known disturbance of the ordinary and established course of events. This is in accordance with the whole tenor of scripture, in which instances of such interposition are given; it is for such interposition that men pray, if, indeed, their prayers have any meaning, more than that of an excellent person, whom I have heard offer this petition: "hasten the time, the set

time," &c. A striking instance of interposition is recorded in the twenty-fourth chapter of the second of Samuel.
The people upon whom God sent the pestilence, regarded
it probably, as being dependant on ordinary causes; but
David, at whose election this particular judgment was
sent, and who saw the visible presence of the angel who
inflicted it, well knew that it was an interposition. This
view of the relations of man to the great First Cause, to
other men, to the universe around him, and, it may be
added, to himself,* is sufficiently intelligible if we suppose
that men *are what they seem;* and that invisible, created in-
telligences, (the existence of which I need not here stop
to prove,) are all just and beneficent. But if we suppose
that the children of men *are not always what they seem*, and
if we admit the existence of a numerous class of spiritual
beings, all around us, who are evil, and who are busily
engaged in planning and causing evil, and who approach
and influence us through the most insidious disguises;
how strangely, and almost hopelessly and irretrievably,
are the interests of men involved and complicated.

What proof is there, derived from scripture or observation, that man is so circumstanced? I. Thes. 2 : 7. *For
the mystery of iniquity doth already work.* The date of this
announcement is A. D. 54. It will be seen by a perusal
of this most instructive chapter, that the *mystery of iniquity,*
whatever it may be, has exercised a most important, and
long continued influence, in the affairs of men. Other
passages in the New Testament, which appear to throw
light on this obscure declaration, perhaps all such, seem
to show, that the mystery of iniquity consists in the introduction, into the church, of the influence of evil angels,
exercised in the guise of the opinions, teachings, and do-
ings of men. In other words, that members of the Christian fraternity had become liable to some or all of the

---

* *I commune with mine own heart: and my spirit made diligent search.* Ps.
77 : 6.

various forms of demoniack possession. Perhaps at first, only that such had been received into Christian fellowship. Has not this mystery of iniquity still wrought, even to the present time, rendering Christianity itself, well nigh a failure, as to any general reformation of manners and morals? How much superior, in these particulars, are Paris, and London, and New York, and other great centres of Christian civilization, to ancient Rome, in the days of Augustus and other emperors! The form of civilization is different in some respects, no doubt. We have it on good authority, that in China, those portions of it that have not been corrupted by contact with Christian nations, there is less crime, than in the most favoured nations of the west.

If the Old and New Testaments are a revelation, written in the ordinary use of the languages in which they are given, there can be no doubt of the reality of demoniack possession. Read attentively, after laying aside prejudice, and see what violence must be done to the language, on any other supposition. Within a few years, Spiritualism has thrown a flood of light on this subject. Spiritualists themselves acknowledge that a part of the obsessing and influencing spirits, to whom the phenomena of Spiritualism are owing, are evil; and it is of little moment whether they are fallen angels, or, as is claimed, the departed spirits of evil men, that continue evil, in the spiritual life. It seems to have been the mission of Spiritualism, *as under Providence*, to prove the reality and frequency, so to speak, the universality of possession—evil possession—a truth, the belief of which will do more to banish that love of pleasure and the world, which is one of the great antagonistick powers to the Christian life, than all the homilies that have been uttered, since the days of Polycarp. It may be added that there is not the slightest *proof* that all the spirits, which have been evoked by Spiritualism, are not evil, but only a transparent *pretence*, that is contradicted by various facts.

It is by no means needful to suppose that in the Saviour's time, all the possessed were like those who obviously required healing; like him who dwelt among the tombs, or the epileptick, &c. Far otherwise. They might have been scribes, doctors of the law, members of the Sanhedrim; men of good report, of grave and austere presence, and most acceptable sanctity of discourse. The *personations* of Spiritualism are evidence of this. *For Satan himself is transformed into an angel of light.* But for some fifteen or sixteen hundred years angels, good angels, *angels of light*, have appeared only in the guise of men. They often appeared thus in earlier times. Is it to this phase of angelick appearance that Satan is transformed? If otherwise, as the greater includes the less, it is reasonable to suppose that he has the power to appear thus. The entire passage from which the above is cited, is worthy of attentive consideration. II. Cor. 11 : 13—15. *For such are false apostles, deceitful workers, transforming themselves into the apostles of Christ. And no marvel; for Satan himself is transformed into an angel of light. Therefore it is no great thing if his ministers also be transformed as the ministers of righteousness; whose end shall be according to their works.*

There is a remarkable and most emphatick passage, that of itself almost proves the justness of the view, given above, of the nature of the mystery of iniquity. Eph. 6 : 12. *For we wrestle* NOT AGAINST FLESH AND BLOOD, *but against principalities, against powers,* AGAINST THE RULERS OF THE DARKNESS OF THIS WORLD, *against spiritual wickedness in high places.*

It will be borne in mind that I have referred to the eighteenth chapter of Revelation, as setting forth the final destruction of the individual form of society. Verse 2: *Babylon the great is fallen, is fallen, and is become the habitation of devils, and the hold of every foul spirit, and a cage of every unclean and hateful bird.*

There is a passage in the Old Testament, which, though referring especially to a distant period, may perhaps be read with instruction. Ps. 78:49. *He cast upon them the fierceness of His anger, wrath, and indignation, and trouble, by sending evil angels among them.*

I will here anticipate to observe that there is a new science, *odometry*, which furnishes unexpected facilities for investigating spiritual phenomena. It is my design to consider the phenomena, those of possession and Spiritualism, so called, in another place, with such aids as the new science affords.

If the condition and circumstances of "the world" be such as I have endeavored to portray, if, in the battle of the ages, our spiritual enemies, instead of assailing us, as has been supposed, from some unknown vantage ground, with the missiles of suggestion, and ill-defined spiritual influence, have found their way into the camp, mingling familiarly with our own troops, clad in the same habiliments, and wearing the same undistinguishable appearance; finding favour with our chiefs, influencing our counsels, and even aspiring to the leadership, we might well nigh despair of the cause of humanity, were it not for the gracious promises of revelation; not a revelation of gifted men, considered merely as such, but a revelation of *divine origin, authoritative and infallible.** At any rate, we might despair of the efficacy of the most perfect social union that man can devise, in accomplishing that reformation, which must precede the blessed state, that seers and prophets have foretold. *Not by might, not by power, but by my Spirit, saith the Lord of hosts.* And this brings us to the point where all reformatory movements must commence — in individual amendment. Here is our only safety. On this condition we may hope for the efficient aid of good angels, who hover around us no less than those that are evil. And indeed, if men could BELIEVE

---

* I propose to consider the sense in which these epithets are to be understood, hereafter.

that they were environed by subtile foes, fraught with the darkest purposes, appearing in the most unexpected of disguises, leading into danger by EXAMPLE, and the profoundest artifices, and endowed with powers, which the mere children of mortality cannot fathom; with what indignant earnestness should we repel the very thought of the strivings of unhallowed ambition, the struggles of emulation and vanity, the dark broodings of malice and revenge, the efforts of useless acquisition, the sordid grasp of avarice, and the weakness of yielding to the allurements of sense. But I will say no more at present concerning possession. I hope to be enabled to place this subject in a clearer light in another chapter.

To return again for a moment, to the subject of the re-organization of society. It is sufficient that this is set forth, in numerous passages of scripture, as an indispensible CONDITION of that momentous change, which only the language of inspiration adequately describes. When God's time for the work shall arrive, when he gives the word, there will be no want of labourers. Hear the prophetick injunction : *Go through, go through the gates ; prepare ye the way of the people ; cast up, cast up the highway ; gather out the stones ; lift up a standard for the people.* Is. 62 : 10. Then we may be sure the enemy will be kept out, either by the direct agency of Providence, by the ministration of angels, or by means entrusted to men, and the application of which being understood, and the result infallible, they may be called scientifick. I decidedly incline to the belief that this last will be the method. But of this hereafter. *And a highway shall be there, and a way, and it shall be called The way of holiness ;* THE UNCLEAN SHALL NOT PASS OVER IT—NO LION SHALL BE THERE, NOR ANY RAVENOUS BEAST SHALL GO UP THEREON, IT SHALL NOT BE FOUND THERE ; *but the redeemed shall walk there.* Is. 35 : 8, 9.

It may be doubted, with the present views and feelings of mankind, and speaking after the manner of the world, though the influence of evil spirits were withdrawn, whether any social union, commencing with those of mature age, would be so far successful and enduring, as to afford an encouraging and reliable model. Those who have been accustomed to the *license* of the present form of society, would find it difficult to make the concessions, and endure the restraints of the most judicious social arrangement; and though it promised, at last, perfect and glorious LIBERTY. Habit, we are told, is a second nature. We are indebted to the Duke of Wellington for a more accurate rendering perhaps, of the general truth, meant to be conveyed, *that habit is twice as strong as nature;* and doubtless the disciplinary experience of his Grace, both as a subaltern and as chief, had afforded him the best opportunities for judging; and in the case supposed, both habit and nature would be to some extent, in antagonism— *nature untrained*—to even the best social arrangements, much as the nature of children is opposed to the salutary restraints of parents and teachers. Men, it would seem, must be educated to the social system. Such an education, commencing at the earliest practicable period, the fraternal sympathies cultivated and encouraged, the right proportion being observed in employment, study, amusement and repose; due employment being found for the more energetick and adventurous, as well as for those of different proclivities; religion taught, as in the apostolic age, in its spirit and its more obvious bearings and tendencies, rather than its metaphysical technicalities; the arts which adorn and embellish life, and serve to render the disposition more genial, more social, more considerate and reasonable, carefully fostered; would form a community, the members of which would be united like the members of a well regulated family; or, the points of antagonism and repulsion, the growth of which, under the fostering dews of individual selfishness is luxuriant, being rounded off, they would dwell together, like the once discordant and hostile members of one of those "happy families," that are sometimes exhibited for the edification of the curious. The members of a community so formed, would have little desire for change, but would regard the world without, somewhat as it might have been viewed by the inhabitants of the Happy Valley; or as the ancients, in the days of early wonder, regarded those unknown regions, fraught with real dangers, and peopled, by fancy, with others, terrible, *but not so terrible as those which actually infest society, as at present constituted.*

The above proceeds upon a supposition, which is not at present tenable, that of the influence of evil spirits being withdrawn. As it was said, more than eighteen hundred years ago, *For the mystery of iniquity doth already work,* so it may now be said, *For the mystery of iniquity doth yet work.* It has worked in all the intervening periods, and contributed essentially towards rendering all the devices and efforts of good men, for the reformation of their fellow-beings, of little avail; and for giving to Christianity, notwithstanding the inestimable gift of salvation, which it conveys, and the purity and excellence of its moral precepts, a savor of death. How have the pious dreams of the founders of monastick orders and establishments, dreams of communities of righteous men and women, living in peace and quietness and plenty, dispersing charity at their gates for Christ's sake; counseling, encouraging, consoling; imparting knowledge; bringing blessings upon the land by their prayers and holy example: how have these dreams been accomplished? And the equally unsubstantial dreams of statesmen; and of warriours who have *fought and bled for liberty?* Is it true of one of the American presidents, and one of the most accomplished statesmen of the entire number, that he pronounced the American government to be the most corrupt on earth? Rome, St. Petersburg, London, New York—how is the millennium flourishing in these great centres of Christian civilization?—say, rather, these representatives of the great Babylon of the Apocalypse.

There have been many—possibly some in all ages—
who have perceived the advantages of combination in the
affairs of men—of a social union, more perfect than that
by families; but have any of the numerous attempts to
realize these advantages met with more than very partial
success? I believe not. The Shaker communities have
perhaps been the most successful, in some respects. In
an economic and *social* point of view, they have been entirely so, though on a narrow plane. Their most considerable communities were established near. seventy years
ago, and they are still flourishing as ever, a circumstance
to be noted. At first they are supposed to have been
nearly all poor, now they are comparatively rich, through
the force of the associative principle. Every one is well
sheltered, fed and clothed, with. moderate labour, and with
considerable means in reserve. Though living somewhat
near one of the most considerable of their establishments,
I have never heard of quarrels, such as are the bane of
many of the New England villages. But with all this
seeming prosperity, the enemy has not been excluded.
They have constant intercourse with very equivocal
spirits—[equivical?] One of these has dictated a new
Bible, a copy of which they were directed to send to all
emperors, kings and chief rulers. I will not affirm that
their views on the subject of marriage, place them without
the pale of common sense; but how will these, together
with their religious belief, and constant intercourse with
doubtful spirits, bear to be considered in connexion with
a remarkable passage in the New Testament, which I will
proceed to quote entire:—I. Tim. 4 : 1—5. *Now the Spirit
speaketh expressly, that in the latter times some shall depart from
the faith, giving heed to seducing spirits, and doctrines of devils;
speaking lies in hypocrisy; having their conscience seared with a
hot iron; forbidding to marry, and commanding to abstain from
meats, which God hath created to be received with thanksgiving
of them which believe and know the truth. For every creature
of God is good, and nothing to be refused, if it be received with*

thanksgiving: for it is sanctified by the word of God and prayer. An acquaintance of mine told me that he mentioned this passage, (or the first verses of it,) to a Shaker, who replied, *That don't mean us*. God knoweth. It would unquestionably be wrong to believe that any considerable proportion of the Shakers, or their leaders, are of those who *speak lies in hypocrisy, having their conscience seared with a hot iron*, without abundant proof. Doubtless with numbers of them, especially of those brought up in the Shaker system, the power of habit is a bond not easily severed. As it appears to have been the mission of Spiritualism, *as under Providence*, to demonstrate the reality and frequency of spiritual influence and possession; so it may have been the design of Providence that Shakerdom should prove to the world, that a well conducted, and successful social organization, in which the visible and generally recognized causes of vice are excluded, is yet not sufficient, of itself, to shut out the enemy. *Not by might, not by power, but by my Spirit, saith the Lord.*

It will be proper to advert to those combinations in which the associative principle is partially adopted, for the purpose of rendering individualism *more scientifick, more advantageous, and more secure*. Such to some extent are "the clubs" of London. Such the vast hotels of American origin, where families, as well as individuals, find a permanent home. I find the following in a newspaper of Jan. 3, '59. "The 'unitary household' established in New York by E. F. Underhill, formerly a reporter on the Tribune, has proved a success, notwithstanding the ridicule heaped upon it at the start, two years ago. It is properly a joint stock boarding-house, where each one pays the actual expense of his keeping, and it is stated that for $5 a week the inmates get as good accommodations in every respect as the first class boarding houses offered for $10. The success is so evident that an establishment for 5,000 persons is projected on the same plan, in which still larger economies can be effected." There are various unions of operatives and operative tradesmen, in some of the large cities, and different manufacturing places, for the purpose of making purchases in the large way, at reduced rates, accumulating capital and reserve funds, and effecting advantageous sales of the products of their industry, accomplishing these and various purposes by the most eligible division of labour, &c. I have seen an account of a remarkably successful combination of this sort in the city of Paris. These unions are very well as evincing, in different modes, and from different points of view, the power of association. They may also answer a good purpose, at a period of transition, in gradually educating to perceive the advantages of the associative principle ; but as permanent institutions would they not be worse than the present individualism, inasmuch as they would intensify and endear that individual selfishness, which is much the same as the *love of money, which is the root of all evil ?*

One of the most successful of the associations of the kind referred to above, has been that of the " Rochdale Society of Equitable Pioneers."* Their statisticks are exceedingly interesting and instructive, but I have only space for a few results. "Fifteen years ago, by hardly saved contributions of three pence a week, some forty working men, *most of them more or less inoculated by the doctrines of Robert Owen,* had amassed a common capital of £28." With this they established a " co-operative store," for the "purchase of flour and groceries for sale among the members." " Their numbers and their capital gradually increased." In a brief period—1849—the capital invested in the store amounted to some £1,200. They extended the co-operative principle to other objects. They have " their butcher's shop, their draper's shop, their shoe-making and tailoring business, their amply stocked grocery and provision shop, their well supplied news-room, their evening school, their library of three thousand vol-

---

* ROCHDALE: " A small town in Lancashire, chiefly noted for woolen manufactures."

umes." " They are the chief authors of the Co-operative Manufacturing Society, in which they have invested £5,000 belonging to the Pioneers, and which has already an additional capital of £30,000." Such are some of the results, shewing the power of the co-operative principle. Without it the " Pioneers " would doubtless still have remained beer drinking workmen, in debt, and spending all their wages every Saturday night.

The article from which the above is extracted, concludes thus :—" We heartily wish them success. The good that they have done in Rochdale and its vicinity we have endeavored to describe. The good which their example may do elsewhere we can hardly estimate. Coöperation in this form, purged from Owenism, and far removed from Communism—recognizing that the laws of political economy are as certain as the law of gravitation—recognizing, too, in direct contradiction to Communism, that, while human nature remains the same, the more direct and personal a man's interest in his work, the better for his work, for himself, and for others—may not improbably prove a most valuable ingredient in our social system. Certainly it has taught the men of Rochdale not only a most intelligent apprehension of their own interests, but a respect for the rights and an appreciation of the good-will of other classes which are too rarely found among working men." The concluding statement of this extract is very well, if rightly understood. It is probable they have become more considerate, that they have less of that impulsiveness, which uneducated men often have, to some extent, in common with children ; but it may be doubted whether, on the whole, there is any essential improvement in their moral sentiments, beyond what may be traced to unadulterated and more wholesome food ; it being indubitable, that the *morale* of peoples and nations and communities depends upon their food, far more than is generally supposed. Is it not possible that they have more of that love of the world, which the Scriptures so pointedly condemn ?

Somewhat, (in the converse,) as the soldier became less brave, after being cured of a disease, that rendered life scarcely desirable. The chief who commanded his cure, expected quite' a different result. It is probable that they have improved in some respects, and deteriorated in others—or at least that they will, as the new influences develope themselves. The good or evil influence of the three thousand volumes of their library will depend very much upon the selection of books. The writer says, " while human nature remains the same," &c., see above. He .seems not to be aware that it is the great, the paramount object of the true, scriptural, prophetical, millennial union, with God's help, entirely to change " human nature," to render it quite a different thing from what it has become, under the transmitted physiological and other influences of a hundred generations of isolated selfishness.

The designs of Providence are sometimes accomplished by the most unexpected means. A few years since it seemed as if, in the older free states of the American confederacy, the entire course of society would be interrupted by the impossibility of procuring tolerable domestick help. As if some form of social life, other than that in families, must be resorted to. Native help was no longer to be had. Just at this crisis the Irish help came in, and the evil was partially remedied. But how long will this last?. The present prospect is, strangely incredible as it seems, that within a few years, in the fortress and citadel of Puritanism in America, the Irish Catholicks will be in the ascendant. They will choose our governors, control our legislatures, appoint our judges. The moment they have the vote, subtile and zealous chiefs will arise, like the invisible warriors of Roderick Dhu, to direct that vote. Heaven knows ' I have none of the popular, or once popular prejudice against our Catholick brethren ; but it is something more than a truism to say that human nature is human nature. Whether Catholick Irish help, with the ultra American, democratick and radical notions of independence superinduced, and with the added consciousness that their leaders have the political power, will serve to render the domestick hearth of Protestants the abode of quietness and peace, the family circle the sacred precinct of the still more blessed society above, is a question which some of those now on the stage may be called upon to assist in determining, before they have passed the meridian of life.

To conclude, the question very naturally arises, what are the signs of the times? Has the morning dawned? Is there evidence that the time has arrived, or will soon arrive, for commencing the millennial social union? I shall endeavour to make some reply to this question hereafter.

EXPERIMENTS ON THE ODIC FORCE.

XI. THE ODIC FORCE EARLY KNOWN BY ITS EFFECTS—THE WORK OF REICHENBACH—PROCESS OF DIVINATION—ARTICLES IN THE JOURNAL OF MAN—COMMENCE EXPERIMENTING—LITERATURE OF THE ODIC FORCE—PENDULUM NOT MOVED BY UNCONSCIOUS MUSCULAR ACTION—PENDULUM MOVED BY OD-FORCE—TERMS EMPLOYED—DEFINITION OR DESCRIPTION OF OD-FORCE—ODIC PROCESSES AT A DISTANCE.

THE odic force must have been known at a very early period, by its more ordinary phenomena. It is supposed to be a very considerable, if not the sole agent, in essential, as distinguished from poetical sympathy, in fascination, and in those processes which are called mesmeric. There is also a kind of divination, it may perhaps be called, and of which I shall speak hereafter, the efficient agent in which is unquestionably the odic force. But it was not till recently, that the power which causes the effects alluded to, was recognized as a separate element or essential principle. Perhaps the best method of introducing this recondite subject, which has elicited much incredulity, will be to give a brief account of my own early acquaintance with it.

I saw a notice of the work of Reichenbach on the odic force, soon after it was published.* I recollect very little about it, except that it appeared to me that the writer was

_____

* Whether after the first publication of the work, in the "Annalen der Chemie" of Liebig, in 1845, or after that of the completed edition in 1848, I cannot say.

11

unreasonably sceptical. He says, rather oracularly, We have doubts of results derived from observations on the sick. Why should he doubt? As if sickness had not its laws, which would enable an observer of tact to discriminate and classify, as well as health. . If this be not so, of what value is the *so called* science of medicine? Besides, it is to be mentioned that although Reichenbach commenced his observations upon invalids and hospital patients, he subsequently obtained similar results from those who were both robust and in perfect health.

During the year 1851 my attention was called to the little process of divination, mentioned above. A small weight being held suspended by a thread, in a tumbler containing water, it was alleged that the thread and weight would commence revolving, the circles enlarging, till the weight would strike the tumbler. This would be repeated so as to indicate the hour of the day. Here was a moving force and intelligence. I knew of no natural cause to which this could be attributed; and being a firm believer in the influence of spirits, I could hardly avoid the conclusion that an appeal, unconscious perhaps, or dimly conscious, but most improper, to some unknown and intelligent being, enabled evil spirits to produce this result; and I resolved never to repeat the experiment.

Some time after, during the same year, I observed in the Journal of Man for November,* an article entitled The Od Force, from Chambers' Edinburgh Journal. The following is an extract. "Mesmer, when ridiculed and defamed by the would-be wise ones of his day, is said to have retorted by declaring that ere 1852 the world would be convinced of the genuineness of his pretensions. The epoch is now at hand, and lo! the prophecy is coming true." Whatever may be the decision respecting the claims of Mesmer, there can be no doubt that the discov-

---

* "Journal of Man," published at Cincinnati, and edited by Dr. J. R. Buchanan.

eries of Reichenbach are genuine, and of great importance. The article above speaks of a few of these, especially that of "dim flames of light issuing and waving from the poles of a magnet, and the finger tips of the human hand, as seen when the light was withdrawn, by numbers of persons of uncommon sensibility. It then proceeds to speak, in connexion, of experiments, described by Dr. Herbert Mayo, and with which he was made acquainted by a German professor of mathematics, Herr Caspari. In these experiments a light weight, suspended by a thread, (as in the experiment described above,) the thread wound around the first joint of the fore finger, would move in various directions, when held over some one of a considerable number of substances, which are enumerated; each basis, (or "Od-subject" as it was called, while the weights, &c., was called an "odometer,") giving some particular movement. The luminous element emanating from the fingers, and to which the discoverer gave the name of *Od*, was supposed to be the efficient agent. The processes seemed to be dependant upon natural causes; and if so my scruples above, might be dismissed. It became my purpose to investigate the matter somewhat, but circumstances prevented, till after seeing, in the Journal of Man for January 1852, a series of articles on the subject. These were very curious and interesting, and I soon made trial to determine whether I had, myself, any of the odical faculty. The odometer moved readily and freely in my hand. For a few weeks I was much engaged in experimenting. My attention was then withdrawn, and it was not till towards the close of the year that I had made arrangements for engaging in a more systematic and extended course of investigation. My earliest memorandum is dated in December. I soon became absorbed in the pursuit, which was continued with a good deal of industry and perseverance, for four or five years. During the years since I have also experimented a good deal, at intervals. I did not have an opportunity to read the work

of Reichenbach till the summer of the next year, (1853.)
In 1857 I saw the work of Sir Benjamin Brodie, entitled
"Mind and Matter." In a note in this work, added by
the American editor, an eminent French savant, M. Chevreuil, *demonstrates* that the *odometer* or pendulum is caused
to move by involuntary and unconscious muscular
motion.* '

The first thing to be proved is that the *odometer* or *pendulum* is moved by some other power than involuntary
and unconscious muscular motion; for even this, as seen
above, has been denied, would perhaps be denied by Professor Faraday. I will give two or three proofs, out of
quite a considerable number that might be mentioned.
1.—The *pendulum* does not move unless the eye of the
operator is fixed upon it. The truth is, three currents of
od are required to effect the movement. One descending
along the arm of the operator; one rising from the *basis* or
od-subject as it is called above; and one proceeding from
the eye of the operator. In my own case, and I have had
little opportunity to experiment with others, if either of
these is cut off, (as can be done by a certain process,) the
pendulum will not move. Instead of the current rising
from the basis however, od thrown into the pendulum, or
into the air around it, will answer. 2.—On holding the
pendulum opposite to either of the poles of a small horse
shoe magnet, and quite near, it revolves with a good deal
of liveliness, making considerable circuits, *though in different directions at the different poles.* On gradually withdrawing the pendulum, keeping it in the line of the magnet,

---

* The above enumeration includes all the literature of the odic force with
which I am acquainted, with the exception perhaps, of the work of President
Mahan on Spiritualism, which however, is conjectural rather than experimental.
I propose to give the minor articles entire, with a few extracts from the work of
Reichenbach, in an Appendix. I think they cannot but prove gratifying to all
who may feel an interest in the subject, in phenomena so little known, and yet
so surprising, so intimately connected with our daily life, and even, may be
added, with our highest interests.

the motion becomes less and less, till at a certain point it is but just kept up. On removing the pendulum an inch beyond this point, the motion entirely ceases. If the pendulum be returned towards the magnet, in the same gradual manner, all this is reversed. The motion again commences, and increases till it acquires the same vivacity as at first. But this is not all. The od which emanates from the magnet spreads out like a brush. But if it be caused to flow in right lines, it will influence the pendulum at a very considerable distance, indeed at the greatest distance, which I have tried. 3.—If the od, produced by the friction of a revolving wheel, in turning another wheel, be thrown upon a neutral basis, it gives a circular movement to the pendulum, towards the right. If the od of the second wheel be thrown upon the basis, the pendulum turns towards the left. If that of both wheels, the action is neutralized, and the pendule refuses to move.

That the movements of the pendulum are caused by the od-force, the visible emanations seen by the ocular sensitives, appears from this, that wherever the sensitives perceive a concentration of the visible appearances, the movements of the pendulum are uncommonly active. And second, by the circumstance that an odical medium can cause the pendulum to move by the action of the will, proving a *spiritual* organization without the body.* The different parts of vegetables affect the pendulum in a manner coincident with the report of the sensitives. There is a method by which the visible flames seem to be dissected, as a ray of light is by the prism. There appears to be good evidence, though I have not the testimony of those who can see. Each of these dissevered principles affects the pendulum, and there is a general resemblance in the different movements, though for the most part, with points of difference.

TERMS. I shall feel at liberty, for the present, to use

---

* This doctrine has been taught perhaps by all the chief leaders in mesmerism.

any of the following terms, as may be convenient. It is probable that hereafter the public taste will settle down upon some one of each class, which will then be commonly employed.

Od, od-force, odic force, odyle, luminous aura. The newly discovered element.

Od-subject, basis, motor. A small plate of some suitable substance, and convenient form and size, to which od-force is brought for examination. Any substance or thing in which od-force inheres, and to which a magnetoscope is applied, to test the same.

Odometer, magnetoscope, aura-test,* pendulum. A string and weight, or small pendulum, to be held or suspended over a motor, for the purpose of testing the properties of its od-force. The term odometer, it will be seen below, has been appropriated, according to its derivation, to another use, and I shall not hereafter employ it in the sense above.

Major, minor. Terms which I have employed to indicate a double *status,* different from negative and positive. There is a large class of substances, which affect an ordinary pendulum, and another, including all poisins, which do not. On giving to a pendulum the odic condition of substances of the second class, it is affected by them, and not by the first mentioned.

Wand, power wand, traction wand, &c. Small wands employed in experimental manipulations on od-force, or for more lasting purposes, and to which suitable odic powers have been given.

Odometer. A basis, wand and magnetoscope, employed for the purpose of determining the impulsive or pendular force of a portion of od. Measured by degrees of convenient force, subdivided in the decimal ratio. Symbols, deg.°, frac.′, (fractional,) ″, ‴, &c.

Odic, odical, odically. I have employed the term odic to

---

* This term has been approved of by high authority. Might not the first word be omitted, and only the other employed?

denote the od-force of any particular substance, as the odic of silk, the odic of cotton. Also, of any particular portion of any substance. The term may be qualified thus, The normal odic, meaning the od-force, which is universally diffused, and in the original or uncombined state. For the most part odics consist of the primary elements, or some portion of them, in a state of combination. The word may also be used adjectively.

Impulsion, induction, &c. These terms require no explanation.

Cataliss. The odo-catalytic state of any substance. Both this and the odic can be changed.

Psychomet. The entire od-psychometric influence or principle, of any writing. This can be detached, and transferred.

Odyla, odylum, odicism. The science of od-force.

If I were requested to give a *definition*, or expressive appellation for the odic force, I should call it SPIRITUAL LIGHT. Imagine a substance as much more attenuated than solar light as that is than hydrogen; and consisting of nine elementary principles, seven of which are coloured and visible. These principles combining and recombining like the rays of light, in endless variety. Radiating from the heavenly bodies, and not only filling all open space, but pervading all solid and liquid substances. Manifesting itself in the different forms of polarity. Important, if not absolutely essential, in the circulation of all vegetable and animal life. Mobile, its equilibrium disturbed by all physiological and chemical, and many mechanical processes. Conceiving of such a substance, one would have a very good general idea of the odic force.

Early in the course of my experiments I acquired the means of producing odic effects at a distance, whether by impulsion, traction or induction, or distant local influence; and also throughout extensive atmospheric and aquarial spaces. Distance of past time interposes no obstacle to the laws of induction. An odic of remote ages, (some of them are exceedingly permanent,) or an exact counterpart, is derived by the tractive process. I need say nothing as to the methods by which these results are accomplished. Any explanations now, would I believe, be ill-timed and injudicious.

•

XII. CIRCULATION OF THE ODIC FORCE IN THE HUMAN SYSTEM.

The apparent outflow of the luminous aura from the human hands, is partly an illusion. Instead of the od being produced in the system, it flows through it. On checking the current of od at the wrist of the right hand of a male, the phenomena with the pendulum, held over the hand, or opposite to the ends of the fingers, are the same, for some minutes, as usual, though with rapidly decreasing force. In a brief period, the od in the hand being dissipated, the hand ceases to influence the pendulum in the least. On checking the od at the left wrist, the pendulum ceases at once to be influenced, when held at the ends of the fingers, but held over any part of the hand, it continues to be affected for an indefinite period. The od, tending upward, remaining in the hand.

With the female this is reversed, the od flowing in at the right hand, and off at the left. With both sexes the od, it appears, flows in at every part of one side of the body, and out at the other; yet the currents, on the two sides, are so similar, in volume and form, and the actual transition being imperceptible, that they both appear to the occular sensitives, to flow outward. Even the currents of the two eyes flow in opposite directions; and there is a line from the top of the head, down through the middle of the forehead, along the middle of the breast bone, &c., where, as at the middle of a magnet, there is no current of od that affects the pendulum.

The circulation of od in a magnet is similar to that in the human body. On checking the current at the north pole of a magnet, the pendulum is not affected opposite, but is affected over every part of the magnet, and opposite the south pole, as usual, but with decreasing force. The od of a small horse-shoe magnet, which I use, is thus discharged in just half an hour. On checking the current at the south, or outflowing pole, a pendulum ceases to be affected opposite, but is affected when held above any part of the magnet, for an indefinite period, the od remaining in the magnet.

The odic force is unquestionably a spiritual substance, as we shall see more fully, hereafter; and doubtless subserves some most important purpose, in the human economy, probably in connexion with the spiritual man. Perhaps as an excitant, perhaps as a nutrient. The outflowing current, in one instance, in which I determined the proportions, was to the inflowing, as 2,224 to 2,374.

Could we see the current, flowing through the body, as clairvoyants of the first class perhaps do, what can be imagined more surprising? Every organ, every tissue of the body, to their minutest parts, and in all their shadings and blendings revealed. Truly we are fearfully and wonderfully made.

There is reason to believe that the odics, which are constantly forming and reforming in the human system, are exceedingly numerous. In disease they become universally or partially morbid, as will be seen more particularly in the next section.

XIII. PREVENTION AND CURE OF DISEASES.

It will readily be admitted as probable, that a power, so considerable as the odic force seems to be, which is so intimately connected with all the sources of life; and, it may be added, which is generally diffused, will have a very

12

considerable influence upon the different and varying states of health and disease. I have instituted numerous experiments for the purpose of determining the rules by which this influence is exercised; and whether in the treatment and prevention of diseases, it could be rendered available. The following are some of the practical results.

COMMON COLDS AND INFLUENZA.

By common colds I mean those, which come, or a large proportion of them, without any particular exposure. Which are epidemick, and sometimes, apparently, contagious. Which have regular stages, and unless renewed, a regular period. Influenzas, for there are probably several kinds of influenza, have the same characteristicks; and in these respects they both resemble the more formidable pestilential diseases. These complaints, (of which there are probably more varieties than is generally supposed,) are all, and in all cases, as I have reason to believe, controled by an odic process. I formerly had two or three colds of this description in a year; but since I have been acquainted with the odic method of treatment, although I have been attacked, much as formerly, (perhaps not so often,) the colds have uniformly been checke'd, and readily dispersed. The remedial process has consisted simply in withdrawing, by means of a traction wand, the morbid odic, and keeping up the *rapport*, so as to prevent any, the slightest, accumulation. There is a morbid odic, proper to every variety of colds and influenza, as appears by the different movements, which they give to the pendulum. These odics are a regular secretion, like any other secretion of the disease; the morbid product is indispensible to the general progress of the complaint, so that if withdrawn, it is at once arrested. On applying this process during the first or second day of a cold, the symptoms are at once abated, and soon cease to manifest themselves.

On looking over my memoranda, since writing the above, I find nothing inconsistent with the idea that the *pestilential colds*, as they may properly be called, can in all cases be checked by an odic process. I find however, that in February 1856, there was a cold or influenza prevailing, which had no regularly developed odic. To this cold I applied, in my own case, a *counteracting* odic, and find minuted the next day, that it had "probably had a favourable influence."

In one instance, when I was informed a "severe cold or influenza was prevalent," I was attacked five times, in less than as many days, but in each instance checked the complaint.

How far any course of odical treatment would be successful in rheumatick colds, those which are caused by exposure to the united influences of cold and damp, and which continue for an indefinite period, I have had little if any opportunity of determining. I have in a single instance, been attacked by a very severe cold, which was obviously caused by exposure. I employed the process of *traction*, as above, and also, if I recollect, (for I find no record,) fasted somewhat, for the cold was very severe. Every thing seemed coming around right, when by reason of untoward circumstances, I was subjected to considerable fatigue, and was a good deal heated. This aggravated, very considerably, what was left of the cold, and from that time it became unmanageable.

During the past winter I have had a cold, different from any which I have observed before. Its approach was so insidious that for some days I regarded it only as a hoarseness. There was at this period no odic. I then coughed occasionally, a light cough, with little or no raising; and still regarded it as not a regularly formed complaint. At last I was taken down, rather suddenly, with symptoms of severe cold, and which continued a considerable time. This cold also was not arrested, though it might have been mitigated, by any odic applications which were made use of. It is now, at the time I am writing, Feb. 27, having continued since September, not entirely cured. Others

in the village have been affected. in a similar manner.
One of my- neighbors, who cured himself by drinking
cider, said it appeared to him to be a distemper, like
whooping-cough, which it is well known, sometimes continues for a considerable period, after the early force of
the disease has gone by. It is not improbable I think,
that during the two first stages, the complaint might have
been checked, by a counteracting odic course.

METHODS OF TREATMENT.

I have spoken above, of two methods of treatment, that
by withdrawing morbid odics, and that by applying counteracting ones. It is proper to explain that the odics of
most or all substances, applied to the human system, produce effects similar to those produced by the substances
themselves, applied in the usual modes. For example,
the odic of a celebrated liniment, excellent for sprains and
bruises, on being thrown into an affected part, has produced a cure, much as a thorough external application of
the compound itself would have done. In addition to
withdrawing morbid odics, there is a process for prevent-
ing their formation. Counteracting odics have been, with
advantage, thrown directly into the lungs, into the stomach, into parts locally affected, into the surrounding atmosphere. There is a curious method of decomposing
morbid odics, extensively diffused in the atmosphere, but
as there are singular objections to this process, which have
been rather surprisingly illustrated, I will say nothing
more of it at present. There are processes, or supposable
processes, which promise much, but which I have not yet
had an opportunity of testing. The odic emanations from
garments, and the walls of apartments, have been an unsuspected source of various complaints. These can be
checked, or their sources removed, and other odics substituted.

• That odic influences are not an illusion, but a serious
reality, in the concerns of health, is proved by the circum-

stance that medicines, carried about the person, in vials, closely stopped, produce very considerable effects, similar to those produced by the medicines themselves, applied in the received methods.

CANCER.

Mrs. S. C. being at my house, I was informed that she had a swelling under her tongue, which it was feared was a cancer. It was a round tumour, of the size of a small hazlenut, with a ridge shooting out on each side. It had been a considerable time in coming on; it hurt her to move her tongue, and when she raised the tongue, it seemed to resist, or hold back. There had been a small open sore on the tumour for about a fortnight, which smarted, and she was much alarmed. It appeared by the odic test, not only that it was a cancer, but that the virus had been taken up into the system. Mrs. C. had probably heard of my pretensions of curing diseases by a new method, but nothing was said on the subject by either of us. I concluded that I could not spend the time, or rather strength, to attend to it. I could not help the feeling however, that this was not quite as I should like to be done by; and considerably more than a week after seeing her, I set a traction wand to withdraw one of the morbid odics, proper to cancer. To make all sure, I set another to prevent its formation. This it appeared afterwards, was practically effective, so that the first was superfluous. Several months later, Mrs. C. (who lives at the distance of about two miles,) was again at the house, and informed me that the tumour was gone, with all the uneasy sensations, she was well. I then procured a note book, and read to her what I had done, of which I had previously given no intimation to any one whatever.

TOOTH ACHE.

Miss E. C., daughter of my housekeeper, had, as was supposed in consequence of a cold, a throbbing tooth-ache, with headache. For two days she had been disabled from her usual avocations. During the second day she had chewed pepper, but without any abatement of the pain, which she expected would continue all night. In the evening, being in another room, and having given no intimation of my purpose, I set a wand to withdraw the odic of inflammation from the tooth. I did not see her till the next morning, when she told me, without being aware of what had been done, that the pain was entirely gone. It appeared that the wand was set about half past six. The pain began to abate at seven, and was gone at eight. Early in the night she was awakened by her mother coming into the chamber, and there was a very slight throbbing; but she slept, and on awaking in the morning, the pain had once more entirely ceased, and did not return.

CONSUMPTION.

I have had opportunity to observe one case of consumption. The patient had had severe night sweats, and was so enfeebled, that on leaving New-York, at the approach of cold weather, to join her friends in the country, her physician, Dr. B., told the family, where she resided, that he should not be surprised if she died in a fortnight.

Miss E. was a daughter of my then housekeeper, and she came to my house. Being pretty sure that the disease would obtain the mastery if she went away, I invited her to remain, which I should not have done, had I not felt a reasonable confidence, founded on a few previous observations, that although my own lungs were susceptible, I could protect them by odic processes. Miss E. came the first of October.

I will here observe that I was not particularly impressed with the idea that she was of the consumptive form, though tall and slender. She had lost a brother by consumption, some time previous.

The weather being mild, she was able for a time to take brief walks, but she soon became extremely liable to catch cold, and was obliged to confine herself to her room.

I was unwilling at first, to engage in any remedial odic processes on her account, and left her to the care of her mother. I observed, October 20, that there were in the sick room, odics of tubercles, general consumptive action, and some minor ones, and set a wand to withdraw and disperse them all, not from the person of the invalid, but from the apartment, and the entire house. This alone was no doubt of great service. What chance have consumptives to recover, breathing constantly an atmosphere that would communicate the disease to some in health?

"Nov. 15.—She has been free from *tubercular action*, or that of *tubercles*, one or both,* but observed, *heri*, she had both. Set a wand, last night, to withdraw both from her person. To-day her pulse better—slower—than I have observed it—78—heretofore, 80 to 95, or thereabouts."

"Nov. 16.—The pulse continues much better—no odic of hectic fever."

"Jan. 18.—Pulse slow enough, and natural—the first time I have observed such a pulse."

"Feb. 9.—Early this month great improvement in Adelaide's complexion—more healthy and vivacious—expression less languid."

When Miss E. left, late in the spring, to return to New-York, she was far from having recovered her strength, though she had blooming health. Her health has continued to the present time, a period of two years. I am tempted to add that I have lately received a message from one of her friends, that she had "married and gone to Washington." Heaven grant that every blessing may be hers.

CHOLERA.

The Asiatic or malignant cholera, which has spread over the earth, commenced, if I remember aright, at a

---

*Tubercular action, that which produces tubercles. Action of tubercles, that of tubercles fully formed. They give different movements to the pendulum, have different odics.

place called Jessore, in India, during the year 1817. It had not been unusual before this, perhaps from an early period, for the cholera morbus, which is common in India, to become suddenly malignant, and to spread extensively. From Jessore the disease spread east and west. It reached the American continent, having crossed the Atlantic, in 1832. It spread rapidly over the United States. The number of deaths at New-York was said to have been three thousand; three fourths as many as died of yellow fever, at Philadelphia, in 1793. Owing to some peculiarity in our climate perhaps, the disease did not subside in this country, as it had done in other regions, but continued to prevail more or less, every year I believe, for the next twenty-three years, or twenty-four years in all. Of its prevalence in 1855, the following are notices. "Last week 381 deaths in New-Orleans, 200 from cholera." Springfield Repub. of June 15. "There were 191 deaths in New-Orleans last week, of which 48 were from cholera." Repub. of July 3. "The cholera is raging fearfully in Morganfield, Ky. There has been some thirty or forty cases, within the last few days, most of which have terminated fatally." I have reasons for doubting very much, the entire accuracy of these reports; but they will serve as specimens of the notices, which were common, during the years above specified.

I will say nothing of my earlier attempts to prevent cholera, except that they were local, and consisting at first, in throwing counteracting odics into the atmosphere, over particular cities or districts; and that I have reason to believe that some of these attempts were successful.

In the spring of 1856, I set a tractive wand to withdraw the odic of cholera from the United States, east of the Mississippi. After the wand was opened, it continued to be traversed by a current of the odic, sufficient to move the pendulum, for eight or ten hours. After this it appeared by an appropriate process, that the odic was all withdrawn. Nothing was gained in the way of compari-

son, by the partial withdrawing of the odic, for the subtile principle tended to an equilibrium, and poured rapidly
across from the west side of the river, not the less that it
was instantly withdrawn, by the traction of the wand.

It will be asked perhaps, how the odic was disposed of.
At first I caused the current to ascend to a considerable
elevation, and probably added a dispersing power there,
though I find no record of it. After a time I discovered
that the odic thus withdrawn, was again accumulating on
the surface. I then directed the current to the crater of
one of the perpetually burning volcanoes, and it was there
thrown into the flame.

A wand set as above, has been a perfect cholera-od-om-
eter for determining the rate of production of the cholera
odic. A current traversed the wand the greater part of
the year, sufficient to move the pendulum, but the force
constantly varying. The following is a record kept in
1857, of the pendular force of the current, on a particular day, in each month from January to September.

	Pendular force.
January, ...	
February, ...	
March, ...	281′′′
April, ...	776′′′
May, ...	7° 352′′′
June, ...	54° plus.
July, ...	112° ——
August, ...	130° ——
September, ...	137° ——

It has been my purpose to note everything of moment,
connected with this important topic, yet I find reports, on
looking over my minutes, of only three cases of cholera,
in the United States, during the six years—1856—1861—
in which I have had a wand set to prevent the disease.
One of a publick man, who it was said had recovered from
the disease, 1856; one of a man who died in Kansas,
1858; and one of a man who was seized while serving as

13

a juror at Covington, Ky., 1860, this also a fatal case. I venture to affirm, from odical investigation, that neither of these was a case of Asiatic cholera ; that they were all cases of cholera morbus. Concerning the last mentioned, I find it minuted that the pendular force of the odic of the disease was 453,''' and add, " of course, cholera morbus." *Of course*, because that although cholera and cholera morbus give the same movement to the pendulum, the least force of the odic of the former, producing the disease, is 710'''. There is still another reason, proving that the disease of this last, though he died in a few hours, was not Asiatic cholera.

During the six years—1856—1861—in which I have had a wand set to prevent the cholera, although there were no cases of the disease, (unless possibly a few might have been brought in from abroad,) the *production* of the deleterious principle upon which it depends, abated but little. The following gives the pendular force in September of each year.

							Pendular force.
1856,	.	.	.	.	.	.	136° plus.
1857,	.	.	.	.	.	.	137° ——
1858,	.	.	.	.	.	.	136° ——
1859,	.	.	.	.	.	.	137° ——
1860,	.	.	.	.	.	.	134° ——
1861,	.	.	.	.	.	.	132° ——

I know no reason to doubt that, should the rapport and traction of the wand that has been set for two years past, be withdrawn, the disease would prevail as heretofore.

XIV. MATTER AND SPIRIT.

Odicism, or the science of od-force, confirms the testimony of scripture, as to the nature of spiritual existence—that it is MATERIAL. The doctrine of immaterialism, I re-

gard as of hurtful, of irreligious tendency. Notwithstanding its claims to transcendent excellence, and superior sanctity, I believe it contributes to render men indif-
ferent and unspiritual. They recoil, naturally and in-
stinctively, from a future existence, unsubstantial, *cold as
moonlight,* and which *appears,* from its very nature, to be
devoid of human susceptibilities. Had those to whom
we are indebted for the modern doctrine of the immateri-
ality of spiritual existence, allowed more scope to common sense, had they paid far more attention to the statements of scripture, and indulged less in ingenious one-
sided metaphysical speculation, the religious world might
have been spared the perplexities and mischiefs of an unsatisfactory and inconsistent theory. It derives its chief
support doubtless, from the theory of matter, which supposes that it consists of massive, solid, impenetrable par-
ticles. A more philosophical and *scriptural* theory on this
subject, would relieve much of the difficulty in appre-
hending the nature of spiritual existence, as according to
the word of scripture.

XV. ILLUSTRATIONS OF SCRIPTURE.

THE SUPREME BEING.

Various passages of scripture, hitherto obscure, are illustrated by a knowledge of the existence and the properties of the spiritual light. Or, these being known to some
extent, the scriptures teach us momentous truths concerning this principle, which could not otherwise be known.

Spiritual light, divinely organized, constitutes the subsistence of God, and of the seven spirits of God. In a
series of lower organizations it constitutes angels, the
spirits of departed men,* of men in the flesh, and of the

---

* Who maketh his angels spirits; his ministers a flaming fire. Psal. 104: 4.

lower orders of the creation. The Bible speaks of the soul and the spirit of animals. Every being endowed with perception, choice and will, has a soul.

Should any one doubt that God is an organized being, let him endeavour to conceive of him as not organized.

Rev. 1 : 4. *Grace be unto you, and peace, from him which is, and which was, and which is to come; and from the seven spirits which are before his throne.* Ch. 4 : 2, 3. *And immediately I was in the spirit: and, behold, a throne was set in heaven, and one sat on the throne. And he that sat was to look upon like a jasper and a sardine stone: and there was a rainbow round about the throne, in sight like unto an emerald.* Ver. 5. *And out of the throne proceeded lightnings and thunderings and voices: and there were seven lamps of fire burning before the throne, which are the seven spirits of God.* Ch. 5 : 6. *And I beheld, and, lo, in the midst of the throne, and of the four beasts, and in the midst of the elders, stood a Lamb as it had been slain, having seven horns and seven eyes, which are the seven spirits of God sent forth into all the earth.* The horns appear to symbolize strength, as the eyes do knowledge. II. Chron. 16 : 9. *For the eyes of the Lord run to and fro throughout the whole earth, to show himself strong in the behalf of them whose heart is perfect toward him.* It will be recollected that it has been observed, that spiritual as well as solar light, consists of nine elementary principles. Need anything be added in explanation of these extracts?

There is an extraordinary passage in Ezekiel, which proves, not only that God is an organized being, but that the *normal organization*, so to speak, is similar, as to external form, (God can assume, it need not be said, any appearance,) to that of man. And it follows that man was literally created in the image of God. Of the eminent writers, I know of but one who appears to have fully adopted this idea, the poet Milton, though there may have been others. And Milton, though principally known as a poet, appears to me to have been more truly philosophical, in treating subjects of this nature, than the great luminaries on these subjects, so accounted, Sir Isaac Newton and Dr. Samuel Clarke, the antagonist of Leibnitz ; who, disregarding the plain teachings of scripture, to say nothing of common sense, resorted to abstract reasoning, and one sided metaphysical speculation. *One sided*, if the converse proposition is equally plausible, and its truth equally probable.

Ezek. 1 : 26—28. *And above the firmament that was over their heads was the likeness of a throne, as the appearance of a sapphire stone : and upon the likeness of the throne was the likeness as the appearance of a man above upon it. And I saw as the colour of amber, as the appearance of fire round about within it : from the appearance of his loins even upward, and from the appearance of his loins even downward, I saw as it were the appearance of fire, and it had brightness round about. As the appearance of the bow that is in the cloud in the day of rain, so was the appearance of the brightness round about. This was the appearance of the likeness of the glory of the Lord. And when I saw it, I fell upon my face, and I heard a voice of one that spake.*

This appearance was unquestionably designed to convey a definite and correct idea, though but a likeness of the ineffable glory of the LORD.

Men, created in the divine image, are still, like the appearance described above, surrounded with spheres, how bright in Eden, but soon, alas, how darkened by sin. And they still have an external organization, resembling that of the seven Spirits of God*.

It is in the first Epistle of John that we are told expressly, that God is light. I. John, 1 : 1—5. *That which was from the beginning, which we have heard, which we have seen with our eyes, which we have looked upon, and our hands have handled, of the Word of life ; (For the life was manifested, and we have seen it, and bear witness, and shew unto you that*

* The nature of the spheres, as in man, has been partially explained. They are fully visible to clairvoyants, and partially so to ocular sensitives. I shall return to the subject of the surrounding spheres, and the external organization, hereafter.

eternal life, which was with the Father, and was manifested unto us;) That which we have seen and heard declare we unto you, that ye also may have fellowship with us: and truly our fellowship is with the Father; and with his Son Jesus Christ. And these things write we unto you, that your joy may be full. This, then, is the message which we have heard of him, and declare unto you, that God is light, and in him is no darkness at all. No one, acquainted with the language of the Scriptures, can suppose that this announcement, so formal and circumstantial, was designed merely to signify that God is a God of infinite knowledge. It has an extensive meaning, and though I am treating more expressly, of the essential nature of God, I will endeavour to give my ideas of its entire purport, or that which is obscure. God is a being of infinite knowledge, wisdom and goodness, of power and of purposes commensurate; He is represented as approving of that which is good, and as disapproving of that which is evil. But this knowledge, wisdom and goodness, the power and purposes, the approval and disapproval, are not abstract entities, they exist only in the conditions of the divine subsistence. That is light, these are light. To those who in sincerity have embraced the faith of the gospel, have obeyed its precepts, and experienced the blessed influences of God's Holy Spirit, these conditions are entirely favourable. They are engaged to bestow upon such eternal life, with all its blessings. Can they desire, or ask, or even conceive of anything more? This message, then, the apostle declared unto all such, THAT THEIR JOY MIGHT BE FULL.

CALL OF ABRAHAM—THE JEWS.

Nothing can be more erroneous than the supposition so often and so confidently brought forward, as if, indeed, it were an unquestionable truth, that at some remote period, the representative men of the human race, were in the state described in the following line of Dryden:

"When wild in woods the noble savage ran."

Precisely the reverse was the fact. Men were reduced to the savage state from one in which the arts and sciences must have prevailed.*

After the dispersion, which took place subsequently to the confusion of tongues, it is probable that the general knowledge brought from the antedeluvian world, by the family of Noah, and the worship of the true God, which had been continued in that family alone, declined more or less rapidly, in all the divisions of the human race, except in one, or a few, of the more favoured ones. The others would find so much employment in preserving their own existence, in maintaining a doubtful strife with the numerous wild animals, almost as powerful as themselves, and in their own dissensions, that little space or opportunity would be left for preserving or cultivating true and useful knowledge, and for keeping out that which was false and hurtful. The inevitable decline of the arts would tend powerfully to destroy civilization.

The dispersion took place or commenced, about one hundred years after the deluge. Somewhat more than three hundred years later, it pleased God to appoint a people, who should be separate from the other nations of earth, who should perpetuate duly, the courtesies and amenities of a true civilization, and practise, not only the useful arts, but those of embellishment; and who should perpetuate a knowledge of the being and character of the creator and governor of the universe; and to whom, in due time, a written revelation would be given, acquainting them with all that was desirable to be known, concerning the origin and history of the human race, the requirements of God, and the methods of achieving the highest purposes of their being.

The patriarch Abraham was chosen to be the progenitor, and common ancestor of this people, the founder of a great nation, a man favoured above others, in whom all the families of the earth should be blessed. The name of

---

* Note (B).

Abraham was originally Abram. It was changed by the divine command. It will be seen that there was important symbolism in the meaning of the two names, and in the change.

It appears that up to the time of the calling of Abraham, all mankind, born after the deluge, were of one race. Different nationalities had arisen, having, no doubt, national peculiarities, but still they remained of one race; a race slightly deteriorated from that of Noah and his sons, which was the same as that of Adam, after the fall. Probably the change in the soil and productions of the earth, and the great changes and irregularities of climate, introduced at the time of the deluge, aided in producing this change. These causes, it is probable, contributed, at a later period, to the division of mankind into a number of races, of characteristicks so variant, that it has been doubted, very unreasonably, whether they all proceeded from a common stock. Unreasonably, because there are known causes, sufficient to have produced all the diversities of race, without supposing that the different races had other than a common origin.

It will here be proper, in view of what is to follow, to say a few words concerning the odic peculiarities of race. Each individual of every race, has an odic of race, which is the same in all, though they have personal odies, which are as diverse as character. The odies of all the different races give the same movement to the pendulum, the differences consist in the force of the movement, that of the higher races being the most considerable. The odic of the Caucasian race gives a movement of the force of 9,° 3', or as it may be written, 93'; while that of the Boshmen of South Africa, and of the natives of Australia is but 25'.* There are various intermediate races. The

---

* The elephant and the black snake of North America, give a movement of the force of 20'; the original difference in the faculties of these extremes, as thus indicated, being not very great; but the one having the faculty of speech, not possessed by the other, and by the exercise of which, their other faculties are very considerably improved and strengthened.

pendular force of the odic of Noah and his sons, and of Adam, was 97'.

Several years after Abraham, or Abram, was separated from his brethren, God made a covenant with him, which was confirmed by signs of a very extraordinary character. The transaction is described in the fifteenth chapter of Genesis. I will cite a part of the description. Ver. 12. *And when the sun was going down, a deep sleep fell upon Abram; and, lo, a horror of great darkness fell upon him.* Whence this *horror of great darkness?* Would it not be disproportionate to suppose that it referred to the bondage in Egypt, mentioned in the next verse? Did it not rather refer, happening as it is expressly said it did, *when the sun was going down,* to a transaction, during which, for three hours, from the sixth hour to the ninth, the sun was darkened? and to a bondage subsequent, far more severe, and longer continued, than that of Egypt? Ver. 17. *And it came to pass that when the sun went down, and it was dark, behold a smoking furnace, and a burning lamp that passed between those pieces.* See ver. 8—10. Whence this symbol? What does it mean? Does it not read thus? *A somewhat, that takes the place of the sun, is in some sort internal to terrestrial creatures. There is also flight.*

It will be recollected that it has been mentioned that the odic force, or spiritual light, consists of nine elementary principles, like solar light. The ocular sensitives have also observed smoke. This, it appears by odic process, is not a separate principle, but consists of a combination of any two or more of those, which may be so denominated. After these preliminaries, the statement, which I am about to make, will not perhaps be deemed so incredible—that immediately previous to these solemn rites, the odic of race of Abraham had a pendular force of 93', and immediately after, one of 97'. Thus when Abraham was constituted the father and founder of a peculiar people, he was also constituted of a superior race, that of Adam and Noah. This superiority of race has continued in the descendants

14

of Abraham to the present time. I have verified it by induction, and I have had an opportunity of verifying it directly. Holding the pendulum over the hand of a German Jew, it gave the movement of 97'. There is not wanting other evidence that the Jews are a superior race. The national vitality under the most unfavourable circumstances, the tenacity with which they hold the native cast of features, in all climes, and under the most depressing influences, the great number of talented men of Jewish descent, in that part of the world where talent is most highly cultivated, their success in the pursuit which actuates the greater part of mankind, their fecundity, &c., &c.

I have observed that there was important symbolism in the meaning of the two names of Abraham, and in the change. Abram means *An high father*, Abraham, *the father of a multitude*.

THE BIBLE.

I have several times, in the course of my writings, referred to the text, Matt. 21 : 43. *Therefore I say unto you, The kingdom of God shall be taken from you*—the Jews—*and given to a nation bringing forth the fruits thereof.* This solemn declaration of the Saviour must be received implicitly, by those who regard the scriptures as of divine origin. The description of the frame of a city, Ezek. 40, seems to prove that this nation is England. Thus much being granted, was it not to be confidently expected that God would provide this nation with an *authentick* copy of the scriptures? By this I mean, not a copy which should necessarily be *accurate*, in the more ordinary sense of the term, but one which should be adapted to all the exigencies and responsibilities of the situation in which the English people are thus placed. As neither of the languages in which the scriptures were originally written, is a spoken language, all copies of the scriptures, designed for general perusal, designed for any but the learned, must be translations; and this alone sets aside all idea of *perfect accuracy*, to say nothing of the changes wrought in all languages by time.

One of the best judges of language* says there is no such thing as a synonym. One of the words will always have a little more force, a little more delicacy. How much more must this be the case, not to mention words of different shades of meaning, in the nearest equivalents, in different languages. Then there are errours of transcribers and of the press. The ancient manuscripts it is said, have in some instances been altered, to suit preconceived theories.

Admitting the original inspiration of the scriptures, by which I mean verbal inspiration, I see no difficulty, considering the imperfection of the beings for whom they are designed, and of the means by which copies have been multiplied, in supposing, in an *authentick* copy, a considerable margin for errours. Even such as result, not only in obscurities, but in inconsistencies. The book will then stand upon the same footing, as respects its origin, as do the ancient classicks, in respect of theirs, which there is no difficulty in receiving, notwithstanding numerous errours. A great objection to a revelation as accurate as a calendar, or a manual of arithmetick, might be rendered, (and which would continue so,) is that it must be limited to a narrow section, in the immense range of human capacity, acquirement and prejudice, or, that it must be exceedingly limited in its topics, or circumscribed in its method of treatment. Again, a book so accurate would be held up as a model, a pattern for men in their own writings, and ordinary transactions.

A *reasonable* margin for errour, (always supposing the book to have been, originally, fully inspired,) is attended with no inconvenience, if the book be approached in the right manner, and in the right spirit. One rule to be observed, and the disregard of which, by expositors and commentators, it is to be feared has been the source of much evil, is to allow obscure passages to remain such, confessedly. Be not in haste to adopt crude and imper-

---

* Lord Chesterfield.

fect explanations, but wait till advancing light and knowledge afford a satisfactory solution. Suspend the judgment in respect of such passages, and even of those which
appear to involve inconsistency. Palpable mistakes, as
discrepancies in numerical statements, will in the case supposed, (of original inspiration,) be regarded as errours, not
of the originals, but of transcribers or of the press. The
provision made by Providence, for obviating the evils,
which it might be supposed would arise from unavoidable errours in multiplying copies of the scriptures, is found
in the promise, Seek and ye shall find. Those who seek
perseveringly, and in a right spirit, will find, if not in all
cases absolute truth, all that is needful for salvation, the
great purpose for which the scriptures were given.

Infidels who object to the scriptures that they are imperfect, and believers, who are *almost* prepared to stoutly
maintain that they are perfect, or who grudgingly and
unwillingly half admit that there are a few unimportant
errours, are entirely one side of the *valley of vision*. They
are beating the air to no purpose, while they imagine they
are assailing the hosts of errour.

I have deemed it proper to make these observations, in
view of the alleged imperfections in the English Authorized Version of the Scriptures, which, as I believe, was
prepared, in the fullness of time, under Providence, to be
the Bible, of the new dispensation, as the Hebrew Scriptures were of the old. The New Dispensation, which
commenced, nearly at the same time as that at which the
old was done away, if, as some have believed, Christianity
was established in England, by one of the Apostles.

Not to insist here upon evidence to be derived from
prophecy, in connexion with civil and ecclesiastical history, and the progress of biblical learning, at the time
when the English version was given to the world, the particular circumstances under which the translation was
made, and the admirable character of the work, in a merely literary point of view, my reasons for the belief above,

are derived more especially from the odic peculiarities of all the copies of the book. These peculiarities are set forth so clearly in a record made in 1854, that I will give the principal portion of it.

"The pendulum, rendered morally sensitive, moves appropriately over printed names of good and bad and possessed, men and women, (giving the sexual, and good and bad movements; and being stationary over the names of the possessed,) in other books than the Bible, in all books so far as I am aware, but with different degrees of force. The same is the case as respects the Bible.

"The Bible also has what may be called a *sacred general odic,* peculiar to itself. When the pendulum is rendered sensitive to this, it moves over any part of the printed text of the English authorized version of the Bible, with a circular movement from left to right, with a force equal to 10′′′. It moves thus over the Hebrew Bible—that used in the synagogues—but not over any other copy of the scriptures, so far as I have been able to determine by induction. Not over the Douay Bible, not over any of the translations of the British and Foreign Bible Society, &c.

"The normal pendulum gives the movements described first above, over the names of men and women in the authorized English and Hebrew scriptures, but not over names in any other printed books or manuscripts. This odic may be called the *Sacred Nominal Odic* of the Bible. This movement has also the force of 10′′′.* There seems no reason to doubt that the *genuineness* and *sacredness* of any copy or passage of the scriptures may be determined in either of these modes.

---

* Whether the ocular sensitives would perceive any difference in the pages of the English and Hebrew Bibles, as compared with other books, I have no direct means of determining. That learned, and gifted, and half-inspired individual, Emanuel Swedenborg, says:—"There is a room in the southern quarter of the spiritual world, the walls of which shine like gold; and in this room is a table, and on this table lies the Bible, set with jewels. Whenever this book is opened a light of inexpressible brilliancy flows from it, and the jewels send forth rays, which arch it over with a rainbow.

"Neither of these odics is derived from the original copies of the inspired authors of the Sacred Books, but is impressed upon all new copies of the scriptures, as specified above, the *general odic*, as appears by odic response, by the immediate power of God; and the nominal odic by the ministry of angels.

"It appears that all the books received as canonical, by the Church of England, are inspired, or have the two sacred odics, but no others—none of the books of the Apocrypha."

The above has been recently verified, by odic appliances, far more perfect and considerable than those which I possessed at the earlier period; and the following particulars added.

I. The English authorized version was adopted by Providence, as the Bible of the New Dispensation.

II. The sacred general odic is derived from the seven Spirits of God, so that it may be said that God is essentially present, in a peculiar manner, in every copy of the authorized English scriptures.

III. This copy of the Bible is the Ark of the Testament, spoken of in the eleventh chapter of Revelation.

It will be recollected that under the Jewish economy, the Ark of the COVENANT was placed in the Holy of Holies, and that over it was a visible light, in which God was present. Under the later dispensation, in gracious conformity with the changed condition of mankind, God is pleased to be present in every copy of his Word; so that every man can have the Ark of the Testament in his dwelling.

There are superstitions, as many would call them, concerning the Bible, one of which is that it is a preservative against evil spirits. I should be unwilling to dwell in a house in which there was not a copy of the Bible. It should always be treated with reverence.

I will cite the entire passage of Revelation, in which the Ark of the Testament is spoken of, and if, in all the writings known as the ancient classicks, there is a single passage comparable to it, for the highest elements of poetick sublimity, I should be gratified to be made acquainted with it.

Rev. 11:15—19. *And the seventh angel sounded; and there were great voices in heaven, saying, The kingdoms of this world are become the kingdoms of our Lord, and of his Christ; and he shall reign for ever and ever. And the four and twenty elders, which sat before God on their seats, fell upon their faces, and worshipped God. Saying, We give thee thanks, O Lord God Almighty, which art, and wast, and art to come; because thou hast taken to thee thy great power, and hast reigned. And the nations were angry, and thy wrath is come, and the time of the dead, that they should be judged, and that thou shouldst give reward unto thy servants the prophets, and to the saints, and them that fear thy name, small and great; and shouldst destroy them which destroy* the earth. And the temple of God was opened in heaven, and there was seen in his temple the ark of his testament; and there were lightnings, and voices, and thunderings, and an earthquake, and great hail.*

While the humblest Christian is permitted to have the Ark of the Testament in his dwelling, it is seen in the temples of God's worship, surrounded by the solemn and magnificent external accessories, and the still more solemn associations, of an Established Religion, ordained by God himself.

The kingdom of God was to be taken from the Jews, and given to A NATION, bringing forth the fruits thereof. Not nations, but A NATION. There is sufficient evidence that this nation is England. May the people of England, and particularly they of the Established Church, who are more especially concerned, receive this truth with adoring thoughts, with right feelings, and with profound humility towards GOD.

---

* Alternative reading, *corrupt.*

What was the design of the Bible? of the varied dis-
pensations of which it gives the history? including the
fall of man, the promises, the account of the deluge, and
the history of the race up to the time of Abraham? The
preservation of the descendants of Abraham, as a separate people, till their numbers were greatly increased?
Their establishment, under the leadership of Moses and
Joshua, as an independent nation? The long succession
of different forms of civil rule, under the guidance of
Providence, the succession of prophets, and of inspired
writings? The machinery, so to speak, of the Mosaic
law, all explained and confirmed by the most sublime and
surprising miracles; and finally, the appearance on earth
of him who was predicted, his teachings and miracles, and
the marvelous circumstances of his death? Surely something more was purposed than the teaching of morality.
Had *that* been the *sole intent*, an amplification of the deca-
logue, with miracles, enough to prove that the book had
the divine sanction, would have been *sufficient*. Will it be
contended that the sole purpose of all this was to teach
men how to behave under the infinitude of ever varying
circumstances—considered merely as men, and not as
prisoners of hope—or, shall we not rather receive the innumerable intimations, and express declarations, in the
writings themselves, that a far higher purpose, a purpose
indispensible to the well being of man, considered in his
entire existence, (first clearly set forth in these very writings,) was in view?

Volumes would be required to give in full, and in regular order, all the circumstances in this connexion, over
which some light might be thrown, by the odic force—
but the limits of the present work will only admit of my
mentioning briefly, a few of the leading particulars.

REGENERATION.

John 3: 3. *Jesus answered and said unto him, Verily,*

verily, I say unto thee, Except a man be born again, he cannot see the kingdom of God. Ver. 5. *Jesus answered, Verily, verily, I say unto thee, Except a man be born of water and of the spirit, he cannot enter into the kingdom of God.* 7, 8. *Marvel not that I said unto thee, Ye must be born again. The wind bloweth where it listeth, and thou hearest the sound thereof, but canst not tell whence it cometh, and whither it goeth: so is every one that is born of the spirit.*

There appear to be intimations in scripture, which prove, that although baptism is ordained, and is to be regarded, when circumstances permit; yet that when this is not the case, a *virtual* recognition and adoption of the rite, will be accepted.

Regeneration is illustrated somewhat, by actual sympathy. But the spirit of God remains permanently, with the subject of the divine influence. It appears by odic process, that the infused Spirit is of the Holy Ghost himself, and not of the seven Spirits of God. That in regeneration there is one effusion, which is not followed by others, or perhaps it should rather be said, by a continued influx.* The presence and influence of the renovator, the comforter, the divine Paraclete, produces, it need not be said, a radical, a vital change in the character, which alone, qualifies the subjects of this gracious ministration, for heaven.

The systems, which encourage exciting revivals, though of less general efficacy than a system more uniform and equable in its influences, are not without beneficent results, and instruction. The exciting influences, which are employed, appear, in various instances, to prepare the heart suddenly, for the influences of the Spirit. When regeneration takes place, under such circumstances, it is believed that it is sometimes accompanied by the phenomenon of a circumambient light, or luminousness. I

---

* This, I believe, has been a question with Divines.

should recommend to those who have opportunity, to make inquiries and observations on this subject.

THE BAPTISM WITH FIRE.

John the baptist says of Christ, Matt. 3:11, *he shall baptize you with the Holy Ghost and with fire.* It is evident, see the entire verse, that the baptism by fire is commensurate with that by the Holy Ghost. The meaning of this obscure passage appears to be as follows. The emanations of the odic current, that traverses the person of every human being, are permanently modified by the thoughts and feelings which they encounter, so that the intellectual and moral history of every individual is written upon the atmosphere, as it were, in symbolic characters of light and fire.* After death these symbolic representatives of thought and feeling, whether good or evil, return to the spirits whence they proceeded, and are united with them; except that the previous evil thoughts of the regenerate, immediately after regeneration, and subsequently, as they arise, are, by the power of Christ cast into the fire, where the odic combinations are immediately resolved into the normal odic. The good thoughts and feelings only, of the regenerate, return, after death, to them, and all, good and bad, to the unregenerate. The next verse, 12, describes the preservation of the good thoughts of the blest, and the destruction of their evil thoughts. *Whose fan is in his hand, and he will thoroughly purge his floor, and gather his wheat into the garner; but he will burn up the chaff with unquenchable fire.* The passage Is. 4:4, *When the Lord shall have washed away the filth of the daughters of Zion, and shall have purged the blood of Jerusalem from the midst thereof by the spirit of judgment, and by the spirit of burning,*

---

* There appears to be another and still more subtile condition of these emanations. They are modified by past thoughts, laid up in the mind. It was by reason of a power, dependant upon some sympathetic or clairvoyant faculty possessed by Tschokke, which enabled him, at times, to read these symbols, that he became acquainted with all the prominent particulars, in the lives of those with whom he conversed.

relates to Jews in Palestine, after the restoration, who are christianized and regenerated, and to the spirits of departed brethren, who had experienced the same gracious influences. See verses 3—6. They evidently relate to a period subsequent to the commencement of the millennium.

The views above, of the nature of the baptism with fire, are strikingly confirmed by Mark 9:43—50. The two last verses read thus. *For every one shall be salted with fire, and every sacrifice shall be salted with salt. Salt is good: but if the salt have lost his saltness, wherewith will ye season it? Have salt in yourselves, and have peace one with another.* This is so clear, in connexion with what precedes, and with the above, that little comment will be required. *Every one* is to be salted with fire, *after death.* Every sacrifice in life, *will be* salted with the same kind of salt, *the outflowing representatives of thought. Have salt in yourselves,* that is, good thoughts, thoughts that have not *lost their saltness.*

THE EUCHARIST.

A number of years since I inquired of the Rev. Mr. H., minister of the Congregational society in this village, whether he would have any objection to my experimenting odically, upon the sacramental bread, for the purpose of determining whether it underwent any change in consecration. He said he should not, and accordingly I procured some of the bread, of the family which prepared it, and to whom that which was left was returned, after the services, and also some of the same, which had not been consecrated. There was a manifest difference, the consecrated bread having acquired an odic. I was enabled, by the tractive process, to experiment in like manner, upon the sacramental bread of other denominations, including of course, that of the Roman Catholick. There was a general uniformity, with special differences. And the results were most astounding; (or rather, it may perhaps be said, would have been, had I not been partially prepared for them,) tending to prove, what is asserted in the New Testament, that Satan is the *prince of this world;* and also, that the *mystery of iniquity* has found its way, by the most unsuspected disguises, into the most unsuspected places. The sacred elements, as dispensed by the English national church, and the Wesleyan church, both in England or its dependances, were alone, on the one hand, free from evidences of evil and possession, and on the other, imbued with divine efficacy, in the form of the substance of the seven spirits of God. There is thus the real presence, as appears to be affirmed by Christ, though not in the way of transubstantiation.

I will not enlarge here, upon the advantages for obtaining spiritual life, in the English national church, though they are very great. They are not a subject for exultation, and God will render to every man, wherever he may be, according to his works. Many are saved in other churches.

On reviewing the above could it well be otherwise? *The kingdom of God shall be taken from you, and given to a nation bringing forth the fruits thereof.* Was it not to be expected that this solemn declaration of the Saviour would be verified, before the eyes of the world.

I will conclude this section by citing two passages from the vision, last of Ezekiel, and referring to others. And let any one who feels an interest in this most important subject, read these passages, and doubt if he can, that the millennium is first to be established in a nation, the government of which is an hereditary monarchy, the king, (or prince as he is called in the sacred text,) being the head of the church.

Ezek. 43 : 1—6. *Afterward he brought me to the gate, even the gate that looketh toward the east : And, behold, the glory of the God of Israel came from the way of the east : and his voice was like a noise of many waters : and the earth shined with his glory. And it was according to the appearance of the vision which I saw, even according*

*to the vision that I saw when I came to destroy the city:
and the visions were like the vision that I saw by the river
Chebar; and I fell upon my face. And the glory of the
Lord came into the house by the way of the gate whose
prospect is toward the east. So the spirit took me up, and
brought me into the inner court; and, behold, the glory of
the Lord filled the house. And I heard him speaking unto me out of the house; and the man stood by me.*

Ch. 44 : 1—3 *Then he brought me back the way of the gate
of the outward sanctuary which looketh toward the east; and it
was shut. Then said the Lord unto me; This gate shall be
shut, it shall not be opened, and no man shall enter in by it;
because the Lord, the God of Israel hath entered in by it, therefore it shall be shut. It is for the prince; the prince, he shall
sit in it to eat bread before the Lord; he shall enter by the way
of the porch of that gate, and shall go out by the way of the same.*

See also, ch. 45 : 7, 8, and to the end of the chapter, and
ch. 46 : 1—15; 16—18.

It scarce need be added that under figures of the Jewish
ritual are described the ordinances of the Christian worship.

SPHERES OF MEN, DEPARTED SPIRITS, AND ANGELS.

Men, the spirits of the departed, and angels, are each
and all surrounded with a spiritual sphere. Clairvoyants
undoubtedly have knowledge on this subject. These
spheres consisting of the odic force, which again, consists
of luminous subsistences, are visible to those who have
eyes to see. And there is no need that men should have
a window in their bosoms: the spheres are sufficiently
characteristick of the internal intelligence. They are
darker as the character descends in the scale of moral
worth, and lighter as it ascends towards excellence.
Would not men be more circumspect, would it not often
alter the whole tenour of their lives, could they realize
that they are surrounded by spirits, good *and evil*, who
know their devices; and that spirits of the departed, look
down from their abode in Paradise, and read their secret
thoughts?

POSSESSION.

Were those who are spoken of in the New Testament as afflicted with possession, really possessed, or only diseased ? On the supposition that they *were* possessed, could the language, considered merely as a narrative, have been more explicit ?

Possession prevails in our own time ? It appears to have been a mission of Spiritualism to prove this.*

There are at least four classes of the possessed. Those who are unconscious of the fact. These are much more numerous than all the others. Those who are conscious of the fact, but not entirely passive. Those who are conscious, and also entirely passive. Those who have not even individual consciousness, their bodies being wielded by the possessing demon.

There is an odic process, which appears to be effectual for expelling the evil spirit, in all cases ; and also to incapacitate him from possessing another.

Possession is much more common than it was a hundred years ago. The following is mainly derived from memoranda made in 1853. Of the forty-six persons who marched to the Lovell fight, 1735, only four were possessed—these were also evil. The remaining 42, (only 34 when the fight began,) including the friendly Indian, who reluctantly went back on account of lameness, and the faint hearted individual, who fled at the commencement of the fight, were all good men. Of the sixteen revolutionary generals, of whom likenesses are given in Headley's " Washington and his Generals," not one was possessed. These however, were very far from having been all under the influence of the principles of moral rectitude. On the other hand, of the fourteen —— —— 1852, eight were possessed, two were evil without possession, and only four were good. Of the nine —— —— publick men,

---

* What are we to think of those who reject the leading facts of Spiritualism ?

1853, five were possessed, one was evil without possession, and three were good.

This increase in the number of the possessed, may well remind us of the passage, (already referred to,) Rev. 18 : 2, *Babylon the great is fallen, is fallen, and is become the habitation of devils, and the hold of every foul spirit, and a cage of every unclean and hateful bird.*

I will conclude by observing, that among the advantages of the English national church is this, that her members, (those who have communed,) are not liable to possession.

THERE IS A RIVER THE STREAMS WHEREOF SHALL MAKE GLAD THE CITY OF GOD. Ps. 46:4.

The entire psalm reads thus. *God is our refuge and strength, a very present help in trouble, therefore will not we fear, though the earth be removed, and though the mountains be carried into the midst of the sea ; though the waters thereof roar and be troubled, though the mountains shake with the swelling thereof. Selah. There is a river, the streams whereof shall make glad the city of God, the holy place of the tabernacles of the Most High. God is in the midst of her ; she shall not be moved : God shall help her, and that right early. The heathen raged, the kingdoms were moved : he uttered his voice, the earth melted. The Lord of hosts is with us ; the God of Jacob is our refuge. Selah. Come, behold the works of the Lord, what desolations he hath made in the earth. He maketh wars to cease unto the end of the earth ; he breaketh the bow, and cutteth the spear in sunder ; he burneth the chariot in the fire. Be still, and know that I am God : I will be exalted among the heathen, I will be exalted in the earth. The Lord of hosts is with us ; the God of Jacob is our refuge. Selah.*

Where is this river? Is it one of those rendered memorable in scripture? the Nilus, the Jordan, the Euphrates, the Chebar? Is it one of the mighty rivers of the ocean? the Gulf Stream, or that river, which pours into the *heart of the seas*, as it is called in scripture, and whose lofty banks have been known, in more modern times, as Calpe and

Abyla? Is it the Tiber, the Danube, the Seine, the Thames? I shall give my reasons for believing that it is a river less known to fame than these, but greatly endeared to those who have the privilege of living upon its banks, even our own Connecticut. Those reasons are founded upon its situation, upon natural features impressed upon it, and upon circumstances which have transpired near.

The Connecticut is the most considerable river of New England, an off-shoot of that Old England, of which I have said so much above. It waters four of the New England states, but rises within the dominions of the British crown, as if to unite countries, that never should have been separated; never would have been, had the leaders of the revolution, been aware of the relations of the parent country, to the best interests of mankind. The Connecticut has a course of upwards of 300 miles, and there are numerous fair and flourishing towns upon its banks. As might be expected, in rocky and mountainous New England, the scenery is diversified. At Walpole there is a remarkable fall in the river, formerly known as the Great Fall, but now called Bellows Falls. Imagine yourself standing upon a bridge, the river perhaps, as was the case in my experience, somewhat swollen by recent rain. Looking toward the north you perceive, at the distance of some twenty rods perhaps, a rocky ledge crossing the stream. Suddenly, near the west bank, the waters pour forth, in mighty volume, with a rush and a roar, giving a surprising idea of material force. This is over in two or three seconds, and the waters again accumulate above, by reason I conclude, of some powerful eddy. In a few seconds the obstacle is again overcome, and again the rush and the roar. This is repeated as regularly as the beats of a pendulum; and is so much like breathing, that were it known that the river had been ordained, as a kind of *secular river of life*, it would be concluded that this arrangement had been made, by the power of the Most High, with express purpose.

I was much struck with the appearance of the west bank of the Connecticut, opposite the mouth of Miller's river, a beautiful tributary stream, which comes in from the east. The low, rocky bank impressed me with an emotion of sublimity, though on a limited scale. I was strongly reminded of the time when the rocks were formed, by the sudden consolidation of the waters.

Near Northampton lofty mountains approach each other, on opposite sides of the river; the appearance of the rocky bank on the east side, resembling that described above. When Madame Jenny Lind Goldschmidt was in this country, she spent part of the summer at the ancient and respectable town just mentioned, and she observed that the view from the hill, west of the town, was equal to any, I am not sure it was not superior to any, which she had seen on the banks of the Rhine.

The falls at South Hadley have the peculiarity of presenting a perfectly regular inclined plane, extending the entire breadth of the river. The descent I should judge to be about fifty feet. Below Middletown lofty mountains, on opposite sides of the river, again approach each other, and so near, in this instance, as to contract the channel to about half its usual breadth, so that at the time of the greater floods, the waters above are sometimes two or three weeks in regaining their equilibrium. This region has mines of cobalt and silver.

As the river has its emblem of life, so it has its emblem of death. At a place called Modus, or Moodus, in the town of East Haddam, there have been heard, from time immemorial I conclude, subterranean noises, sometimes attended with shaking of the earth. The Indians formerly resorted to this place to hold their *Pawaws*. "An old Indian being asked what was the reason of such noises in this place?—answered, 'The Indian's God was very angry because the Englishman's God came here.'"

As if nothing were to be omitted, there are tokens, on the borders of the Connecticut, sufficient of themselves to

16

prove the correctness of the Mosaic history of the creation and deluge, and the untruth of the "enormous" figment, that ages interminable as it were, have been employed in fitting this poor earth, to become the abode of men. I allude first to the bird tracks found in the rocky strata, near the bed of the river. These were so inconsistent with the received theories, that it was denied at first, if I am rightly informed, that they were or could be bird tracks. My own theory of the bird tracks is this. That they were made by antediluvian birds, of large size, aquatick, or semi-aquatick, who had been enabled to preserve their existence, through the deluge, by resting upon the bosom of the flood, or upon such floating masses as they would be likely to observe in their long flights.* That a flock of these birds were in the neighborhood of the Connecticut, when the land first appeared. They would gladly improve the earliest opportunity to disport themselves upon a firm or sustaining surface. Thus the tracks were made. Almost immediately the yielding surface was hardened into one moist, but comparatively solid. By some of the casualties which must have happened amidst the rushing waters, which were subsiding at a vast rate daily, the depression of the strata themselves, the damming up or breaking away of the waters, the newly formed strata were again submerged, and other strata were formed above them. The strata, when impressed, may have been in a rapidly forming state, neither plastick earth on the one hand, nor completely formed rock on the other. The idea of a *very gradual* hardening of the strata, in a climate like that of the valley of the Connecticut, and of other strata forming *very gradually* over them, is not feasible. There is not often a fortnight, scarce ever, if ever, a month, in which the impressions would not be obliterated.

---

* Gen. 7 : 21. *And all flesh died that moved* UPON THE EARTH.—Ver. 22. *All in whose nostrils was the breath of life,* OF ALL THAT WAS IN THE DRY LAND, *died.* This would not preclude amphibious animals from surviving the deluge; nor such as sought and pursued their food in the waters.

The lone, the solemn and the grand Ashcutney affords similar testimony. Imagine a mountain of solid rock, rising above the surrounding surface, to an elevation of over 1700 feet, in the form of a perfect cone. The level summit may have an area of two or three acres. The sides very steep. Will it be credited that this mountain, so perfect in shape, so accurately poised, was produced by upheaval, either in a solid or semi-liquid state? The idea of a crystalizing process, on a scale of commensurate grandeur, from a liquid element, (I do not say menstruum,) while it is not only consistent with scripture, but eminently conformable to it, seems to afford the only reasonable explanation; if indeed, the mountain were formed by a *process*, and not by the more direct power of the Most High.

As was to be expected, the poets have not been unmindful of this beautiful river, and its tributary streams. I remember to have seen, many years since, some very pleasing lines on Westfield river; and wondering much, who, *about here*, could write such poetry. It read like selected English poetry. This, it is to be recollected, was before the rise of the modern school of American poets. I have since had reason to believe that the lines in question were written by St. John Honeywood, who, in the early part of his life, was occasionally at Westfield. Barlow thus describes the Connecticut in the vision of Columbus.

> Thy parent stream, fair Hartford, met his eye,
> Far lessening upward to the northern sky,
> No watery gleams through happier vallies shine,
> Nor drinks the sea a lovelier wave than thine.

But it is time to speak of those circumstances, which have happened near the Connecticut, and upon which, if aught, will depend its claim to have been distinguished, in scripture, above other rivers.

The work entitled Millennial Institutions, composed in one of the villages on the banks of the Connecticut, was published in 1833. The title sufficiently indicates its general scope. In this work it was first made known to the world, that England was the nation in which it had been ordained, that Millennial Institutions should first prevail. Heaven forbid that I should say this with any feelings of exultation. Far different are my sentiments. Yet I humbly trust, that the work has been graciously and mercifully accepted, as a sacrifice, seasoned with salt. Other writings followed, making, with the above, an irregular series, treating upon kindred and congenial topics. Comment on the twenty-third chapter of Isaiah. Seventh Vial, Aerial Navigation and the Patent Laws, Theological Mystery. Of the present work, after an interval of eleven years, during which my odic investigations have been mostly conducted, nothing need be said.

I will now mention a circumstance, that has happened on the banks of the Connecticut, within a comparatively recent period, which, according to present appearances, tends to prove that this is indeed the river, that was to make glad the city of God. The Prince of Wales, as is universally known, visited the American Continent in 1860. He arrived at St. John's, New-Foundland, July 23. After travelling extensively in the British Provinces, and in the United States, where he was received with a decent recognition of his exalted rank, and a hearty good will, highly creditable to the inhabitants, he turned his course towards the distant city, where he was to embark for Europe. On his way he crossed the Connecticut at Springfield, Oct. 17. He spent the preceding night at Albany. On the morning of the 17th, there was an earthquake, very severe for this region, which shook the northern part of New England, and Canada. Was this coincidence accidental? The Prince, on the 17th, pursued his course from Albany to Boston. While at Springfield, to gratify the curiosity of the numbers, who had assembled to see him, he appeared to view, for a few moments, supported by some of the distinguished individuals of his suit.

Probably I shall gain little credence, but I affirm, on the testimony of odic response, that while the Prince thus stood, in the presence of thousands of witnesses, a large proportion of them dwellers in the Connecticut valley, he was anointed, in anticipation, by an angelick being, even as David was anointed, in anticipation, by Samuel, king of that nation to which the kingdom of God is transferred, and which has been ordained to prepare the way for the millennium. The times and the issues are in God's hands; and may the blessing of God, the God of Israel and of the millennium, rest upon this prince.*

I will conclude by addressing a few words to the Mother of the Prince. Queen Victoria, Though a humble and obscure individual, you will admit that I have some claims to your attention. Those claims I will not now specify nor insist upon. But I wish to be absolved in your mind, and in the minds of all, of even the suspicion of having unfriendly or disrespectful feelings towards yourself. Such feelings do not exist. I should not dare to indulge in feelings inconsistent with the word of God.

I will now proceed in the performance of a duty, which I believe devolves upon me. It is to advise your Majesty, to abdicate. I will not be too strenuous in respect of the rule laid down in the Christian scriptures—I. Cor. 14 : 34, 35 ; I Tim. 2 : 11, 12—which forbids women to speak in the churches, and inferring thence, that a woman cannot perform the duties of head of the church ; but read, I beseech you, the passages, which I have cited, above, from that prophetick vision—verses 1—6 of Ezek. chapter 43, and 1—3 of chapter 44—in which, under figures, derived from the ritual and circumstances of the Jewish nation, while yet the kingdom of God was with them, are set forth the ordinances of the church of the millennium. Who knoweth how soon the glory of the God of Israel will come from the way of the east, his voice like a noise of many waters, and the earth shining with his glory, to re-

---

* Note (C.).

ceive and inaugurate his prepared millennial church? He will enter by the way of the gate whose prospect is towards the east. Had it been foreseen, by the Spirit of inspiration, that thereafter a *woman* should sit in the east gate, to eat bread before the Lord, would there not have been some intimation of the circumstance, however veiled and obscure? It is remarkable, that while, in the description of the *frame of a city*—Ezek. 40—the queen is recognized, under the figure of the left hand pillar of the east gate, as being, in some sort, and as companion of the king, one of the secular heads of the nation;* there is not, in the description of the temple, the slightest allusion to the queen, or to women of any rank or condition whatever, as appointed to fill a station in the church. Again, while particular instructions are given to the prince, respecting gifts, which he may render to his sons—Ezek. 46 : 16—18— the daughters of the royal house are not even mentioned. This silence does indeed, assign to women, of every rank and degree, that place, in the arrangements of the millennial church, which is given to them, by the apostle to the Gentiles, in the passages referred to above. Is not the evidence conclusive? But I must cease. I will only repeat, with such emphasis as I may, the advice, which I have given above. QUEEN VICTORIA, earnestly, solemnly, in all sincerity, and friendliness, and honour, I advise, I exhort you to abdicate.

And Heaven grant, that you may be enabled, so to comport yourself, in this exigency, that the peace and the blessing of the God of peace, may descend upon the present Majesty of England.

* See plan.

XVI. MISCELLANEOUS.

CHEMICAL CONSTITUTION OF THE HEAVENS.

The observations of Reichenbach prove that od radiates from the sun, moon and stars, from all solid and fluid substances, that it is a principle " that extends over the entire universe."

Each of the heavenly bodies appears to have what may be called a *general odic*, proper to itself, somewhat as the magnetic fluid is proper to this earth; and also a *collective odic*, consisting of radiations from all the chemical substances, of which they respectively consist, intimately blended, but not in a state of combination. The presence of any element with which we are acquainted, even in the remotest fixed star, and the proportion in which it exists, may be determined, *it is exceedingly probable*, by receiving the rays on a surface so prepared that all the emanations from any particular substance, will be concentrated at a point. This condensation may be continued for an indefinite period, and the sensitiveness of a pendulum can be increased, over that which is normal, to an indefinite degree.

COMMUNION WITH DEPARTED SPIRITS.

In a former publication, I have spoken of a translucent, concentric sphere, which it was supposed surrounded the earth, and the refraction from which, it was believed, caused the zodiacal light. It was also believed that this sphere was Paradise, (not heaven,) the abode of the separate spirits of the just, after death, and previous to the final judgment. This hypothesis is confirmed by odic response. It will be seen by the following, what success attended an endeavor to hold communion with one of the blessed inhabitants of this sphere.

Matthew, of the Apostles of the Lord Jesus Christ, and first in order of the Evangelists, Art thou a blessed spirit, inhabiting the external sphere of the earth, or Paradise, and art thou able and willing to commune with a child of clay, dwelling on the earth? If so, be pleased to give to the pendulum a circular movement towards the left.

The psychomet of this writing was sent to the apostle Matthew, and after a brief interval, a pendulum was held over a prepared basis. It directly acquired a circular movement towards the left.

Wilt thou be pleased to give a similar movement, for an affirmative, the contrary movement for a negative, and an oscillating movement, to the right and left, to signify that it is your pleasure that a question should be withdrawn.

Answer: Yes.

Has Jesus Christ come in the flesh?

Answer: Yes.

To explain the reason for proposing this question, I will cite the three first verses of the fourth chapter of I. John. *Beloved, believe not every spirit, but try the spirits whether they are of God; because many false prophets are gone out into the world. Hereby know ye the Spirit of God: every spirit that confesseth that Jesus Christ is come in the flesh is of God: and every spirit that confesseth not that Jesus Christ is come in the flesh is not of God: and this is that spirit of anti-christ, whereof ye have heard that it should come; and even now already is it in the world.*

Wilt thou commune with me on future occasions, God willing?

Answer: Yes.

Farewell.

This seemed a favourable commencement of an intelligent intercourse with an inhabitant of one of the celestial spheres. On another occasion the following questions were proposed, and answers received.

Matthew, of the Apostles and Evangelists, and dwelling in Paradise, wilt thou again hold converse with an inhabitant of the earth?

Ans.: Yes.

Am I permitted to inquire respecting the conditions of life, and the circumstances, of the separate spirits?

Ans.: Yes.

Does the separate spirit consist of the mind, soul and spirit which he had, when united to a mortal body on the earth?

Ans.: Yes.

Is your individuality preserved, so that you are known to one another?

Ans.: Yes.

Are spirits, as they are called in terrestrial language, of a material subsistence?

Ans.: Yes.

Does Paradise present a surface, diversified with hill, and dale, and stream; and adorned with trees, and living green, and plants, and flowers, like the earth, but incomparably more beautiful?

Ans.: Yes.

Does an earthly view, seen in sun-light, through the sides of a prism, give a faint idea of the glories of the celestial scenery?

Ans.: Yes.

Is the distance of the external sphere from the earth, more than three thousand, and less than four thousand Jewish miles?

Ans.: Yes.

Does the external sphere extend over eighty-five degrees of north latitude, and eighty-three of south?

.Ans.: Yes.

Are the inhabitants of Paradise much interested in all that relates to the spiritual concerns of men?

Ans.: Yes.

Can you behold the inhabitants of the earth when you choose?

Ans.: Yes.

Is each one surrounded by a spiritual sphere, some light, some dark?

Ans.: Yes.

Are the virtuous, and the evil, and the regenerate, all readily distinguishable by their spheres?

Ans.: Yes.

Are the spirits in Paradise waiting in confidence, having passed by the assurance of hope, for the day of the final judgment?

Ans.: Yes.

Are the bodies of the ransomed of the Lord to be then raised, as spiritual bodies, incorruptible, and to be reunited to their spirits?

Ans.: Yes.

Farewell.

FRAME OF A CITY.

ENGLAND

APPENDIX.

———————•◦•———————

The following is from the Journal of Man for November, 1851:

[From Chamber's Edinburgh Journal.]

THE OD FORCE.

It is nearly a century ago since Mesmer began his remarkable career, and six-and-thirty years have passed since he descended unhonored to the grave. But when ridiculed and defamed by the would-be wise ones of his day, he is said to have retorted by declaring that ere 1852 the world would be convinced of the genuineness of his pretentions. That epoch is now at hand, and lo! the prophecy is coming true. Within the last few months there has been a stirring in men's minds. Not a year ago, Mesmerism was still laughed at by the vulgar, and scouted by men of science; and the few who in heart gave heed to it, were careful how they let the quizzing public into their secret. Now all this is changed; since winter commenced, a revolution has been all but accomplished. Poor Mesmer is no longer vilified as a charlatan; he is about to win his long-deferred laurels.

A new truth, it has been well said, has to encounter three normal stages of opposition: In the first it is denounced as an imposture; in the second—that is, when it is beginning to force itself into notice—it is cursorily examined, and plausibly explained away; in the third, or cui bono? stage, it is decried as useless, and hostile to religion. And when at length it is fully admitted, it passes only under a protest that it has been perfectly known for ages! As mesmerism has now reached at all events the third stage of belief, it may prove not uninteresting to glance at its present aspect.

Mesmer declared that he had discovered a cosmical (or world-wide) power, by means of which he could induce sundry startling phenomena in his patients; but his whole system was regarded as a piece of daring charlatanism, until lately a laborious and inquisitive German stumbled upon a something somewhat similar. Von Reichenbach, in the course of his researches, became aware of a certain power, undreamed of by modern physiologists, pervading both living beings and inert matter, to which he gave the arbitrary name of *Od*. Whatever this was, it could be both seen and felt, though only persons of a certain (relaxed or irritable) temperament were capable of perceiving it. In the dark, such persons saw dim flames of light issuing and waving from the poles of a magnet; and if a hand were held up, the same luminous appearance was visible at the finger-tips. When Reichenbach, to test the reality of this, had a powerful lens so placed that it should concentrate the light of the flames (if flames there were) upon a point of the wall of the room, the patient at once saw the light upon the wall at the right place; and when the inclination of the lens was shifted, so as to throw the focus successively on different points, the sensitive observer never failed in pointing out the right spot. Reichenbach also found that when slow passes were made with a strong magnet along the surface of the body, his subjects experienced sensations rather unpleasant than otherwise, as of a light draught of air blown upon them in the path of the magnet. When the northward pole of a magnet was employed, the sensation was that of a cool draught; while the southward pole, on the contrary, excited the sensation of a warm one. He soon discovered that the whole body possessed these Od qualities, and that the one side of a person was *polar* to the other; that is to say, one's right side bears the same relation to his left as the negative and positive sides of a horse-shoe magnet; so that when two persons take hold of each other's hands *normally* (left to right, and right to left), the Od current passes through both persons unobstructedly, but sometimes attended by uneasy sensations. But by changing hands the circle is broken, and the opposite currents meet: so that if the two persons be equal in odylic power, no effect is produced, the rival currents mutually repelling each other: but if unequal, a sense of inward conflict ensues, which quickly becomes intolerable. We have ourselves experienced this.

'But what does all this testimony to the reality of the Od force amount to?' says the sceptic. 'The subjectivity of your evidence renders it worthless. All that you can say is, that you and a few others see and feel so-and-so, and as we, and the great majority of men, see and feel nothing of the kind, we must just set you down as very fanciful persons, who are the dupes of your own imaginations.' This, in truth, is a very damaging line of argument, and, coupled with the charge of collusion brought against all platform exhibitions of mesmerism, was deemed sufficient to shelve it altogether. The only obvious way of overcoming this argument was by exhibiting so many severely-tested cases as gradually to overwhelm scepticism, by making it more astonishing that so many honest and sensible men should be deceived by impostors, or duped by their fancy, than that the marvels which they avouched should be true.

Fortunately a more speedy and satisfactory remedy for scepticism has at length been found. An objective proof of mesmerism has just been discovered ; and it is so simple in its nature that any one can try it for himself. Dr. Herbert Mayo, well known both in the literary and medical world, has of late been residing as an invalid at Boppard on the Rhine ; and anxious to while away the long tedious nights of winter, he resolved to engage in the study of the higher mathematics, and with this view sent for Herr Caspari, professor of that science in the gymnasium at Boppard. It was on the last night of December last, that the German professor entered the room of his invalid pupil, and after the hour's lesson was over, they entered into desultory conversation. 'I am told you have written something on the divining-rod,' said Herr Caspari, 'and as I have two or three experiments possibly akin to it, I thought it might not be uninteresting for you to see them.' He added that, so far as he knew, they were original, and that, though he had shown them to many, he had never yet received any explanation of them. He then attached a gold ring to a silk thread, wound one end of the thread round the first joint of his fore-finger, and held the ring suspended above a silver spoon. After a few seconds' quiescence, lo and behold ! the ring began to oscillate backward and forward, or to and from Herr Caspari. At the suggestion of the operator, the maid was then summoned and directed to place her hand in his unengaged one ; and forthwith the oscillations of the ring became *transverse !* Herr Caspari next took a pea-like bit

of something which he called *schwefel-kies,* and which he
said exhibited another motion: when held suspended
over either of the fingers, it rotated one way; when held
suspended over the thumb, it rotated in the contrary direction. The professor then took his departure, promising to
return on the morrow to assist in any explanatory experiments which his pupil might think fit to make.

Before detailing these, let us explain his terms. Any
article of any shape suspended either by silk or cotton
thread, the other end of which is wound round the nail
joint of the forefinger or thumb, he calls an *odometer.* The
thread must be long enough to allow the ring, or whatever it is, to reach to about half an inch from the table, upon which you rest your elbow, to steady your hand. As
soon as the ring becomes stationary, place under it on the
table what substances you please—these he calls *Od-subjects.*
A good arming for the odometer is gold, or a better still,
a small cone of shell-lac about an inch long; the best od-
subjects are gold, silver, and one's fore-finger. All od-
subjects do not act equally well with each odometer: for
instance, an odometer of dry wood remains stationary over
gold, while it moves with great vivacity over glass; and
over rock-crystal shell-lac acts very feebly, while a glass
odometer oscillates brilliantly. We may add that, in our
own experience, the *transverse* oscillations are never so
strong as the longitudinal; doubtless because the former
act against the attraction of the body, while the latter act
with it. The following are a few of Dr. Mayo's experiments:

" 1. Odometer (we will suppose armed with a shell-lac,)
held over three sovereigns heaped loosely together to form
the od-subject; the odometer suspended from the forefinger of a person of either sex. *Result*—Longitudinal
oscillations.

2. Let the experimenter, continuing experiment 1,
take with his or her unengaged hand the hand of a person of the opposite sex. *Result*—Transverse oscillations
of the odometer.

3. Then the experiment being continued, let a person
of the sex of the experimenter take and hold the unengaged hand of the second party. *Result*—Longitudinal
oscillations of the odometer.

4. Repeat experiment 1, and the longitudinal oscillations being established, touch the forefinger which is en-

gaged in the odometer with the forefinger of your other hand. *Result*—The oscillations become transverse.

5. Repeat experiment 1, and the longitudinal oscillations being established, bring the thumb of the same hand into contact with the finger implicated in the odometer. *Result*—The oscillations become transverse.

6. Then continuing experiment 5, let a person of the same sex take and hold your unengaged hand. *Result*—The oscillations become again longitudinal.

7. Experiment 1 being repeated, take and hold in your disengaged hand two or three sovereigns. *Result*—The oscillations become transverse.

8. Continuing experiment 7, let a person of the same sex take and hold your hand which holds the sovereigns. *Result*—The oscillations become longitudinal."

The following experiments, with results exactly parallel to the preceding, possess the greatest physiological interest:—

" 20. Hold the odometer over the tip of the forefinger of your disengaged hand. *Result*—Rotatory motion in the direction of the hands of a watch.

21. Hold the odometer over the thumb of your disengaged hand. *Result*—Rotatory motion against that of the hands of a watch.

22. Hold up the forefinger and thumb of the disengaged hand, their points being at two and a half inches apart. Hold the odometer in the centre of a line which would join the points of the finger and thumb. *Result*—Oscillations transverse to the line indicated."

The development thus given of the few isolated and long hoarded experiments of Herr Caspari was by no means so simple an affair as it may seem to be. For several days Dr. Mayo was in doubt as to the genuineness of the results, so capricious and contradictory were they; and it was only when he discovered that approaching the thumb close to the other fingers of the odometer hand had the same effect as bringing it into contact with the odometer finger, that he succeeded in obtaining unvarying results.

"The interest of these experiments," says Dr. Mayo, " is unquestionably very considerable. They open a new vein of research, and establish a new bond of connexion between physical and physiological science, which cannot fail to promote the advancement of both. They contribute a mass of objective and physical evidence to give support and substantiality to the subjective results of Von Reichenbach's experiments. They tend to prove the existence of some universal force, such as that to which he has given theoretical shape and form, under the designation of Od. And such a universal force, what other can we deem it to be than the long-villipended influence of Mesmer, rendered bright, and transparent, and palatable, by passing through the filter of science ?"

For his other experiments, especially those with the odometer and magnetic needle, as well as for a list of some other substances suitable for experimenting with, we must refer to the book itself. Our readers will find the odometer treated of in a supplementary chapter (the twelfth) to the new edition, just published, of Dr. Mayo's "Letters on the truths contained in Popular Superstitions"—a work of the most absorbing interest, in which a number of astonishing material and mental phenomena are systematically treated, and the latest discoveries of science are made to shed light on the old horrible legends of Vampyrism, on True Ghosts, on the mysteries of Trance and Somnambulism, and lastly, on Mesmerism, and the higher trance-phenomena of prevision and clairvoyance. It is no secret that Sir William Hamilton and Sir David Brewster (two of our most distinguished men of science) are now converts to the new doctrines, so that there is now no risk of these not obtaining the fullest investigation ; and of the few good books at present published on this subject, we know of none so curious, so full, and so dispassionate, as this of Dr. Mayo's. We cannot at present enter on so wide a field of inquiry as his little volume opens up : we must content ourselves with a few further remarks on his latest discovery—the odometer.

In concert with a fellow-dabbler in the black arts, we first repeated Dr. Mayo's experiments, and then began examining for ourselves. Knowing that when a person wishes to consult a clairvoyant at a distance, he supposes he can do so without being brought into personal contact with the clairvoyant, by simply sending a lock of hair, a handkerchief, or anything that has been long worn about the person, it was natural to suspect that these articles might be impregnated with the peculiar Od of the sender. At any rate, we found that if we suspended a gold ring by a woman's hair, a transverse motion ensued, as if a female had been actually brought into contact with us. In like manner, if a woman were using the odometer, by making a man's hair part of the suspending cord, a change immediately ensued in the oscillations, as if a man had laid his hand upon hers. All we can as yet say further is, that the odometer oscillated with more than usual vivacity when suspended over the spinal cord of a boy; while over a well-developed female head, a similar action took place—with this difference, that it was the *transverse* oscillations that were most energetic. We propose for ourselves, and particularly recommend to others who are better fitted for such inquiries, a course of experiments with the brain and eye of men and animals. Von Reichenbach thinks he has now identified his Od force with diamagnetism: and the electrometer has already shown that muscular action is produced by a kindred agency.* The brain, itself, indeed, has been likened to an electric machine, and in part the parallelism is correct; for there is a waste of brain in thinking, and a waste of zinc when electricity is evolved.

The experiments with the hair remarkably corroborate Dr. Mayo's (No. 2), in establishing the *sexual* difference of Od; and we doubt not some more delicate odometer will soon be discovered, by means of which the *individual* varieties of Od will become distinguishable. That such varieties exist is already known. It has often been remarked that people mesmerically entranced are differently, sometimes most disagreeably, affected by the different persons who then approach them. A gentleman had a brother in delicate health, and exquisitely sensitive to Od, whom he used to mesmerize himself; for of several

---

* An anatomical inquirer asserts, that the muscles of the human body are evidently capable of exerting (or rather transmitting) an enormously greater force than we ordinarily see them do: all that is requisite to attain this being a greater evolution of electricity by the brain; or, in other words, a greater intensity of volition. The astonishing influence of the volitive process in producing strength, is evident from the prodigious muscular power occasionally exhibited by persons when inordinately excited by passion—still more remarkably from the supernatural strength of fever-frenzy or of maniacs. It is worthy of notice, also, that the gigantic strength of Sampson came by *accesses*, or impulses. We may add in connexion with this subject, that a person has just patented a new motive power, which acts by passing electricity along a fibrous substance—that is to say, just as our muscular system does.

who had been tried, there was but one other person whose hand (in mesmerizing) the brother could bear at all. This was a maid-servant, who was herself highly susceptible; and she said that she perceived, when entranced, the suitableness of her influence, and that of the brother, to the patient—using the singular expression that they were *nearly of the same color.* She said that the patient's od-emanation was of a pink-color, and that of the brother's was a brick-color—a flatter, deeper red; and she endeavored to find some one else with the same colored Od to suit her master. "In some experiments made at Dr. Leighton's house in Gower street," says Dr. Mayo, "I remember it was distinctly proved that each of the experimenters produced different effects on the same person. The patient was one of the Okeys, of mesmeric celebrity; and the party consisted of Dr. Elliotson, Mr. Wheatstone, Dr. Grant, Mr. Kiernan, and some others. Mr. Wheatstone tabulated the results. Each of us mesmerized a sovereign; and it was found that on each trial the trance-coma, which contact with the thus mesmerized gold induced, had a characteristic duration for each of us." Thus it seems as if every one had a spiritual effluvium peculiar to himself, and more or less affecting those with whom he comes in contact—even as every one has a peculiar bodily effluvium, by which you see a dog track one's footsteps in the grass.

May we not discern in this a clearing up of some of those mysteries which have so long baffled thoughtful inquirers? May we not see in this an explanation of those unaccountable predilections which sometimes seize us?— of that "love at first sight," so long derided, and yet so true? A child in its nurse's arms will cry instantaneously when some persons approach it—persons whom it has never seen before—and often the instinctive feeling of aversion proves permanent; while to others, equally strangers to it, it will stretch out its little arms delightedly, as if to well known friends. And which of us cannot recall some case in his lifetime when he has been fascinated on first sight—he knew not how—often without ever exchanging a syllable with his charmer? It is a phenomenon that happens every day, and is not less powerful in its influence than frequent in its occurrence, yet it has never been accounted for. Plato sought to explain this mystery by the notion, that souls were united in a pre-existent state, and that love is the yearning of the spirit to reunite with the spirit with which it formerly made one, and which it discovers on earth. How often has this beautiful idea inspired the poet's strain! The Od force clears up Schiller's "Mystery of Reminiscence" (as he titles his love poem) much more simply and satisfactorily than do the dreams of Plato.

Another thing worth noting is, that the Od force exists in, and is given out by, inorganic bodies, as well as by living bodies. One instance of this will be seen in No. 7 of Dr. Mayo's experiments, where it is evident that the sovereigns give out Od in the same way as if another person had taken hold of the operator's unengaged hand. But this power is by no means confined to gold; silver, lead, zinc, iron, copper, coal, bone, hair, horn, dry wood, charcoal, cinder, glass, soap, wax, shell-lac, sulphur, earthenware, and some other substances, have already been found to exhibit Od qualities when tested by the odometer; and probably *all* other substances will be found to possess more or less of the same power; and the few experiments already made (the odometer is not yet six weeks old) seem to show that each substance, as well as each individual, has a quality of Od peculiar to itself.

This strange force, in fact, is cosmical, as Mesmer long ago affirmed his to be. It extends throughout space, and reaches us even from the stars. Von Reichenbach's patients were quite sensible of the influence of the heavenly bodies—the sun and fixed stars being Od-negative, and the moon and planets Od-positive: in other words, the former causing the sensation as of a cool draught of air— the latter of a warm one. May not this exhibit the germ of astrology—of the ancient and almost universal belief in the influence of the heavenly host upon the destiny of man? although, doubtless, much of the basis of that old doctrine still remains lost to us. How does attraction act? May we look for a solving of this mystery, too, in the new powers which the researches of the mesmerists are now beginning to disclose? But there is no limit to conjecture here. An ocean of new and strange things spreads out before us, brooded over as by the clouds of the dawn; and as here and there the faint light of morning penetrates the haze, it reveals a prospect that makes the boldest hold his breath, and the most daring imagination confess its feebleness.

One word more, and we have done. The subjects of the electro-biologists (so self-styled) are made to *mesmerize themselves* by fixing their eyes intently for some time on a piece of bright metal placed in their hand. That the Od force of the metal may assist the result is probable; but even the metal itself is by no means indispensable to the success of the experiment. We have heard of at least one person who could entrance himself by gazing fixedly on the cornice of his room; and we could show how the same thing has been accomplished for three thousand years in India, simply by a steadfast concentration of thought. But in our own day, and on the testimony of numerous travellers, we find the feats of the electro-biologists exactly paralleled on the banks of the Nile. The present magicians of Cairo take a boy (the young, be it recollected, from their delicate susceptibility, are most readily affected by mesmeric influences,) making him stoop down and gaze steadfastly into a little pool of ink in the hollow of his palm; and after continuing thus for a little while, the youth is said to describe to the stranger any absent person or object as he is commanded. Nay, the stranger himself is sometimes subjected to the experiment; and forthwith, on command, beholds armies, processions, &c., in the inky mirror which he holds in his palm. With some travellers the Cairo magicians are unsuccessful; but the electro-biologists are liable to similar failure—the result in both cases depending on the more or less susceptible organization of the persons experimented with.

The following articles are all from the Journal of Man for January, 1852.

NEW DISCOVERIES—THE AURA-TEST—ODOMETER —MAGNETOSCOPE, &c.

I have received several communications from correspondents who have been engaged in repeating the experiments with the odometer mentioned in this Journal. My correspondents are quite sanguine in the opinion that they have discovered and demonstrated very important laws of nature, and have proved that MIND CAN ACT ON INORGANIC MATTER, by a direct effort of the will, which is one of the most important and interesting propositions that could be added to our existing stock of knowledge. It would seem really that if spirits can *rap* when out of the body, they ought to be able to do as much before leaving the body.— Why not? I would invite the careful attention of my readers to the discoveries of my correspondents, and, also, to the report of similar discoveries in England. After reading which, they will be prepared to consider my own statement of the apparent philosophy of these phenomena.

The name suggested by my Illinois correspondent, of *Aura-test* is better than either of the terms " *Odometer* " and " *Magnetoscope*," as the experiments are really a test of the *aura*, or influence which appertains to the nervous system.

LETTERS FROM A LADY OF ILLINOIS.

"Dec. 18. Yesterday I received your November Journal. The article on Od Force much attracted my attention, reminding me of something I discovered, or rather *thought* I discovered nearly a year ago. But, to-day, or more properly speaking, *yesterday*, I began, in the evening to try experiments—experiments which lured me on through midnight to morning, and now I will, before retiring, give the result according to my convictions.

1. The relation which man stands to the earth (and outward universe also) causes the rotations and vibrations of the odometer to be affected by his position as to the points of the compass. With me the experiments 20 and 21, on page 4 of the Journal, resulted as here given, when tried by a *male* facing north or south ; but with a woman, when she varies her position to the different points of the compass, the changes of movement are such as given here.

[The drawing here given shows that, when the individual faces north or south, the vibration is in the north and south line ; when she faces east or west, the vibration is on the east and west line ; when facing the intermediate points, those on the western side produce rotations like the hands of a watch : those on the eastern side produce rotations in a direction opposite to those of the hands of a watch.—ED.]

When a male holds it the vibrations and rotations change places.

Held over inferior animals, I discovered a diagonal vibration; from north-west to south-east over females; from north-east to south-west over males.

Suspended over *both* male and female, the blended aura gives a rotary motion to the odometer. My odometer was a pair of steel-pointed dividers. I like this odometer better than any other I tried. I am disposed to call the acting essence "aura," and the odometer an "aura-test." Sex ascertained by suspending over a footprint—that of males taking a longitudinal motion from north to south— females the same motion from east to west. The aura-test seems to play more freely when the experimenter faces the north. Tried experiments to see if the aura arising from manuscript could be made perceptible to the senses; tried an innumerable quantity of various manuscripts with the *greatest success*—could test the sex of the writer with no difficulty, the manuscripts of males giving the north and south vibration, females the east and west; both together, a circle more or less perfect, according as the force of character of the two assimilated. Manuscripts 54 years old gave as brisk a vibration as those of yesterday.

My father was much interested in these manuscript experiments—the aura-test does not play so freely with him. He would seem to paralyze many, so that there would be but a trembling of the suspended steel. He thought it was because he despised the writers. When father had tobacco in his mouth, there was no vibration, but on removing it the aura-test would again play. When father suspended the steel over tobacco, there was a brisk rotary movement; but, if I or any of my brothers tried it in the same position, the poor aura-test stood and trembled with disgust. Hardly had the rest of the family retired for the night, when I hastened to get my Charles' letters, in order to test them. It has been my custom, ever since he left me, to go to his grave, and frequently write letters to him there. I receive happiness and benefit from so doing; and in taking his letters from their deposit, I also took my roll of these spirit letters of mine to him. Feeling a hesitancy to test his letters, notwithstanding my but now earnest desire to do so, I took up this roll, and suspending my odometer over it, discovered the movement was a *circle*. Oh! that moment of intense rapture! I quickly sprang to the conclusion (since I had not before discov-

ered a circular movement over manuscripts, excepting
from the blended aura of male and female letters,) that
his spirit was with mine when I wrote these letters, and
you can imagine my feelings. But on testing his letters
to me, I found that, without exception, his letters gave the
circular movement too, only contrary to mine; mine revolving *against* the hands of a watch, and his *with* them.
Then I concluded that the loving and friendly sentiments
perhaps gave the circular movement to the aura; and I
went over other letters, holding the test close to the paper
sentence by sentence, and the aura would give the circle
over all those passages where the kindly feelings were in
immediate action, in other places the longitudinal movement was given as before. Over an ordinary letter, when
I held the steel so as to be suspended, say three inches
above the manuscript, the motion was that longitudinal
or transverse one, which merely gave the sex; but all letters actuated by the enthusiasm of love, even at that
height of the aura-test, still gave the male or female circle.

Dec. 19.—To-day, I found that all stimulants gave an
aura which produced the same vibration as that peculiar
to male manuscripts—while sedatives gave the female.
Over poisonous substances, there is more or less of a
trembling paralyzation. I tried a very pretty experiment thus: I wrote a word with my right hand, and
wrote it again with my left hand, and then with both
hands. My right hand writing gave the female movement; my left the male; both together the circle. I
could tell, by the test, what sex last occupied a seat or
bed;—circles over the clasped hands of two individuals.
Experiment where the aura-test is suspended over the
head of a subject, while the operator stands behind, both
facing to the same point of the compass—the movements
are the same as when the test is suspended on the right
forefinger of the subject. It is interesting to see how the
action of the steel is increased by others of the same sex
as the subject touching his person.

I begin to think I have discovered a key to the cause
of the "rapping" phenomena. I told father so: he says
he does not doubt it, and thinks, through a knowledge of
the laws of this force, which the aura-test makes visible,
that "perpetual motion" may be arrived at.

Dec. 20th.—To-day I discovered beyond the possibility
of doubt, what I thought I found out months ago, viz.,

that we can *will matter*. I found I could will the suspended aura-test to take whatever movement, rotary or otherwise, I would. Father ridiculed the idea, said I must move my finger involuntarily, but I pressed the finger, holding the test against my forehead, so that it could not possibly move, and I could move with my will more readily than before. Father then tried it himself. He has to hold the test in his hand awhile after I have been experimenting with it, before it will move with him—after thus magnetizing the steel, father found he could indeed will it, and he was convinced, while I in this discovery found an explanation of the cause why the test will not vibrate with sceptics, they involuntarily perhaps, will it not to move. I run off into a wide range of thoughts and speculations on the cultivation of the will faculty. Believe it is the magnetism of their will which makes men great— am reminded of Kossuth's adopted sentiment, "there is no obstacle to him who wills,"—think faith and will identical, and think that it was the cultivation of the will faculty Christ would teach when he says, "by faith we may remove mountains."

Tried experiments to make the aura-test move without having it suspended from the person—not satisfactory. The experiments work the same whether one is "isolated" when trying them or not. Reichenbach, you remember, conjectures the force is not identical with electricity at all.

I thought the aura-test played better when the end of the finger suspending it was elevated to about 60 degrees above the horizon. Is not that near the dip of the magnetic needle? Indulge in various speculations here.

The test plays more freely sometimes than others with me.—When my mind is disturbed, it does not act so well. An unembarrassed frame of mind and an empty stomach I think most favorable requisites.

Dec. 21.—Notice the beautiful play of the aura-test when acted upon by the will, to change from one circle to the other. (All such experiments I make when facing the north.) The motion is first north and south for a few vibrations; then it comes round like the hands of a watch from the north, after making this circle two or three times. Sometimes when on the east side of the circle, it suddenly runs across to the west, then turning towards the south, rotates against the watch hands. And it returns to the other circle once more by running across from the south to the north, and then turning again like watch hands.

I perceive there are two great aura forces, and that they act at right angles to each other. One of them, I am convinced, comes from the north. I am not determined whether the other comes to us from the west, or falls vertically. When they act equally, they produce circles; and circles are formed when anything is created—be it a thought, a substance, or an animal. I find I can apply this (I believe) truth very successfully to the better prosecution of my household duties, especially culinary ones. The more healthy food is a combination of the two forces, and the test over it, therefore, gives a circle. I am more than ever convinced that men and women should unite in all action whose aim is the advance of our race.

When the solitary man receives a high thought, it is, I think, reasonable to conclude that the necessary positive or negative he received in order to produce this circle, came to him from a higher sphere.

But let me restrain my pen, for it was not speculation, but the results of experiments merely I intended to communicate.

Dec. 22.—Went to-day to see my cousin, in order to ascertain the reality of my experiments. She always receives the Journal at G. some days before we do here. The aura-test plays well in her hands also: and I was deeply gratified to perceive the results of her trials of it were the same as when I held it. I tried her with manuscripts, daguerreotypes, the points of the compass, sedatives and stimulants. All was very satisfactory. After all this, I told her she could will the steel. She did so to her great delight—then informed me she had thought several times before that she could give it any movement she pleased. I found L., in her experiments previous to my visiting her, had also discovered the test played better when she faced the north. She had also discovered that one of another sex could change the movement, by merely touching her person with a long wooden rod, and that distance made no perceptible difference. She had never thought of trying manuscripts; but when her experiments had been the same as mine, she had arrived at like results. When one of opposite sex touches the person holding the aura-test, if the holder *wills*, the contact will not change the motion as usual.

Dec. 23—I make no further discoveries with the odometer—feel a strange desire to give you some of my *speculations*, but forbear. My mind is still occupied with circles, and the earnest desire to know from whence these two forces come to us which form them. I have long thought the Deity was a Universal Spirit, rather than an individualized being; and I find myself wondering if these two forces may not be his attributes—Himself. But since I have given what I consider the most important of my *experiments*, I break away from the subject, for I ought not to intrude upon you anything which I am unable to prove.

But one thing I think these experiments satisfactorily make evident, viz: that in every individual, male or female, both stimulant and sedative forces act—that when one is well, their action produces that circle in the bodily atoms we call 'health'—that disease is a disturbance or inactivity of one of these forces; and the action of judiciously applied stimulants and sedatives may restore the circle again.

P. S.—I thought I discovered that *colors* affected the aura-test; but I was not satisfied, because I came to this conclusion after I found I could will the test; and therefore I was not always sure but my will affected its motion. I have proceeded all along through these experiments with great caution. I have endeavored that my enthusiasm and my imagination should be restrained, so as to keep me within the bounds, not merely of fact, but of *evident* fact.

SECOND LETTER FROM THE SAME, JAN. 17, 1852.

You have doubtless received my letter mailed Christmas—also one from L., forwarded since, containing statements of some of our experiments on the Odic Force.

I thought from the natural point to which all who were stimulated by your article on Od Force would send the result of their investigations—that receiving such, you would have them so tested that the true would be sifted from the false; for many of your readers beside L. and myself have but limited opportunities of testing our experiments, by trying them in the hands of a *great number* of different individuals, and have thus, I doubt not, in some cases received for truth what if further tried might prove ill grounded.

I hoped you would be the first to present the public with the discoveries on this new force, and that, therefore, it would be done in a careful and scientific manner. I believe L. shared with me in this earnest wish.

But yesterday, the St. Louis Daily Republican, of Jan. 5th, fell into my hands; and lo! an article headed "Spiritual Communications—Odic Force," which was forwarded to that sheet by W., her father.

"The Odic Force can be readily tested by any one. Almost any substance will answer the purpose; but a pair of gold ear-rings, or a piece of steel two or three inches long, *suspended by a string from the first joint of the forefinger*, with the elbow resting on a chair or table, will show the power. Let the person face to the north, and the instrument will begin to vibrate. The motion that it takes is usually north or south, but not always so. In some hands it vibrates strongly, making an angle of nearly forty-five degrees with the horizon, but in most cases it is less. Placing mineral or vegetable poisons beneath it, paralyzes the motion. A single Homœopathic pellet of nux arrests the motion—so of sepia, the two hundredth potency. Tobacco in the mouth of the operator, or snuff in the nose, arrests the motion. Over some substances it takes a transverse motion—over others a rotary motion. Manuscript affects it, and in some instances very actively. The manuscript of a deceased friend giving it vitality that was perceptibly diminished in the hand of a stranger. Touching different organs of the brain changed the motion. The intellectual organs giving increased activity and diversity to the motion, whilst over the organs of crime it becomes paralyzed and motionless.

"But the most astonishing discovery relative to this power, and which is original here, and so far as I know, before undiscovered, is, that *it can be controlled by the will*. The mental command that it shall abandon a state of rest, and take a forward, transverse or rotary motion, or that it shall return from any motion to a state of rest, is promptly obeyed; and as soon as the effort of the will ceases, the odometer returns to a state of rest, or to its natural and spontaneous action. This fact need not be doubted, for it is in the power of any one to prove it.

"Many of us have seen, or have imagined that we saw an astonishing influence exerted upon the animal frame by mesmerism; but here we have an immediate and incontrovertible evidence of the *power of the will over inani-mate matter!* This fact is the more valuable, because open to the practical experience of all, both "the learned and the unlearned," and must prove an important aid to phys-ical science, to say nothing of spiritual or of psychological investigation. I have made an experiment with a bar of iron weighing ten pounds, which took the north and south vibration spontaneously, and then obeyed my mental call for a rotary motion without the delay of one second. The weight and magnitude of the body which may thus be set in motion, are probably illimitable." W.

LETTER FROM L. W.

You have probably, ere this, learned from my cousin the interest which the article on the newly discovered Od force, in your last Journal, has excited in our minds. We, or at least I, have been so deeply absorbed in the subject that I have thought of little else for the last two or three weeks. It opens so illimitable a field for thought and imagination that the mind is lost in the effort to compre-hend its immensity. Even were there no more discov-eries to be made in it, it would still be productive of great good, for these are experiments which any or every one can prove. Many who cannot be made to understand and believe anything that is not made evident to their senses, will, in making these experiments, see and feel the dark cloud of doubt which has shut out from them the invisible world, suddenly dissipate, and forever. Upon the minds of several in our immediate neighborhood, to whom the subject has been broached, and who are naturally very skeptical upon such subjects, a beneficial effect has already been produced.

But the rapid development of the laws which govern this force, and the nature of the discoveries made, seem to indicate that science, and especially human science, is to receive from it new light, and that it may be applied at a future day to some practical use. It is in the full belief that this will be the case that my cousin and myself are prosecuting our investigations. It is quite probable that you or some of your correspondents may have made the same discoveries, but as there is a possibility that they may be new to you, I beg leave to submit the results of my experiments.

My cousin tells me that she has given you an account of our observations up to the date of her last letter. Since comparing notes with her, my experiments have been based principally upon the following ascertained facts : First, the odometer when suspended over stimulants takes the longitudinal vibration, over sedatives the transverse motion, and over deadly poisons is entirely paralyzed. Second, when suspended over the manuscript of a male, the vibrations are longitudinal, and over that of a female transverse. Manuscript expressive of affection or of benevolent feelings produces a circular motion. In my experiments I am generally careful to face one of the cardinal points. If the intervening points are faced, the result will be a circular motion, where a longitudinal vibration was obtained in the former position, and vice versa. Whilst experimenting with manuscripts, it struck me that the different regions of the brain, the intellectual and the region of affection, might produce an effect upon the odometer corresponding to that of manuscript. You can imagine my delight when I found the correspondence perfect. When the odometer is held above the head of a person of my own sex, the regions of the intellect and of energy produce the longitudinal vibration, the region at the side of the head, comprehending reverence, modesty, &c., gives the transverse, and the moral region produces a perfect circle, whilst the region of hatred and fear paralyzes the odometer completely. I wished exceedingly to try a manuscript expressive of violent anger or of some of the baser passions, but unfortunately (for my experiment) possessing none such, could not ascertain whether the correspondence would be complete in this particular. There is no reasonable doubt, however, that it would be so. You, perhaps, will be able to ascertain. When suspended above the head of a person of the opposite sex, the odometer takes the circular motion at the regions of energy and the intellect, the moral region gives the longitudinal vibration, and the region of crime paralyzes as before. This fact seemed at first to set aside the idea of a correspondence between the effects of the brain and of manuscript, and troubled me not a little, till I found that if the odometer be suspended by the left hand over manuscript, the result is the same as that obtained when it is suspended from the right above the head of a male, and that if the left hand be used as the odometer hand in experimenting with the head of a male, the result will be the same as that obtained from the head of a female when the right ·hand is employed. These facts seem to be an additional proof, if any is needed, of the idea which I first saw advanced in your journal, that every one, whether male or female, combines two opposite sexes in his or her own person.

There exists not only this correspondence in their effects upon the odometer between the brain and manuscripts, the productions of the brain, but there appears to be a remarkable correspondence between it, (the brain) and the inanimate creation. Thus, the intellectual and energetic regions correspond to stimulants, the side regions to sedatives, and the region of crime to poisons. A stimulant and a sedative united produce the circular motion. How will this correspond with the effect of the moral region?

The influence of medicinal substances upon the odometer is certainly very wonderful. It seems as if this little quivering piece of metal, connected with the human system but by a thread, is endowed with life, or a mysterious sympathy, and with an unerring sagacity, which enables it to detect almost instantly the nature of whatever may be brought within its sphere, and the presence of anything that might be injurious. It occurred to me to try medicines homœopathically prepared. The result was most astonishing. A single pellet of any medicine exerts as powerful an influence as one ounce of the same substance. One pellet of Sepia of the two hundredth *potency* produces entire paralysis. Having none of a still higher potency, I was not able to ascertain the exact point at which an infinitesimal quantity would cease to act. My father found that immediately after taking a dose of Nux Vomica, the odometer was paralyzed. By exerting his will he could move it a little, but a very little. The fact that the odometer can be controlled by the will, renders extreme caution necessary in conducting these experiments. I therefore employed another person to select the medicines, not knowing myself what they were until the trial was over. Does not this experiment prove beyond controversy, 1st that the system is operated upon through the nerves, and 2nd, the power of homœpathic medicine to act in this way, and that as far as medicinal action is concerned, mere quantity is entirely unimportant, or rather that an infinitesimal dose is as potent to produce this action as many grains can be. Being somewhat enthusiastic in the cause of Homœpathy, this proof of its power has given me especial pleasure; and my enthusiasm will, I trust, be my excuse for speaking to you, in too decided a manner, perhaps, upon a system which, if I mistake not, you regard as fallacious.

Since the discovery of the power of the will, we have sometimes amused ourselves in willing against each other. One person holds the odometer, and wills it in a certain direction, while another places a hand upon the head of the person, and wills a contrary direction. Ordinarily no effect is produced, but I have been making a trial with my father, which shows the astonishing power of the will over matter, and is also an experiment in Neurology. I seated myself with the odometer, and willed it to take the longitudinal vibration, while my father placed his hand on the top of my head, and willed it in the contrary direction. No change was produced. At my cousin's suggestion, he then placed his hand upon the organ of Pliability. The struggle was long and severe, but I was finally obliged to yield in spite of myself. I experienced afterwards the same feeling of lassitude, with slight trembling, which long continued bodily exertion occasions.

A singular fact elicited from the experiments with manuscripts is, that Odic force, or fluid, or whatever it may be, arising from manuscript, may be communicated by contact to metals, and probably to other substances, and affects the odometer in precisely the same manner that the manuscript·itself does. I have tried gold and tin only.

We have used various substances for odometers, but gold and steel appear to be the best; and what is very strange, size and weight seem of very little consequence. My father tried an iron bar of ten pounds weight. It moved as readily and was as easily controlled by the will as an odometer of a few inches in length. There is apparently no limit to the power. Various theories have passed through my mind as to the nature of this force, but a new experiment—a new fact, puts them all to flight."

H. J. CHURCHMAN, of Baltimore, writes as follows, under date January 6, 1852:

"Some of us have been experimenting pretty extensively with the 'odometer,' and unless we have mistaken a *seeming* for a *reality*, we have attained to a further development of its powers. The oscillations seem to me to be subject to the will. It will become nearly stationary—vibrate longitudinally, transversely, or in a circle, in obedience to my *will*, without any other impulse that I can discover. If this is mere conceit, I would like to be convinced of it. Please make the experiment. If this seeming *is* reality, it is certainly very curious, and in the hands of some of your philosophers perhaps may lead to something further."

Dr. B. A. PENN, of Camden, Carroll county, Indiana, sends the following account of his experiments, under date December 25, 1851:

"Within the last five days I have been engaged in a series of experiments, which have resulted in some of the most singular phenomena I have ever witnessed; and which open a new field of investigation to the philosopher,—especially to those engaged in adding new truths to establish animal magnetism. The person principally engaged besides myself in these experiments, is Simon F. Landry, without whom I should probably have remained ignorant of the discoveries which I have made, and which I believe are original. I was led to those experiments from the perusal of the article headed Od Force, in the November number of the Journal of Man; but, as some will probably read this who have not read that number, I shall give some of my experiments, and the results.

I tried several before I succeeded, and was about resigning it all, along with the balance of popular humbugs.

Experiment 1.—I took a hair; to one end I attached a vial cork, and wound or looped the other end around the joint of the fore finger above the nail: so that the cork would swing about six inches. I then stood a board on end, and placed the finger on it as steadily as I could; the cork then hung about an inch over my knee. I then placed under it a round piece of glass (top of a bottle stopper;) in a short time the cork began to oscillate and describe small circles over the glass in the directions of the hands of a watch; which circles gradually became larger. Another person then took hold of my hand, and the oscillations ceased, and the cork commenced vibrating right and left, like the pendulum of a clock. A third person was then added, when the first described oscillations were again repeated, but more rapidly or with larger circles. These experiments I varied in a great many different ways. I found that the odometer, as it is called, moved more freely for some persons than for others; I also found that taking hold of the person's disengaged hand with my right hand, changed the course of the odometer, and taking my left hand changed it another way. And taking a plate of metal in one hand, also changed it in another direction. The best subject I found was Simon F. Landry; the odometer moved much more freely for him than any other person, and, at that time, he was slightly under my influence, by animal magnetism. After performing various experiments, I was standing some distance from him; the odometer was vibrating to and from his body (which was a natural direction,) when I remarked I would turn it north and south.

To our mutual astonishment, before I touched him the odometer changed of itself and went in accordance with my wishes. I do not recollect of ever being so astonished before in my life. I did not say anything for some moments, during which time the odometer continued to move from north to south; I then said I would turn it round with the hands of a watch—when to astonish us still more it almost instantly obeyed—I then told it to run round in the opposite direction, and it instantly obeyed— I did this more than fifty times, and in every instance it went in exact accordance with my will. And sometimes Landry, misunderstood what I said as well as some others, but the odometer never misunderstood me, it always went as I directed it to go. A great many would no doubt destroy all my experiments by saying that the young man turned the odometer as I directed—that might be done and I thought at first must be the case. But I have proofs to the contrary, we had his hand and finger held by an assistant, and a third person placed so as to make a sight post of his finger, and still the odometer went as before. But we have still another proof, I suspended the odometer from the end of my own finger, yet it would not vibrate but very slightly, I told Simon to put the end of his finger against the end of mine, he did so and immediately the vibrations commenced and were as perfectly under the control of my will as before. But another proof still, we placed the odometer on the finger of a young man, I then took him by the hand so as to run a current of electricity through him, but the odometer would not act as I wished.

I then told Simon to hold his hand under the other gentleman's. He did so and the odometer oscillated as usual; we had it going on finely—when the young man's hand lagged down so that the odometer touched the glass—I told him to raise it, he did so—but let it drop again—I asked why he did not hold up his hand—he said he could not, he was too sleepy—I then looked at his eyes and discovered he was mesmerized. I have several other experiments and their results, but I will be brief. I wish you to philosophize on this subject, and let us have the result of your reasonings."

Mr. R. R., of Newark, Illinois, writes, January 23d, as follows:

"In the November number of the Journal of Man is an article on the Od force, from Chamber's Edinburgh Journal. Feeling some interest in the experiments there detailed, a few evenings since I concluded to try them, and succeeded, much to my satisfaction, in accomplishing the results as described by Dr. Mayo. In continuing my experiment on number 20 and 21, I happened, in using my forefinger as an od-subject, inadvertently to bring my thumb and forefinger together, and found the rotary motion to continue the same as when the fore-finger alone was held up; this did not seem to agree with the theory laid down. I supposed that the effect of the thumb would be to counteract that of the finger; it then occurred to me, possibly the motion might be caused by the thought or the power of the *will*. I then proceeded to test it by experiment, and succeeded in producing a rotary motion, either with or against the hands of a watch, or a longitudinal or transverse, or a state of perfect quiescence, by a concentration of will, or thought, wishing or willing either of the motions; let the string be held by the forefinger, by the thumb, or by the thumb and fore-finger together. I had tried as an odometer, a gold ring, but found a cone made of shell-lac, as described by Dr. Mayo, to answer the purpose full as well, and more convenient. I found it not necessary to have an od-subject; the motion could be produced by holding the odometer over the table, or by suspending it at a distance from the edge. I think the motion can be produced more readily by having a mark or point under the odometer, from which the direction of the motion can be more easily determined by the eye; for it seems to be necessary for success in the experiment, that the eye should be placed on the odometer, and, as it were, to catch the first sign of motion, to produce it in the required direction. I have thought the motions were produced quicker by using the fore-finger as an od-subject than a mark or point; and it has appeared, at times, as if there was a feeble current of air blowing upwards from the end of the finger after holding the odometer for a few seconds, causing a sudden shaking or vibrating motion to be produced, and then the desired motion would immediately commence.

I think the reason the experiments of Dr. Mayo are reproduced is, that the experimenter expects the motions, such as he describes them, to be produced, and thinking so, they follow, as a matter of course. It makes no difference whether the odometer be suspended from the forefinger or thumb, or if they be held together; it acts equally well. I was not certain at first but the motion might be produced by a motion of the hand, given to it by the impulse of the mind, but I have convinced myself of the truth of the phenomena, by placing some article on the table, against which I could lean or bear my hand to steady it; yet still the same effect was produced. There is no voluntary motion of the odometer in my hands, and the cause, no doubt, of Dr. Mayo's difficulties in his first investigations arose from an uncertainty in his mind of the motions to be produced. When he had settled in his mind the motion attending a certain combination, the effects were uniform. I give you my experience and the facts, and shall leave speculations alone. I sincerely hope that you receive sufficient encouragement for the Journal of Man. I should not know how to do without it."

Mrs. A. T., of New York, writes, January 28th:

"There is another power in the 'oscillations of the odometer,' which is not alluded to in the article upon the 'Od Force' in your November number, taken from Chambers' Edinburgh Journal—namely, the action of the *will* upon the odometer—powerful to reverse the natural movement of it. Last winter I was shown the experiment of suspending a ring in a tumbler, and having it strike upon its side the hours of the day; which it did correctly.

I concluded that, as I *knew* the time of day, it must have something to do with the mind. I commenced willing it to strike, and found that I could attain any number; and then changed the oscillating motion to a circular one, &c."

Dr. Madden, Dr. Quin and others, have brought forward this subject in England, and late English papers give the following report of experiments with what they call the MAGNETOSCOPE:

"A gentleman, Mr. Rutter, of Black Rock, Brighton, has recently invented a magnetoscope of such extreme delicacy, that it is capable of indicating plainly to the sight the existence of magnetic currents which would appear to be constantly traversing the human frame, and the various modifications of them which are produced by circumstances apparently of a totally insignificant character—such even as contact with the dead objects and living people around us.

The invention of the instrument is undoubtedly Mr. Rutter's, so far as it is an invention at all. However, many of the phenomena produced by the apparatus, and the principle of the arrangement, were introduced to the notice of the English public several months ago, by Dr. Mayo. No doubt many who read his work thought too contemptuously of the apparently fabulous phenomena there said to be producible, to take the trouble of putting the matter to the test of experiment, even though nothing was required, if I remember right, than to string a gold ring on a silken thread, let it hang loosely and freely from the human hand, and watch the results. In this form, however, it was a mere toy. Mr. Rutter has made of it a philosophical instrument.

The following account is drawn up from notes taken at a lecture on the instrument given in London, by Dr. Madden, of Brighton.

1. From a stand fixed firmly to the table there rises perpendicularly a rod of wood, say eighteen or twenty inches high, having a brass knob on the top. From the knob projects at right angles with the upright, a brass arm, say nine inches long, tapering to a fine end.

2. A fine silken filament is attached to one end of a small spindle-shaped piece of sealing wax like a fisherman's float—but the shape is not material. This is hung from the extremity of the brass arm—and the line being merely a raw thread taken from the cocoon, there is no twist or

tendency to turn in it, but the plumbob hangs free to vibrate or circulate, or adopt any motion in obedience to the infinitesimal influences which are to act upon it.

Immediately underneath the centre of the bob is a small circular wooden plate, say four inches in diameter, so made as to be fixed in a horizontal position, higher or lower: that is, nearer to, or farther from the lower point of the bob. On this is placed a glass dish, rather less than the tablet it rests on, and about as deep as the bob is long. The tablet is then moved upwards until the lower end of the bob *almost* touches the centre of the glass dish. The bob, thus hanging down into the dish, is protected from the accidental movements of the surrounding air. If thought desirable, however, the whole line and bob can be surrounded with a glass shade, such as are placed over artificial flowers or small statuary, having a hole in the top for the string to pass through.

The apparatus being thus prepared, and the sealing wax bob hanging dead from the brass arm, and all parts at rest, the operator placed the finger and thumb of his right hand upon the brass knob, and almost without any perceptible interval the bob was evidently moved; in a few seconds it was decidedly making an effort to swing round, and in less than a minute was steadily careering in a circle parallel to the sides of the glass dish, the lower end of the bob tracing a circle of perhaps two inches in diameter, or the size of a crown piece, from left to right, as the hands of a watch move. The lecturer said he would call this the *normal* motion, being that which was invariably produced, at least after some practice ; but it was a curious fact, and as yet unaccountable, that many of the movements were different with different individuals ; that they were often even different with a given individual on first experimenting and after considerable practice ; but that there came a time when an operator could depend on the movement peculiar to himself occurring without exception.' This left-to-right movement invariably occurred, however often the experiment was made, the bob invariably beginning to swing with the sun a few seconds after the application of the finger and thumb to the knob. He stated, too, that many experiments which at first were difficult, or gave dubious results, became sure and unvarying as the operator increased in delicacy by practice.

The mode of stopping the movement is by taking a

piece of bone in the left hand, when the motion gradually slackens and ceases. With Mr. Rutter the bob will stop almost immediately, but with Dr. Madden the time occupied is tediously long, and, therefore, more forcible means were, on the present occasion, employed when it was wished to commence a new experiment. The lecturer, however, showed an equally satisfactory experiment. Placing the finger and thumb of the right hand to the knob, and holding a piece of bone in the left, no movement whatever could be produced: on dropping the bone from his palm, the bob was instantly *stirred*, and in a few seconds once more traced out the normal circle.

When only the *finger* was applied to the knob, the bob set up, not a circular, but a to-and-fro movement, like a clock pendulum. On stopping it, and applying the thumb only, a similar pendulation was produced, but in a direction directly across and perpendicular to the former. The direction of the swing for finger and thumb respectively, was always the same, however often the experiment might be tried: that is, calling the direction for the finger north and south, that for the thumb was east and west; and if, while the finger was producing the north and south swing, the thumb was substituted, the bob was instantly affected —staggered, so to speak—and shuffled itself into the east and west direction.

While the lecturer held the knob by his finger and thumb, a person standing by touched the operator's left hand with his own right, when, instead of a circular motion, an oscillatory one was produced, but in a direction different from the other two. On this, a chain was formed by the gentlemen present joining hands, and as the chain increased, the arc of oscillation increased until the bob swung as far as the sides of the dish; the contribution of a few more hands, and it must have struck the glass. If the bystander touched the experimenter with his finger (index) only, the same effect was produced as if the experimenter touched the instrument with his finger only, and so with the thumb.

Now came an extraordinary and mysterious part of the subject. The lecturer stated that if, while the operator's finger and thumb were producing the left-to-right movement, a woman were to touch his left hand, the bob would immediately refuse to proceed in the normal direction, and be carried round in the opposite direction—right to left. No ladies were present, but the lecturer stated that anything which had been worn or carried about by a female for a length of time, or even a letter written by one, would do as well. Incredible as this may seem, it was put to the proof and succeeded. The instrument being at rest, the operator placed his right hand on the knob, and a letter written by a lady was laid in the palm of his left, when the bob immediately commenced a circular movement from right to left: This was tried with several documents, one of which was of the date of September 26th, twenty-four days previous. One of these experiments was startling, and touches on a disputed and much-vexed question; but we may venture to state what really occurred. One letter placed on the hand produced an apparent indecision on the part of the bob to such an extent that the lecturer "gave it up;" he could not tell what sex the writer was. It proved to be a woman; but the writing had been penned while in the mesmeric sleep, on which the lecturer remarked, that Mr. Rutter had already ascertained the fact of the disturbing influence exerted by a somnambulist.

The remainder of the experiments were performed with a particular object, as it was imagined that the phenomena now first exhibited had an important bearing upon the homœopathic law and practice of healing. But the interest of the experiments is not confined to those who have this in view; and the most anti-homœopath, at all events, must be indebted to the heterodox practice for the means of performing some of the most curious of all the experiments—means unattainable elsewhere, and which were provided for a purpose altogether different from the present, and therefore all the more beyond suspicion. We allude to the homœopathic globules, attainable in any quantity from the chemists. These are simply little pills of white sugar, over which has been poured a tincture of that medicine with which it is desired to saturate them. The tincture may be of any potency or dilution, and the globules are named accordingly. Thus, a drop of the strong, or original, or mother tincture, say of belladonna, is diluted and thoroughly mixed with ninety-nine drops of fluid.—One drop of the mixture is taken out, and of course contains a 100th part of a drop of belladonna. This is diluted and thoroughly mixed with ninety-nine drops more of fluid. One drop of this mixture is taken out, and of course contains a 100th part of a 100th part of a drop of belladonna—that is, the 10,000th part of a drop. This is diluted and thoroughly mixed with ninety-nine drops more of fluid. One drop of this mixture is taken out, and of course contains the 100th part of the 10,000th part of a drop of belladonna—that is the 1,000,000th part. Suppose this process proceeded with to the twelfth, or still more, to the thirtieth time, and it may be understood how many were impressed with the idea that a drop of such a preparation could not possibly contain any appreciable quantity of belladonna,—certainly none that could act, for good or ill, on the animal economy. But these preparations are gross and material compared with the dilutions or potencies often resorted to, where thirty is left behind, and the chemist manipulates up to the hundreds, and even thousands.—No wonder that men pohpoohed, and declared that in a drop of such a fluid, and still more certainly in a globule of sugar moistened with a very small portion of such a drop, there could be no belladonna at all.

With globules of this character the lecture proceeded to experiment.

First placing his hand on the knob, a few globules of pure sugar were placed on his left palm; but no effect whatever was produced by the sugar, the direct circular movement taking place as usual. For the sugar was then substituted one globule of sulphur, 30th dilution, and the motion was at once reversed. In consequence of a question from a gentleman present, as the lecturer was about to proceed with a new substance, he made the following curious statement: that he had been trying the magnetoscope with gold, and it struck him as strange that the gold ring on his left hand appeared inert, while that which he held acted. But on putting by the ring for a short time, it was found to influence the instrument like any other specimen. He had found, too, a similar difference with newly adopted garments and such as had been long worn—as though articles in time became saturated with an individual's electricity, and became part of himself.

A globule of the 20,000th and another of the 65,000th sulph. produced no effect; but one of the 7,000th acted immediately.

A trituration was then tried. One grain of arsenic had been rubbed down with ninety-one grains of sugar-of-milk. A small portion of this was placed on the left palm, and caused the plumbob to stop; but on a bone counter being also placed on the palm, the normal movement from left to right ensued, as if nothing had been there. It will be remembered that the effect of the bone is to stop the circulation of the plumbob, and that of the arsenic is also to stop it. The arsenic alone succeeds in doing so; yet when the effect of the bone, *in the same direction*, is added to it, they nullify instead of assisting each other, and the influence of the right hand is exerted as if the left held nothing at all. This is certainly curious, whatever we may think of its bearing on the homœopathic dogma, '*similia similibus curantur,*'—of which more anon.

A globule of arsenic of the 40,000th dilution was tried, and stopped motion.

On placing a globule of bryonia (20th) in the left palm, a pendulum motion was produced in a line running north-west. Calcareo-carbonica produced a north and south pendulum; iodide of potassium a north-east; muriate of ammonia, an oscillation in a long, narrow ellipse lying north and south; sulph. and mercury both give a *reverse* circular motion.

Be it remembered, 1st, That, however the direction and character of these movements altered, yet they were invariably the same for the same substance—insomuch that the operator having one of the globules taken at random from any box, placed by a bystander on his left palm, could, from the figure described by the bob, and its direction, pronounce what medicinal substance the sugar contained; 2nd, That the vibrations here spoken of were not mere incipient agitations of the bob, to which a wish to believe gave positive character, but *bona fide* swingings to and fro, so that the arc described by the lower end of the bob was perhaps more than two inches long.

It will be seen that this new branch of magnetology, though here shown in more or less connexion with homœopathy, and with what has hitherto been known as animal magnetism, has no necessary dependence on these proscribed subjects; neither are there the difficulties of proof, and the apparent openness to fraud, and the consequent disinclination of many to experiment, which attend the latter. The opponents of these systems are apt to regard every thing which succeeds as a collusion or an accident, and every failure as a damnatory proof; and the repugnance even to experiment is extreme. Here the

21

student may acquaint himself with phenomena as curious, and at first thought as incredible, as any that have aroused the indignant incredulity of the wise, jealous for the honor of the human intellect and the dignity of the established authorities—phenomena produced by the unassisted experimenter, consisting in gross, material movements, leaving no room for delusion or illusion.

———

The foregoing statements are not only interesting and curious, but appear to indicate discoveries of the highest importance. So great a number of seemingly harmonious and curious facts, cannot be entirely devoid of instruction ; but what they indicate, must be ascertained by a more thorough examination than the facts have as yet received. In the American experiments, it is to be observed that the odometer, or aura-test, was always suspended from the person of the experimenter, which connexion was supposed to be necessary, for the purpose of rendering it sensitive to the auric force. Here is at once a source of fallacy. It is easy to produce any number of vibrations and gyrations, by suspending a weight from the finger ; and it would be extremely difficult to prevent it from manifesting motion. If the movement of the suspended body was really produced by the substance placed underneath it mechanically influencing the motion, it would be very easy to make the requisite experiments with a gold ring, or a bit of sealing-wax, suspended by a fixed mechanical support, independent of the human body. But no such experiments have been made—or if made, they have proved entire failures—thus demonstrating that the suspended body or odometer is not really influenced by the object over which it is suspended ; and that all the movement which is really produced, is produced through the agency of the human being who is concerned, and not by means of inorganic matter. It is true that in the English experiments, the odometer was suspended from a brass rod, attached to an upright support, upon which rod the finger of the experimenter was placed. Such a contrivance would possess all the mobility necessary to put the suspended body in motion. If instead of a brass rod and wooden upright, a solid iron frame be substituted, resting on an immoveable basis, from a projecting arm of which the moving body is to be suspended, the requisite conditions would exist, but no movement would be produced. In other words, the whole of the movements which have been described as taking place, belonged to the movement of the hand and arm of the operator alone. Consequently they are proofs, not of a mysterious force acting upon dead matter, but of the influences that operate upon the living constitution of the experimenter. Hence, individuals who are highly impressible, are apt to prove successful in such experiments where those who are defective in impressibility fail.

When impressible persons hold the odometer or aura-test, over the various organs of the brain, they are themselves affected by the proximate organs, and the unconscious movements of their hands, which are imparted to the suspended body, are produced in accordance with the pathognomic laws; hence, the record of such experiments becomes interesting, simply as an illustration of the laws of muscular movements, governed by the brain; and a beautiful and decisive demonstration is produced, while the operator is unconscious of the law which he is obeying.

The influences of medicinal substances, when held by the hand, are transmitted through the nervous system, and are thus made to excite the muscular system, producing movements in accordance with their constitutional influence. Medicinal substances which excite the basilar organs, produce basilar movements; and those which excite the anterior and coronal region of the brain, produce a corresponding class of movements. Hence, the explanation of the various movements which have been produced, requires a knowledge of those pathognomic laws which I am now developing in the Bremer correspondence. Why the results should vary according to the position of the individual, in relation to the points of the compass, appears at first inexplicable; but a clue to this mystery may be obtained by a knowledge of the relation which man bears to the globe. I would simply announce that the pathognomic laws bear a fixed relation to the points of the compass, and consequently that the various lines—north and south, east and west, and their intermediates, correspond in their character and influence with the pathognomic lines of the brain. Hence, the attitude in relation to the points of the compass must have its influence, as well as the impressions of medicinal substances, which may be swallowed or held in the hand.

As the movements of the suspended body are produced by the hand of the experimenter, it is not at all myste-. rious that they should appear to be governed by the influence of the will. The influence of the will, or a strong mental impression, is quite capable of producing move-ments, when the individual is unconscious of having called his muscles into action. The limbs of mesmeric subjects, under the control of operators who rely upon imagination and commands emphatically uttered, readily perform the movements which he suggests, even when the subject is reluctant, or makes decided attempts at resist-ance. The impression on the mind becomes realized in the muscles, without the consent or even knowledge of the subject. It is not strange, therefore, that the mesmeric subject should exhibit these odometric movements at the command of the operator's will, or that they should be produced unconsciously by other influences, or even by the idea the subject entertains. In short, the whole of these experiments, while they fail to develope any new laws as to the relations of mind to inorganic matter, af-ford a beautiful illustration of the laws of muscular move-ment—the delicate impressibility of the human constitu-tion, and the relations of man to the universe.

I have repeated a few of these experiments, showing that with impressible persons they may be successfully performed, but with a sufficient degree of firmness and steadiness, no such movements occur. A detailed expla-nation of the movements might be given, but space for-bids.

———

[From the American edition of Mind and Matter, by Sir Benjamin Brodie.]

In connexion with the subjects discussed in this chapter by Sir Benjamin Brodie, the following letter addressed by the eminent French savant, Chevreuil, in 1833, to his friend Ampere, the celebrated electrician and physicist, will be read with interest. In this letter, M. Chevreuil discusses the influence of the mind on muscular and nerv-ous action, particularly in reference to the asserted fact that a pendulum formed by a heavy body and a flexible string would oscillate, when held by the hand over certain substances, although the arm should remain perfectly stationary.—*Am. Ed.*

" The pendulum I used was an iron ring suspended by a flaxen thread; it had been arranged by a person who was very anxious that I should verify for myself the phenomenon which appeared when it was placed over water, a block of metal, or a living being—a phenomenon which I saw appear in his hands. It was not, I confess, without surprise that I saw it reproduced when, having taken hold with my right hand of the pendulum's string, I placed it above the mercury reservoir of my air-pump, an anvil, several animals, &c. I concluded from my experiments that, as I was informed there were only a certain number of bodies apt to determine the oscillations of the pendulum, it might be that, in interposing other bodies between the former and the pendulum, the oscillations would cease.

" Notwithstanding my presumption, my astonishment was great when, after having taken with my left hand a plate of glass or a cake of resin, &c., and having placed these bodies between the mercury and the pendulum which oscillated over it, I saw the oscillations diminish in length and then wholly cease. They recommenced when the intermediate body was taken away, and again ceased upon its re-interposition. This succession of phenomena was repeated a great many times, with a really remarkable constancy, whether the intermediate body was held by me or by any other person.

" The more extraordinary these effects seemed to me, the more necessary I felt the importance of verifying that they were foreign to all muscular motion of the arm, as I had been informed they were, in the most positive manner. This induced me to lean my right arm, which held the pendulum, upon a wooden support, which at intervals I gradually advanced from my shoulder to my hand, and brought back from my hand to my shoulder. I soon noticed that in the first circumstance the motion of the pendulum decreased in proportion as the support was placed near the hand, and that it ceased when the fingers which held the thread were themselves supported, whereas in the second case the contrary effect took place.

"This induced me to think that it was very probable that a muscular motion which took place unknown to me determined the phenomena; and I was the more inclined to take this opinion into consideration as I had a souvenir, vague in truth, of having been in *a certain state* when my eyes followed the oscillations described by the pendulum which I held in my hand.

"I made the experiments spoken of above over again, my arm being entirely free, and I convinced myself that the souvenir just spoken of was not an illusion of my mind, for I felt very distinctly that, while my eyes followed the oscillations of the pendulum, there was in me a *a disposition or tendency to the motion*, which, involuntary as it seemed to be, was the better satisfied as the pendulum described larger arcs; consequently, I thought that if I had repeated the experiments, first taking care to blindfold my eyes, the results would be very different from those observed. It happened so exactly. While the pendulum oscillated above the mercury, a blindfold was placed over my eyes; the motion soon diminished; but, although the oscillations were feeble, they were not sensibly diminished by the interposition of the bodies, which seemed to have arrested them in my first experiments.

"Lastly, from the moment the pendulum was at repose, I still held it for a quarter of an hour over the mercury without its moving. During this interval, and totally unknown to me, the plate of glass and cake of resin had been interposed and withdrawn several times by persons in the room.

"This is the interpretation I give to these phenomena: When I hold the pendulum in my hand, a muscular motion of my arm, although insensible to me, moved the pendulum from its repose, and when once the oscillations had commenced they were soon augmented by the influence exercised by the sight, so as to put me in that particular frame of disposition or tendency to the motion. Now, it must be acknowledged that the muscular motion, even when it is increased by this same disposition, is nevertheless weak enough to stop, I will not say under the empire of the will, but when it has simply the thought of trying to see whether this or that will stop it.

"So then, there is an intimate connexion between the execution of certain motions and the act of the mind relative to them, although this mental act is not the will which commands the muscular organs. In this regard, it seems to me that the phenomenon I have described is interesting in connexion with psychology, and even the history of sciences; they prove how easy it is to take illusions for realities, whenever we turn our attention towards a phenomenon wherein our bodies play a part, especially in circumstances which have not been sufficiently analyzed.

"In truth, if I had contented myself with making the pendulum oscillate above certain bodies, and with the experiments where these oscillations were arrested when glass, resin, &c., were interposed between the pendulum and the body which seemed to determine its motion, then certainly I would have had no reason not to believe in the divining rod, or any other thing of the same sort. Now, it may be easily conceived how honest and educated men are sometimes led to recur to very chimerical ideas to explain phenomena which are not in reality removed from the physical world we know.

"Consequently, I conceive without difficulty that an honest man, whose whole attention is fixed upon the motion a rod which he holds in his hands may take from a cause unknown to him, may receive from any the least circumstance the tendency to motion necessary to superinduce the appearance of the expected phenomenon. For example, if that man seeks a spring, and he has not his eyes blindfolded, the sight of a green plot of grass over which he is walking may, unknown to himself, determine in him the muscular motion capable of disarranging the rod by the established association between the idea of active vegetation and that of water.

"The preceding facts, and the interpretation above given of them, have led me to connect them with others which we may daily observe. From this connexion the analysis of them becomes both more simple and more precise than it was, at the same time that they form an *ensemble* of facts, whose general interpretation is susceptible of a great extension. But, before going further, let us distinctly remember that my observations present two leading circumstances :

"First. To think that a pendulum held in hand may move, and that it moves without our having the consciousness that the muscular organ gives it the least impulsion. *This is the first fact.*

"Secondly. To see this pendulum oscillate, and its oscillations become longer from the influence of the sight upon the muscular organ; and this, too, without our having the consciousness of it. *This is the second fact.*

"The tendency to motion, determined in us by the sight of a body in motion, is found in several cases. For example:

"1. When the attention is wholly fixed upon a bird flying, a stone thrown, running water, the body of the spectator is directed more or less towards the line of motion.

"2. When a billiard player follows with his eye the ball he has just put in motion, he places his body in the position he would see the ball follow, as if it were still possible for him to direct it towards the mark whither he sought to direct it.

"When we walk upon a slippery place every body knows with what promptness we throw ourselves on the side opposite to that whither our body is carried in consequence of losing its equilibrium; but a circumstance less generally known is, that a tendency to the motion appears even when it is impossible for us to move in the sense of this tendency. For example, in a carriage the fear of being upset makes us lean in a direction opposite to that which menaces us, and from it result efforts which are so much the greater as the fright and irritability are greater. I believe that, in ordinary falls, the falling is less painful than the effort made to prevent the fall. It is in this sense that I understand the justness of the proverb: *Il y a un Dieu pour les enfans et pour les ivrognes!*

"The tendency to motion in a determined sense, resulting from the attention given to a certain object, seems to me the prime cause of several phenomena generally ascribed to imitation. Thus when we have seen or have heard a person gape, the muscular motion of gaping generally takes place in us in consequence. I may make the same remark about the communication of laughter, and, besides, this example presents more than any other analogous one, a circumstance which seems to me to support the explanation I have given of these phenomena. For laughter, feeble at first, may, if kept up, become accelerated (pardon the word), as we saw the oscillations of the pendulum held in the hand augment in amplitude, influenced by the sight; and laughter, in being accelerated, may go to convulsions.

"I do not doubt but that the sight of certain actions proper, so act forcibly upon our frail machine, that the relation of these same actions animates with the voice or gesture ; or, further, the knowledge communicated of them by merely reading about them does induce some individuals to do these very same actions, in consequence of a tendency to motion, which thus mechanically determines them to an act of which they never would have thought, had not some circumstance, extraneous to their will, presented it, and to which they would never have been led, but by that which we call instinct in animals.

"In here terminating the exposition of facts which seem connected with my observations, I think I should make a remark which is certainly contained in the foregoing paragraphs, but which may escape some reader ; it is, that this tendency to motion, to which I attribute the prime cause of a great number of our actions, takes place only when we are in a certain state, which is exactly that which magnetizers call *faith.*

"The existence of this state is perfectly demonstrated by my experiments. So long as I believed the motion of the pendulum which I held in my hand *possible*, it took place ; but, after having discovered the cause of it, it was impossible for me to reproduce it. It is because we are not always in the same state, that we do not constantly receive the same impression from the same thing.

"Thus the gaping of another does not always make us gape ; laughter is not always communicated from the laugher to his neighbor, &c. The great orator who wishes to make the crowd share his passion does not reach at one leap his object ; he commences by disposing his audience to it, and it is only after he has made himself master of them, that he gives his last argument, his last trait. The great poet, the great writer constantly resort to the same artifice ; they first prepare their reader for their final impression.

"Nothing is more curious in the study of the causes which determine man's actions, than the knowledge of the means employed by the shopkeeper to attract and fix the buyer's attention upon the qualities of the article he would have him take ; or the knowledge of the means employed by the 'necromancer ' to have one rather than another card drawn from a pack, or to divert the spectator's attention upon one thing so as to withdraw it from

22

another, a diversion without which the 'necromancer' would cause no surprise, which is the great object of his art. It results from these considerations that the most different professions employ quite analogous although excessively varied means to attain the same end, that of first fixing man's attention so as afterwards to produce on him a determined effect.

"I think my observations are connected with the history of the faculties of animals; that some of their acts attributed to instinct are really of the class just spoken of. This seems to me especially true of gregarious animals; and it seems to me that it would be very interesting to study in this regard the influence of their leaders upon the subordinate members.

"Do not the instances above mentioned throw some light upon the cause of the fascination one animal exerts over another?"

EXTRACTS FROM THE WORK OF REICHENBACH.

"If a strong magnet, capable of supporting about ten pounds, be drawn downward over the bodies of fifteen or twenty persons, without actually touching them, some among them will always be found to be excited by it in a peculiar manner. The number of people who are sensitive in this way is greater than is generally imagined: sometimes three or four are met with in such a number as above mentioned: indeed, I know an establishment where the experiment was tried, and of twenty-two young ladies who were collected there, no less than eighteen felt more or less distinctly the passage of the magnet. The kind of impression produced on these excitable people, who otherwise may be regarded as in perfect health, is scarcely describable; it is rather disagreeable than pleasant, and combined with a slight sensation either of cold or warmth, resembling a cool or gently warm breath of air, which the patients imagine to blow softly upon them. Sometimes they feel sensations of drawing, pricking, or creeping; some complain of sudden attacks of headache. Not only women, but men in the very prime of life, are found distinctly susceptible of this influence; in children it is sometimes very active."

" The magnet thus declares itself as *a general agent upon the vital principle ;* a property of it which individual physicians have indeed endeavored, though as yet without solid results, to bring into more extensive application, in reference to the possibility of deriving from it a curative treatment in cases of disease,—which, however, has not yet been received by natural philosophers into the realm of physics; and from the uncertainty of the observations, hitherto, has been altogether passed over by natural science generally. Nevertheless, magnetism, when more closely examined, presents an infinitely varied and exalted interest on this side. If a portion of the phenomena here assert an influence upon life, this occurs exactly and especially at the point where the boundaries of the organic and inorganic are intermingled. Since a doubt exists whether it shall be attributed to the domain of physiology or of physics, it is neglected on both sides. Thus it is left over to medicine, and has not always fallen into the best hands there. I hope, in the following pages, to disentangle some of the threads of this knot, and to combine a number of phenomena under a common point of view, at the same time arranging them under fixed physical laws."

The work gives an exceedingly interesting account of the first experiment in which the author was enabled to verify a previous conjecture, that there were sensitives, who would be able to see luminous appearances at the poles of a magnet. The sensitive, in the experiment described, was " a young woman of 25 years of age, who had suffered for several years from increasing pains in the head, and from these had fallen into cataleptic attacks, with alternate tonic and clonic spasms." The magnet employed in the experiment was one of great power, " capable of supporting about ninety pounds of iron, with the armature removed."

" The magnet was placed upon a table about ten yards from the patient, with both poles directed toward the ceiling, and then freed from its armature. No one present could see in the least; but the girl beheld two luminous appearances, one at the extremity of each pole of the magnet. When this was closed by the application of the armature, they disappeared, and she saw nothing more ; when it was opened again, the lights reappeared. They seemed to be somewhat stronger at the moment of lifting up the armature, than to acquire a permanent condition, which was weaker. The fiery appearance was about equal in size at each pole, and without perceptible tendency to mutual connection. Close upon the steel from which it streamed, it appeared to form a fiery vapor, and this was surrounded by a kind of glory of rays. But the rays were not at rest; they became shorter and longer without intermission, and exhibited a kind of darting rays and active scintillation, which the observer assured us was uncommonly beautiful. The whole appearance was more delicate and beautiful than that of common fire; the light was far purer, almost white, sometimes intermingled with iridescent colors, the whole resembling the light of the sun more than that of a fire. The distribution of the light in rays was not uniform; in the middle of the edges of the horseshoe they were more crowded and brilliant than toward the corners, but at the corners they were collected in tufts, which projected further than the rest of the rays."

At the close of various sections of the work there is a "Retrospect," specifying briefly, the points supposed to be proved by the particular division of the work. Some of these specifications are as follows.

"A strong magnet exercises a peculiar action upon the senses of many healthy and sick persons; it is an agent upon the vital force.

Those who manifest this sensibility in a high degree frequently exhibit a great exaltation of the acuteness of the senses, and are then in a condition to perceive light and flame-like appearances upon the magnet. The strength and distinctness of this perception increases with the sensibility of the observer and the obscurity of the place.

The pole—M gives the larger, the †M the smaller flame, in the northern latitude of Vienna. Its form and color change according as the magnet is open or closed,—a magnet made by touch, or an electro-magnet,—free, or under the influence of other magnets.

Positive and negative flames display no tendency to unite.

The flame may be mechanically diverted in various directions, just like the flame of a fire.

It emits a light which is red, that acts upon the daguerreotype, and may be concentrated by a glass lens, but is without perceptible heat.

Magnetic flames and their light exhibit such complete resemblance to the aurora, that I believe myself compelled to consider the two as identical.

"Every crystal, natural or artificial, exercises a specific exciting power on the animal nerves, weak in the healthy, strong in the diseased, strongest of all in the cataleptic.

The force manifests its abode principally at the axes of the crystals, most actively at its opposite extremities: it therefore exhibits polarity.

It emits light at the poles visible to acutely sensitive eyes in the dark.

In particular diseases, it attracts the human hand to a peculiar kind of adhesion, like that of iron to the magnet.

"The sun's rays carry with them a power to affect sensitive patients, which agrees perfectly with the force residing in crystals, the magnet, and the human hands.

The greatest influence in reference to a force corresponding to that of crystals is manifested in the outer borders of the red and violet-blue rays of the solar spectrum.

The light of the moon possesses the force now under consideration in a strong degree.

Heat is a source of it.

It occurs with friction, and

It appears as a result of the light of flame.

"Chemism is a widely-comprehensive source of magnetic-like force, both when simple and when produced by combustion and the voltaic pile.

"Not only magnets, crystals, hands, chemism, &c., but all solid and fluid matters without exception, produce sensations of coolness and tepid heat equivalent to pleasure and inconvenience.

The effective force, therefore, does not appertain to particular forms or especial qualities of matter, but it dwells in matter in and by itself.

This force not only manifests itself in contact, but also at distances,—as from the sun, moon, and stars; so, also, from all matter.

Finally this principle is one that extends over the entire universe."

NOTES.

I have never been a member of any Legislature, and I know next to nothing, by personal observation, about their proceedings. Such knowledge as I have is derived mostly from the publick journals. These affirm persistently that our legislative assemblies, including the Congress of the United States, are exceedingly corrupt. So much so that publick virtue, if it exist, is deprived of influence. "The lobbies of the legislative halls are filled with a class of men called agents, whose business it is to work private bills through Congress, or publick bills in which, like—private interests are deeply concerned, by means of influence upon members—or, in plain terms, by some form of corruption. This is no secret matter, for indeed secrecy is little known in American affairs; the power of the lobby is alluded to in every debate." This is extracted from a writer who seems to be distinguished by candor and moderation. And while it describes the chronic state of the evil, the following is indicative of one of its periodical developments. It is from a manifesto of an assemblage of distinguished politicians, chosen to designate a presidential candidate. "The people justly view with alarm the reckless extravagance which pervades every department of the Federal government; a return to rigid economy and accountability is indispensible to arrest the systematic plunder of the publick treasury by favoured partisans, whilst the recent startling developments of frauds and corruption at the Federal metropolis show that an entire change of administration is imperatively demanded." The party, represented by the convention above, succeeded in electing their candidate, who came into office in March 1861; and in the daily paper of to-day,* (friendly to the present administration,) and received since commencing this paragraph, I observe an article which commences thus, "The plunderers and speculators, who have made such frightful inroads upon the federal treasury the last year, &c., &c. This need not implicate the present administration—it only proves that the evil is well nigh ineradicable.

---

* April 30, 1862.

This state of things, which the most ardent admirers of the American form of government do not deny, and which it may be presumed affects, more or less directly, most of the departments and processes of the government, suggests a number of very grave considerations. And first, while human nature remains as it is, and the individual constitution of society furnishes temptations for all, is there any probability of a reform? especially as the evil appears to be increasing. If not, in what sense can our government be held up as the chief hope, the last hope of oppressed humanity? Is it sufficient to have a government by the people, without regard to its answering the purposes of a government? Again, did a similar state of things exist in the colonial legislatures, previous to the revolution? or in the early periods of the present government; during the administrations of Washington, Adams and Jefferson?* I believe it will be found that the declaration of war against England, in 1812, (soon followed by the memorable "Baltimore mob,") will mark, as nearly as any considerable publick event, the commencement of the present era, of the downward course. Previous to that event, the government had been administered, and influence wielded, by men who were formed under English institutions and traditions. The influence of American, democratick and Anti-English principles, and feelings, was then clearly manifested. American institutions, administered by genuine Americans, have had free scope for fifty years.

It has been a period, notwithstanding very considerable checks, of great material prosperity. Yet will not statistics prove that we have not increased faster, comparatively, in numbers and wealth, than for fifty years previous to the revolution? Not faster than that portion of British America, which remained loyal; while taxes are much higher than they were before the revolution, or than they now are in Canada. If so, and taking into account the losses and privations of two wars, (for the second war with England is to be taken into the general account,) and of twenty years of commercial depression, at times of almost entire stagnation, what have we gained by the revolution? Had its leaders been aware of the prophetical relations of England, would it have taken place? What has caused the rapid decline in the purity of our government, during the last fifty years?

---

* I have heard a distinguished Federalist, conversant with affairs at Washington, admit that Jefferson's administration, having especial reference perhaps, to the first term, was an economical and good one.

The last question is one of great practical importance. If the cause can be clearly apprehended, there may be some hope of finding a remedy. In attempting a brief and imperfect consideration of this question, it will be proper to notice the circumstance, that in twelve years after the establishment of the constitution, the power and prestige of the government passed away from the friends of Washington, the party with which he was identified, and have never since been regained. The very name by which they were known, became a term of reproach. At the same time a shadow of infidelity passed over the land. Mr. Jefferson, the idol of the hour, was known to be an unbeliever in revelation, to say nothing of the cordiality of the democratick party towards France. It had been predicted that in a few years the Bible would be an obsolete book; and there is reason to believe that many, who had thought very little, seriously, upon the subject of religion, affected an unbelief, or a leaning towards it, which they did not feel. Infidelity, or something resembling it, was the fashion. These particulars are worthy of notice, as marking the first considerable step in that downward progress, which has continued to the present time.

The popular theory of democratick government, which at present prevails, is very different from that of the founders of the American union. Their theory, from what we know of the men, was unquestionably this. That the great mass of the people, from want of time, of opportunities for acquiring information, and in many instances, of education, would be unable to judge intelligently, of publick affairs; but at the same time they were good judges of character. In choosing professional or other aid, in the management of their private affairs, they would, for the most part, select judiciously. It was obviously for their interest to have a good government; and they would, with the same discretion and caution, select men to manage the affairs of the nation. To them, to their judgment and probity, they would be confided. The fathers of the constitution little dreamed of a condition of the body politick, *and social*, in which affairs of state would be decided in primary meetings, and by their organs of the press; while little would be left for the representatives of the people, at the seat of government, but to settle the question of their own pay, to make speeches, not for convincing, nor throwing light on the subjects discussed, but for effect, hearkening to the lobby, and recording the edicts of the constituency. It will not be required to consider the question which is the best form of republican or democratick government, that which prevailed in the first years of the constitution, or that which pre vails at the present time. The progressive changes in the administration and accidents of the government, have been owing, in a very considerable degree, to more complete political organizations in the later periods. That corruption has been organized, and rendered surprisingly efficient and influential, seems to be conceded on all hands. *Can it be a good tree that produces such fruit?* Yet I am not aware that those Divines who hold that man is *totally depraved*, are less patriotic, less eulogistic of the American constitution than others.

Do not all theories of democratick or republican government, suppose more virtue, and less waywardness, less *selfishness*, than have yet been found in any people? Is it not true that in forming theories of popular government, practical considerations, essential to the result, have been disregarded, or too vaguely estimated? The obliquity and perverseness of the human mind, since the fall. The fact, (of important practical bearing,) that distance lessens the force of *moral* considerations, as is seen in the little care that men often bestow upon their spiritual concerns. They will sometimes sacrifice private interests, when temper and feeling are enlisted, would they sacrifice publick considerations less readily? at least men of the hard, worldly stamp. What scope is afforded here for likings and dislikings, for the influence of the irrepressible conflict between the different interests of society. Men appear to be more readily excited, when conversing on political than on other topics. Is this owing to personal feeling, or to a consciousness of imperfect statisticks? At at any rate it is a curious psychological fact. They find it difficult to avoid attaching themselves to some party; then come party trammels, and division of responsibility, a disturbing cause of no little efficiency. Secret societies, with their selfishness, and invisible but potent influence. The arts of the demagogue are seldom wanting. Alas, are not our government, and the tendencies, social and individual, under it, *of the earth, earthly?* A zealous and patriotick poet exclaims:—

"Thy reign is the last and the noblest of time."

But *that* nation, as we have seen abundantly, has a religious establishment. Should it be alleged that in consequence of circumstances attending the origin of the collective American people, the diversities of religious belief, the national and other antipathies of its various populations, it is impossible America should have an establishment, that only proves that she cannot be the nation which the poet describes.

How instructive history might be, *had it ever been written*, and had we been prepared to receive it. But have either of these conditions ever been fulfilled? Doubtless many important and interesting facts have been chronicled, which it was of consequence to preserve, as part of the history of the race, and of the progress of the human mind; but have publick men ever been so communicative, that the initial moving forces could be recognized? There have been two classes of men, and there is reason to fear that they have often been publick men, whose motives are not communicated: those who are passively and absolutely possessed. It is fearful to think what influence they may sometimes wield. Were the purposes and motives of those not possessed, actually made known, it would illumine but a small portion of the *darkness of this world.* When the devices of the great enemy are known, and his influence in the affairs of men, history may be written.

It may be profitable here, to advert once more to the subject of possession. It is one of transcendant importance. If men believed in this momentous fact, they would realize the danger of departing from the right way, and the comparative vanity and worthlessness of the things of time, except as they subserve the concerns of another state of being. They would be ready to obey the injunction, Ephes. 6 : 10, 11. *Finally, my brethren, be strong in the Lord, and in the power of his might. Put on the whole armour of God, that ye may be able to resist the wiles of the Devil.* The verse which follows the above, can not be cited too often, or its substance kept in mind too steadily. *For we wrestle not against flesh and blood, but against principalities, and powers, against the rulers of the darkness of this world, against spiritual wickedness in high places.* Here is no remote, mythical contest ; it is instant, present, urgent, practical. When will the fashionable incredulity, concerning spiritual influences, (especially those which are evil) and what may be termed the cognate branches of knowledge, mesmerism, clairvoyance, actual or physiological sympathy, presentiment, and latterly, the odic force, which appears to have originated, or principally, with the infidel writers of the last century ; which seems well nigh invincible, because current in certain ranges of society, because it ministers to the gratification of vanity, as being superiour to popular belief, because its votaries, in their imaginary superiority, will not investigate the subject, be swept away, and a more scriptural and rational belief succeed? Rational, because supported by the most abundant evidence, aside from well grounded faith in the testimony of scripture. Perhaps more effectual with such, than any evidence or any reasoning, would be a suspicion, (if such could find its way to their minds,) that instead of being leaders of opinion, they are really behind the times, that they combine, with the most absurd rejection of testimony, a marvelous facility in receiving the dogmas of a belief, which is rapidly passing away, and becoming obsolete.

I have observed, above, that it appears to have been a mission of spiritualism to prove the reality of possession, in our own time. If those who speak with such entire self-complacency and assurance of the delusions of spiritualism, mesmerism, &c., while they have not honestly and impartially investigated the several subjects, could realize in what a false position they place themselves, they would practise more reserve, unless, indeed, they happen themselves, to be subject to influences, which either they are not conscious of, or would not acknowledge. Should any, who may read these pages, wish to know more concerning the matters spoken of, I would recommend to their attention Capron's "Modern Spiritualism," especially chapter 7, in which he speaks of the Manifestations in the family of the Rev. Dr. Phelps, "Footfalls on the Boundary of Another World," by Robert Dale Owen, and Mrs. Crowe's "Night Side of Nature." The first mentioned work was written by one who was neither fanatical nor credulous, and who appears to have been influenced by a commendable spirit of impartiality. The manifestations in the family of Dr. Phelps, are, alone, decisive of the question. Mrs. Crowe says : "Many German physicians maintain that, to this day, instances of genuine possession occur, and there are several works published in their language on the subject ; and for this malady they consider magnetism the only remedy, 'all others being worse than useless. Indeed, they look upon *possession* itself as a demono-magnetic state, in which the patient is in rapport with mischievous or evil spirits." "They particularly warn their readers against confounding this infliction with cases of epilepsy or mania." And again "This disease, which is not contagious, was well known to the Greeks ; and in later times Hoffman* has recorded several well established instances." It is to be observed that the cases here referred to, and those which Mrs. Crowe describes, (some of which were cured by magnetism,) were distinguished by palpable, and very remarkable symptoms, from which it may be inferred that they resembled the cases described in the New Testament. Mrs. Crowe says : "Among the distinguishing symptoms, they reckon the patient's speaking in a voice

---

* One of the most distinguished of the German physicians.

that is not his own; frightful convulsions and motions of the body, which arise suddenly, without any previous indisposition; blasphemous and obscene talk; a knowledge of what is secret, and of the future; a vomiting of extraordinary things, such as hair, stones, pins, needles, &c., &c."* That far more numerous class, in which there is nothing to distinguish the patients from ordinary individuals, does not seem to have been contemplated. This class, in which, as has been said, there are several gradations, is the class which is dangerous. Think of an acquaintance, a companion, a friend, in whose mind, (as in one of the lower stages of possession,) the normal flow and sequence of ideas is interrupted by suggestions of an indwelling and hostile spirit, and that, without the consciousness of the possessed. The advantages possessed by evil spirits, who wield the bodies of men in the higher forms of possession, for misleading, deceiving, tempting, influencing those around them, need not be dwelt upon.

Haunting is a different affair from possession, but if the reality of cases of haunting can be established, it will go far, by parity of reasoning, to show the possibility of possession. There are two cases, attended with extraordinary and uncommon circumstances, which I should judge no intelligent court or jury, if the cases were subjected to judicial investigation and decision, could avoid deciding, (whatever their prepossessions,) were cases of *haunting*. That is, cases in which intelligent agents, not of the human family in the flesh, applied themselves, for considerable periods, to disturbing and annoying individuals, who were. I allude to the cases of M'lle Clairon and of Capt. Barton. The first mentioned is generally known; that of Capt. Barton was published in the Dublin University Magazine, I believe for 1843, perhaps a year later. Both cases appear to be perfectly well authenticated, names and dates are given. The one was, for a considerable time the wonder of the city of Paris, the other, of the city of Dublin. The case of Capt. Barton presents a most thrilling narrative; and I should think its general dissemination might be highly useful. There is another case, as well attested as the above, as to the facts, though perhaps there is not quite the conclusive proof (though there is no reasonable doubt,) that the disturbances were caused by spirit influence. I speak of the case of a British officer, described by Mrs.

---

* I have known of a case of delirium tremens, or some similar affection, in which hairs suddenly came into the mouth; and the patient was impressed with the idea that they were *snares* of the evil one.

Crowe, page 409, New-York edition. The same case is described by Mr. Owen, with an important additional circumstance, an admission by the sufferer, that "perhaps he deserved it." Both had the particulars from Mrs. S. C. Hall, the authoress, who was acquainted with the family.

There is another form of spirit influence, or that which appears to be such, which perhaps I should mention; that which is exhibited in feats of legerdemain. The uneducated, or many of them, believe that the performances of jugglers are accomplished by the aid of evil spirits; while the educated, highly respectable writers even, affecting to disbelieve this, speak of ingenious deception, trick, &c. This is sufficiently pitiable. The uneducated have much the better of the argument. If the feats are the result of trick, deception, &c., it is deception on a much higher plane than is contemplated, in the ordinary and legitimate use of the language, so that they are *not* deceptions, &c. To illustrate my meaning. At an exhibition of legerdemain, in an open arena, one of the performers takes a small bag, full of brass balls, which he throws into the air, one by one, to the number of thirty-five. None of them are seen to return. After an interval of a minute he makes various motions with his hands, and utters a kind of barbarous chant. After a few seconds they descend in the same manner, one by one, till all are replaced in the bag. This may be real, or it may be an illusion of the eye or mind of the observer; but whichever it is of the three, it results from agencies, influences, which are unknown to science, which are not mentioned in books of natural philosophy. I think it would be well for performances of legerdemain to be regulated, somewhat in this manner. No one to be permitted to perform in publick, without a license. A suitable board to be appointed to grant the licenses, but to such only, as will give an intelligible and satisfactory explanation of all the feats which they perform. Such explanations to be recorded, and the commissioners to be bound to secrecy for a considerable number of years. Such an arrangement would, I imagine, produce one of these results. Either the jugglers would be banished from the land, or a number of interesting, and perhaps valuable scientifick truths would be elicited. I have little doubt which it would be.

I can say little concerning the rationale of my own observations on the subject of possession. I will mention however, that none of the possessed, so far as I have observed, are odic mediums. The pendulum remains motionless in their hands. There are other causes however, which prevent the movement of the pendulum, so that this is, by no means, of itself, an infallible test of the actual fact of possession. I was led to a knowledge (in part at least,) of the means of expelling evil spirits, and of rendering them harmless thereafter, so far as possession is concerned, by the study of some of the most obscure passages of scripture.

As has been repeatedly intimated, a belief in the reality of possession would have a tendency to alter men's opinions and sentiments on various topics. It would render them less worldly minded, more honest, more careful of giving our spiritual foes an opportunity of inflicting injury. It would lessen the heat of political strife. I cannot say that a president of the United States has ever been possessed. I believe no one has. Yet what, but a merciful providence, can preserve us from such a calamity. I have reason to believe that several governors of states have been possessed. It were needless however, to multiply instances and reflections. The more important practical considerations will readily suggest themselves.

Note (B), P. 103.

The history of the rise of the useful arts, in the antediluvian period, seems to have been designed for instruction; indeed, to enunciate a law of God's government of the world; but I do not learn that the instruction has been elicited and set forth, heretofore. The sons of Lamech, it appears, were ingenious persons, who became founders in various branches of the useful arts:—see Gen. 4:17—24—It is exceedingly probable that the father was employed, perhaps as an overseer, in some process of those which his sons were carrying on. While thus engaged he had the misfortune to cause the death of a young man. He thus announces the event to his two wives: Gen. 4:23, 24. *And Lamech said unto his wives, Adah and Zillah, hear my voice; ye wives of Lamech, hearken unto my speech: for I have slain a man to my wounding, and a young man to my hurt: If Cain shall be avenged sevenfold, truly Lamech seventy and sevenfold.* It does not appear precisely in what sense it was said by Lamech he had *slain a man to his wounding, and a young man to his hurt.* He might have been conscious of carelessness, or haste; or he might have feared the misconception or ill feeling of those around him. Perhaps the iteration, *a young man,* renders the latter probable, especially in connexion with what follows: *If Cain shall be avenged sevenfold, truly Lamech seventy and sevenfold.* To understand this it will be necessary to inquire why Cain was to be avenged sevenfold. Commentators seem to have misunderstood the character and position of Cain. He was a murderer, but was he a murderer at all in the present sense of the term? He probably did violence to his natural feelings, in slaying his brother; but on the other hand he was prompted to the act by powerful feelings; and his moral training was probably, from the circumstances of the case, far more limited and imperfect, than that of the most ignorant, in civilized communities, at the present day. It does not even appear that homicide had ever been forbidden. It is probable that the prohibition would have been alluded to, if it had. Cain had doubtless witnessed death in the inferiour animals, but never, probably, in a human being. Hence he could never have experienced that indescribable horrour, which the presence of death inspires; and he could have known little about the subject, as well as many others, which elicit and educate the moral sentiments, by tradition. He had doubtless heard of the tree of life, and probably something of a future state of being, and it is not impossible that he imagined that Abel, in a brief period would be restored to consciousness, and the former, or some change of existence.

For reasons of this nature God mercifully forbore to inflict the death penalty upon the sorrowful, and possibly repentant murderer; and not only so, he extended to him the divine protection, to which, indeed, Cain seems to have felt that he had some claim: see Gen. 4: 14. God was pleased to set a mark upon him, not as a sign of reprobation, but as a token to over zealous persons, who might be disposed to slay Cain, under a mistaken idea of rendering justice, that he would be memorably avenged. Cain was a *fugitive and a vagabond* for a time, but he had descendants, and after a period, like the other patriarchs, builded a city, which, as well as his son, born after he became a fugitive, he called Enoch, meaning *dedicated* or *disciplined*.

The application of this to the case of Lamech is sufficiently obvious. Lamech, while engaged in an employment, which was not only useful, but indispensable to the welfare, and future progress of the race, without evil intention, caused the death of a fellow being. There were probably those, in the infancy of the useful arts, (it could scarcely be otherwise,) who put the worst construction upon the event. But Lamech was so confident of the rectitude and propriety of his course, that he spoke with assurance, indeed he seems to have spoken under the influence of a prophetic fervor, in saying that as the favorable circumstances were far more considerable, than with Cain, so, should any one malignantly, and urging the erroneous plea of justice, inflict death upon him, he would be avenged, far more than Cain. Thus, at the very commencement of the useful arts, the great principle or fact, seems to have been expressly recognized, that there is a dark side to useful improvements, that the same powers, which, properly employed are of such beneficent tendency, may be applied, by accident or design, to uses, proportionately hurtful; but that notwithstanding, advancement in a knowledge of the powers of the elements around us, which can minister legitimately, to the well being of man, is both our privilege and our duty.

Various circumstances were exceedingly favorable to great and rapid progress in philosophical knowledge, and those arts which are governed by its principles; and I can have little doubt that when it is said there is nothing new under the sun, allusion is made to the antediluvian period. That the principles of government were well understood, that the most ample protection was afforded to persons and property, notwithstanding the great wickedness that prevailed, appears from the immunity enjoyed by Noah and his sons, during the long period in which they were engaged in an enterprise, which must have been exceedingly repugnant to the feelings of those by whom they were surrounded.

Note (C), P. 125.

The following articles, describing the earthquake of Oct. 17, 1860; and the journey of the Prince of Wales from Albany to Boston, on the same day, and his reception at Boston, are extracted from the Springfield Daily Republican, of various dates.

An Earthquake in Springfield.—Two memorable events occurred in Springfield on Wednesday; namely, the passage of the Prince of Wales through the town, and the passage of an earthquake under it. A few minutes before six o'clock in the morning, while the writer of this was lying in his bed, supine and wide awake, there came a gentle, vibratory motion of the bed, from west to east, apparently. The motion was so unusual as to attract immediate attention, and to excite curiosity to learn the cause. It was not like the jar which would be caused by a heavy walk in an adjoining room; but seemed like the result of a vibratory power, applied horizontally to the whole house. This passed away, and was succeeded at brief intervals by three or four similar shocks, which sometimes began and sometimes ended with a kind of tremulous thrill. As nearly as we can remember, it was the fifth shock which declared the genuine earthquake, and settled the question. Windows and doors responded to the vibration in all parts of the house, and left no doubt as to the character of the phenomena. In the third story of the Republican Block, a gentleman was so much startled that he ran to the window to see what could be the matter. Earthquakes are very rare visitors in this latitude.

The earthquake extended over all the northern part of New England and through Canada. At Boston and vicinity, it seems to have been lighter than here; at Manchester, N. H., about the same; while at Saco, Me., there was a loud report, a perceptible rocking of buildings with the ringing of the bells. It grew in severity as it extended up the Connecticut Valley; we hear of it through Vermont, at Barton, St. Johnsbury, Northfield, Woodstock, Windsor and Littleton. At Barton, fastened doors were unlocked and the church bells rung by it, and at Northfield, a church-spire was shaken out of its propriety, and left standing obliquely. The Connecticut, Albany and New York papers do not mention the phenomenon as observed in those sections.

THE RECENT EARTHQUAKE.—The earthquake of the 17th seems to have been more violent at Quebec, Canada, and in that vicinity, than in any other part of the country. Some describe the sensation produced by it there as that of immediate proximity to some extensive steam manufactory, whose wheels were revolving with that degree of velocity which gives a thudding sort of sound and strong vibratory motion. In others, the action was oscillatory, with an occasional vibration; but in all, everything moveable and immovable was shaken more or less; many things of a light nature being thrown down, and glass and china ware, furniture, light and heavy, were rattling and jumping in the most extraordinary manner. In some instances the plaster of the ceilings and walls was shaken down, and the jointings of wooden buildings opened. In the frame buildings of the suburbs, especially St. Roques, along St. Vallier street and by St. Sauveur, the shock seemed to have been very severe, men, women and children rushing from their dwellings half-dressed, with terror depicted in their countenances, asking one another incoherent questions, and receiving equally incoherent replies. On the plains the effect was very great, old soldiers resident in them stating that the shock exceeded in intensity those experienced by them in the East and West Indies. At Beaufort Asylum all the inmates that could ran out of the building, while those who had not

24

such opportunities ran shrieking through the wards and corridors. In several rooms the plaster was shaken down, and strong joints were forced open by the motion given to the building. The engineer of the establishment, while superintending the machinery, heard the boilers of his engine clatter together in such a manner that, apprehensive of an explosion, he ran out of the engine-room. Indeed, the shock seems to have been felt with greater violence in the open country than in the city. Farmers from the neighborhood of Laval, when on their road to market, had halted their horses for a little rest, and themselves gone into a house in the bush for the same purpose, felt the shock so severely that they rushed terrified from the house, imagining that it was coming down about their ears. At Lorette, doors were shaken from their places, and crockery in cup-boards smashed to pieces. At Point Levi the motion of the earth was violently felt, and fear and terror prevailed everywhere. On the river, too, the trembling, vibratory motion was communicated to the shipping.

THE PRINCE OF WALES IN MASSACHUSETTS.—HIS TRIP FROM ALBANY TO BOSTON.—The Prince of Wales, now about to complete his American tour, and with face turned homeward, made his promised entree into New England, on Wednesday, passing through Massachusetts from the West to Boston. The program had been of long standing, and was unchangeable; and there was no lack of preparation on the part of the railroad managers that it should be carried out with eclat. And so it was, the weather adding its full share of favoring circumstances. It had been hoped, indeed, that now that. the royal party had visited the principal cities of the North and West they would improve this opportunity to see somewhat of our interior New England life, and that Springfield would be chosen for this purpose. But the brief time remaining, and the necessity of an early arrival at Boston, Wednesday afternoon, not only prevented this, but denied also any prolonged stop at stations along the route.

The excursion train consisted of a baggage and two passenger cars. The tourists, according to their established usage in this country, chartered it as to running expenses, at a cost of some four or five hundred dollars for the through trip. They allowed the corporation, however, to furnish cars according to its own choice, and the opportunity thus given was well availed of by the railroad managers, who had the satisfaction of being often complimented by the Prince and his party for the good taste and liberality displayed in this respect. The forward car, designed for the attendants and invited guests, was not changed from its usual wear, except by the addition of a strip of carpet in the aisle between the seats. The rear car, prepared especially for the Prince, and the costly refitting of which we have already described in detail, was divided into two saloons, the forward saloon retaining the usual car seats, but now newly and handsomely upholstered, while the other was furnished with sofas and a centre-table. Both the cars were selected from those heretofore in use on the road, and both will be returned to their former service. The train was drawn to Worcester by the favorite locomotive Addison Gilmore, now, with the cars, appearing fresh from under the hands of the decorators, who had completed their work by a display of the flags of England and America. William E. Granger presided at the throttle valve of the engine, which has been his special charge for years, assisted over the western division of the road (with which he was not thoroughly conversant) by Mr. Bolton. Conductor John B. Adams of this city had the active charge of the train to Springfield, and James Parker took it thence to Boston, both being chosen for these complimentary positions on account of their long time and faithful service on the road in this capacity.

The party, having passed the night at Albany, left their hotel at eight o'clock, Wednesday morning, under escort of the Burgess corps of that city. Great numbers of people were gathered at points along the way to witness the departure. At the cars the Prince bade adieu to Gov. Morgan, Senator Seward, Mayor Thatcher, and Capt. Kingsley commander of the escort, and withdrawing hastily into his own saloon to avoid the crowd, the train moved out of the depot at 8.49, only four minutes behind the special card time arranged for it. The party numbered some thirty persons, including from the start Lord Lyons, the Duke of Newcastle, the Earl St. Germain, Gen. Bruce, and others of the immediate suite, with the twelve or fifteen under officers and attendants; also, president Chapin and superintendent Gray of the Western railroad, Dr. Robert Campbell of Pittsfield, one of the directors of the same, and several representatives of the press. Gov. Morgan's aids accompanied the party as far as the state line, and Colonels Thompson and Sargent of Gov. Banks' staff came on board at Springfield. Other additions were made along the line, of whom were James D. Colt of Pittsfield, attorney to the railroad, directors Tinker of North Adams and Shaw of Boston, alderman Willis of Boston, and, at Worcester, a considerable delegation of the Boston committee of reception.

The Prince and his party were dressed plainly in the style of travelers, wearing neither jewelry nor ornament. The Prince himself appeared in a blue pilot cloth coat, with drab pants, and black hat and maroon colored gloves. Taking his seat in the forward saloon of his car, he kept it quite closely to the end of the route, devoting himself to smoking and reading as a means of passing the time. The Albany papers were first devoured, and then a selection of railroad literature was taken up. While other members of the party preferred the after saloon and its easier accommodations, with conversation or sight-seeing, he himself adhered to his straight seat, his cigar and solitude. Except when spoken to he said little or nothing. The romantic scenery along the Berkshire portions of the route, which others noticed with expressions of surprise and delight, were passed by almost unheeded by him. He seemed to wish that he might be left alone and unnoticed, not that he disdained other people, but that he is tired out and surfeited with their attentions. When spoken to, however, he was always affable and polite, entering easily into conversation and his countenance brightening up with an expression of intelligence that added much to his handsome features. He shrinks especially from being gazed at by the crowd. Only at Pittsfield, Chester, Springfield, Palmer and Worcester was he coaxed upon the platform that the people might see him. At these places the large numbers gathered made it imperative and he submitted with good grace. There were a thousand or more at Pittsfield, and the train stopped but for a moment. At Chester, where there was a longer delay for wood and water, a small crowd compelled his appearance by their uneasiness to see him. Westfield can have the satisfaction of knowing that he got so far as to rise from his seat before concluding not to show himself. At Springfield and Worcester there were crowds of several thousands; and while in the one place people had to look quick, in the other he was kept on the platform full fifteen minutes, wearing an air of painful unrest, while a needless delay was being made to attach a third car in the train for the Boston committee that had come up to meet him. Soon after leaving Springfield, Colonels Thompson and Sargent of the Governor's staff were presented, and the former made a neat impromptu address of welcome, saying in substance :—"I am commanded by his excellency to welcome your royal highness to the commonwealth of Massachusetts ; to conduct you to its capital ; and to tender you all the facilities which your visit may require." The Prince bowed his thanks, speaking his grateful acceptance in his countenance even though he said nothing.

The run was made from Albany to Worcester, 154 miles, in five hours and twenty minutes, including fully twenty minutes for stops. The time made was thus a little better than 30 miles an hour. At all the stations along the line there were numbers of people gathered, and at nearly every crossing there were some to see the bright train pass swiftly by. The train was run under the established rules of the road, and was not given any preference above its own time-card. Exact time, almost to a second, was, however, made at every station, and none of the regular trains were delayed. The running of the train was acknowledged by all on board to be the perfection of railroad equipment; cars never moved more smoothly or with less jostle and jar. The starting, halting and running were alike performed with an evenness of motion that could not but be noticeable, and the engineer, though unseen, was not forgotten.

At Worcester the Addison Gilmore was replaced by a locomotive of the Boston and Worcester road—the "Dispatch," now bearing its new name as the "Prince of Wales." The car of the Boston committee, which was here added, was placed between the two Western railroad cars, and the Prince was invited to honor it by his personal presence inside, which we believe he consented to do for a while. This car is entirely new, built expressly for this occasion, and furnished elegantly. The train left Worcester at 2.22, and arrived at Longwood, a few miles out of Boston, in a run of little more than an hour for the forty miles. The party were here received by a large delegation from Boston of military and citizens, and escorted into the city by way of Roxbury and the neck :—

[BY TELEGRAPH.]

Mayor Lincoln, with the committee of the city government, received the Prince and suite cordially, but with little formality. The party at once entered open carriages, and under escort of the Lancers and Light Dragoons proceeded to the Revere House. The sidewalks, balconies and windows on either side of the route were thronged with people, whose welcome seemed hearty but was not noisy.

The public reception of the Prince in Boston takes place to-day, and the day will be observed as a holiday, all the schools being suspended, and most of the stores closing at or before noon. The grand military review takes place on the common at 1 o'clock, followed by a collation to the royal party in the State House. A grand musical festival of 1200 children with an orchestra of sixty performers, at Music

Hall, completes the exercises of the afternoon, and a ball at the Boston theatre, in the evening, and for which tickets to admit 1000 gentlemen and 1500 ladies (the full number) have already been sold, fills out the day. On Friday the Prince visits Harvard College and afterwards departs for Portland, where the embarkation occurs on Saturday for England and home. The city is full of strangers, distinguished people, military guests, and a miscellaneous crowd of spectators.

THE PRINCE AT BOSTON.—After his arrival at the Revere House, Wednesday afternoon, the Prince was allowed to pass a quiet evening. Edward Everett and a few other distinguished men were introduced, and the Prince was once or twice called to the balcony by the crowds that packed Bowdoin square to see him, but otherwise the privacy of the royal party was not broken. Wednesday night and Thursday morning crowds of people, military, etc., were pouring into the city to witness or participate in the display of the afternoon, and Thursday morning the city had put on a truly festive appearance. The stars and stripes and the royal cross of St. George floated together everywhere; decorations, public and private, were being put up in the streets; the shipping showed all the bunting it had; the streets were swarmed and crowded; and long before the hour people by the tens of thousands were moving towards the common to witness the military review at 1 o'clock. Meanwhile the Prince kept his apartments, receiving distinguished visitors, and showing himself occasionally at the windows to the crowds in Bowdoin square. Among those presented to him was Ralph Farnum of Maine, the veteran and sole survivor of Bunker Hill, who is now stopping at the Adams House. This interview was very pleasant to both parties. A ride about the city, incognito, had been talked of for a part of the forenoon, but this was given up. At twelve o'clock the Prince and suite, dressed in uniform, the Prince as a colonel in the English army, were escorted to the State House by the National Lancers, an immense crowd following and lining the way. None but those who were so unfortunate as to be engulphed by the human tide can estimate the pressure about the State House at this time. Inside the governor, council, state officers, members of the two houses, etc., with many ladies, were in waiting. The arrangements within were admirable, and the few decorations were elegant and tasteful. The Prince was received in the council chamber by Gov. Banks, who said to him :—

It is with great pleasure that I welcome your highness to the commonwealth of Massachusetts, and extend to you the most cordial greeting of its people. They have regarded with profound gratification your visit to this continent, so auspicious in its opening, so fortunate in its progress, and now, I regret to say, so near its termination. Be assured, sir, you will bear with you the united wishes of the people of Massachusetts for your safe return to your friends and your country, to which we are attached by so many ties of language, law and liberty. In their name I bid you welcome.

I welcome with unfeigned pleasure the distinguished and honorable gentlemen of your suite.

Permit me to present to you my associates in the executive department of the government—his honor the lieutenant governor, gentlemen of the executive council, the secretary of state.

The royal party was then introduced by the Prince, and afterwards they passed through the hall of Representatives, the Senate chamber, and the Doric hall to the southern entrance, where horses were in waiting. They here mounted for the review, the Prince riding a splendid black stallion with his own caparison at Gov. Banks' right. The military had been formed on Shawmut avenue at 11 and were now drawn up on the Common. There were forty companies in the line, composed of the first and second brigades with companies from Springfield, Haverhill, Worcester, New Bedford, Lawrence, Lowell, Plymouth, etc., attached to one or the other. The military counted 2089 bayonets, and with officers and music there were probably 2500 in the ranks. The first brigade, Gen. Bullock, occupied the Charles street mall from Boylston street entirely across to Beacon. The second brigade, Gen. Pierce, reached up the Beacon street mall. The Ancient and Honorable Artillery, counting 250 men, had the city government in escort and were formed in front of the first brigade. The Governor and party took up their position on Flagstaff hill, in front of which was a group consisting of field and staff officers on horseback, and among the distinguished guests Robert C. Winthrop, Edward Everett, Gov. Dennison of Ohio, Hannibal Hamlin, Commodore Hudson, the mayors of Lowell, Montreal and Gardiner, and Major-Generals Sutton and Morse and staffs. Amid the thunder of artillery and music by the bands the cavalcade then passed along the lines, and afterwards the troops themselves marched by in review. The military now formed in column, and with the royal cavalcade under escort of the Lancers the line of march through the city was begun. The route was down

Boylston, Washington, State and Commerical, then back by way of
Faneuil Hall, Dock Square and Washington street to Court, through
Tremont to Beacon, and through Beacon to the State House, where
the troops were dismissed.   Everywhere along the route the sidewalks
and windows were packed with people, and the display was brilliant
beyond the power of a brief narrative to describe.   Arrived again at
the State House a collation was served, at which there were among the
thirty or more invited guests Senators Wilson and Sumner, Gov. Dennison of Ohio, Hannibal Hamlin of Maine, Edward Everett, ex-Chief
Justice Shaw, President Felton of Harvard College, the judges of the
supreme court, etc.

Following the collation, and at about 5 o'clock, the party now as-
suming citizen's dress, took carriages at the State House to attend the
musical festival of 1200 children at Music Hall.   The hall was elaborately decorated, and the royal guests occupied a raised platform in
front of the gallery.   The exercises seemed to afford the visitors much
satisfaction.   The principal piece in the program were the following
verses, composed by Holmes, though at first erroneously credited to
Longfellow.   We repeat them corrected from a former publication :—

OUR FATHERS' LAND.

God bless our fathers' land,
Keep her in heart and hand
   One with our own !
From all her foes defend,
Be her brave people's friend,
On all her realms descend,
   Protect her throne !

Father, in loving care
Guard Thou her kingdom's heir,
   Guide all his ways:
Thine arm his shelter be
From harm by land and sea;
Bid storm and danger flee,
   Prolong his days !

Lord, let war's tempest cease,
Fold the whole earth in peace
   Under Thy wings !
Make all Thy nations one,
All hearts beneath the sun,
Till Thou shalt reign alone,
   Great King of Kings !

The ball at the Boston Theater in the evening closed the festivities of the day. The extensive arrangements for it were carried out in the most thorough manner, and a spectacle was presented which far eclipsed any similar gathering of the kind ever witnessed in New England. Not less than three thousand people, representing the chivalry and beauty of Massachusetts, were present, and the dance went on merrily until a late hour in the night. The ball, like all other parts of the day's proceedings, was a gratifying success, honorable alike to the city and its distinguished visitor.

The prince takes to-day for quiet visits to places of interest in and about Boston, including Harvard College. There will, however, be no further public display in his honor, and he will depart for Portland in a special train Saturday morning, there to embark immediately for home.

Note (D).

I propose, in this note, to add something to what has been said concerning useful and economic applications of odic processes. Some of the most valuable of these, it will have been seen, consist merely in removing or withdrawing native odics.

Whencesoever derived, whether from the normal odic, which appears to be universally diffused, from the solar and stellar radiations, or from some other source, there is, it would seem, an unfailing supply of the odical elements ; which are naturally elaborated into innumerable combinations; and which may be elaborated, in a similar manner, by artificial processes. I have made some progress, in a considerable number of odic processes, (whether of application or withdrawal,) which promise to be useful, but which circumstances have not permitted me, in most instances, to bring to that degree of perfection and certainty, of which they are apparently susceptible. A few of these, and some of which, even in their present state, promise to be useful, I will here mention.

The Diffusible Stimuli.—It was supposed, from the nature of these substances, and the mode of their operation upon the human system, that they might probably be imitated, or in some sort reproduced, by concentrating their odical or spiritual elements, in some inert medium. If opium, morphine, hyosciamus, musk, and other articles of that general description, and those allied to them, as quinine ; or good

25

substitutes, perhaps better articles, could be produced at a moderate rate, and under circumstances that would well nigh insure their being of uniform quality and strength, it need not be said it would be a great acquisition to the healing art. I suppose that the failures of the most skillful practitioners are sometimes owing to the want of perfectly reliable medicines, the effect of which can be accurately calculated. I have not experimented much in this direction, partly it is probable, for the want of good subjects to experiment upon. I am myself, several years past the allotted term of human life, and frail; so that I am not much disposed to experiment upon myself, except with very considerable caution; and good subjects, those endowed with the faculty, or who have acquired the habit, of introspective observation, and who are gifted with the requisite degree of patience, are not, in this age of excitement, so readily found. That something like what has been described can be accomplished, is certain, but whether to the extent of realizing the idea, or any considerable approach to it, may be doubtful; at any rate if so, it is yet to be determined.

I have recently, with the more powerful odic appliances, which I have had at command for about a year past, made some attempts to imitate or reproduce some of the articles referred to, but with doubtful success. One of these was the herb which, as is said, cheers but not inebriates; though a physician informed me that he once saw two young women, who, upon some wager or strife, had drank immense quantities of tea, sufficient to produce a singular kind of inebriation, which continued two or three days. By concentrating the odical elements of green tea in powdered rusk and in sugar, an artificial tea was produced, which in one of the subjects, caused, in every instance, several hours of wakefulness; in another it produced, once, unmistakably, those phantoms, with which the tea drinkers, (of this kind of tea,) are familiar. But neither of these subjects had had sufficient experience of the exhilerating effects of tea, to judge whether these were produced; and indeed, they partook of the infusion but in small quantities.

THE MATERIALS OF TEXTILE FABRICKS, EMPLOYED FOR CLOTHING.—The only materials of which these fabricks consist, that need be mentioned here, are the common ones of linen, cotton, silk and wool. These differ very much in their mechanical structure, but their different physiological effects, (in addition to warmth,) are probably owing, for the most part, to their more occult properties. Silk is supposed to be tonic or stimulating, cotton is an irritant in various kinds, woolen is an irritant, when new, or newly washed, but this, as it wears off, is probably owing to mechanical structure; linen alone, appears to be cool and healthful. The extraordinary preference given to linen for use on sacred occasions, both in the Old and New Testament, is quite remarkable. It is remarkable in connection with the circumstance, (at least such was the case in my own early experience, and no change has been observed since,) that cotton gives, normally, to the odic pendulum, the same movement as the right hand of an evil man, and linen the same as that of a just man. But the physiological effects of cotton are such, in the normal state, as to render its use of very doubtful propriety. It produces in some an eruption of the skin, in others, there is reason to believe, chronic inflammation of the eyes, in others, a chronic irritation of the lungs, predisposing to consumption. Numbers cannot sleep well in cotton, it produces restlessness and wakefulness. It is considered to be totally unsuitable for dressings for wounds. In my own case, used for socks or sheets, it produces intolerable itching of the feet and ankles; but this I have some reason to believe, is partly at least, an induced state; I have not known of it in others. Is the hurry which every body is in, in this fast age, owing, in part, to the general substitution of cotton for linen? Is the greater prevalence of possession in recent periods owing, directly or indirectly, or perhaps both, to the same cause? I fear that each of these questions would have to be answered in the affirmative. Yet cotton has become so considerably a part of the system of the world, that it would be extremely difficult to relinquish its use. Under these circumstances it is gratifying to know that cotton can be linenized; that is, deprived, by an easy process, of its odical elements, and those of linen substituted. Whether the change will be entirely permanent, under all circumstances, and whether the physiological and *moral* effects of the linenized cotton will be equal to those of linen, will not be established, to the satisfaction of all, without numerous and varied experiments. In a recent experiment linenized cotton has been washed many times, with the usual application of soap, and of scrubbing on the wash board, without the slightest change; and there is reason to believe that at least, it will not produce the physiological symptoms described above.

But this is not all. Both cotton and linen, when worn by those affected with chronic diseases, scrofula, erysipelas, gout, &c., imbibe the morbid odics of the several diseases. These react upon the system, &c. But by an appropriate process they can be occluded, and rendered insusceptible of these morbid influences.

INHALATION—SPIRITUAL OXYGEN.—Odicism affords great facilities for the practice of inhalation. The spiritual elements of every article in the pharmacopœia, can be presented to the lungs, in the most appropriate form, and in any quantity. I have made a few experiments of this kind, especially with spiritual oxygen. In a case of palpitation it afforded extraordinary and unexpected relief. Should its general antispasmodic powers equal those in this instance, it would be an antispasmodic of more efficacy than any at present known ; unless, indeed, some circumstance should preclude its employment in large doses. In the instance mentioned, (or instances, for it was employed several times for the same purpose,) it was only of the pendular force of 5′′′. This might be increased many thousand fold. I have surmised that, as the heart and lungs are probably its more appropriate sphere of action, in numerous cases of disease, where death is about to take place from exhaustion, the skilful and bold application of this substance, might keep up the action of the heart, carry the system by the crisis, and thus—alas—put off the approach of death for a time.

CLIMATE.—For several years the climate of the United States has been entirely changed, so far as it was productive of cholera. Other changes equally extensive, might doubtless be produced. It is believed that influenzas and pestilential colds might in a great measure be prevented. Differences of climate are attributable, in some degree, to different proportions, in the atmosphere, of spiritual oxygen and spiritual ozone. The former of these is combined with the atmosphere, the latter is free. These proportions, there is little or no reason to doubt, can be regulated. The polarization of the normal odic can be determined, and this, if an inconvenience which has hitherto attended its use can be obviated, has a most important influence upon diseases.

www.ingramcontent.com/pod-product-compliance
Lightning Source LLC
Chambersburg PA
CBHW030548040726
47497CB00008B/2626